D0097973

REDEMPTION

Also by Mark Walden

In the H.I.V.E. series

The Higher Institute of Villainous Education

The Overlord Protocol

Escape Velocity

Dreadnought

Rogue

Zero Hour

Aftershock

Deadlock

In the Earthfall series

Book 1: Earthfall

Book 2: Retribution

REDEMPTION

Book 3 of the Earthfall Trilogy

MARK WALDEN

Simon & Schuster Books for Young Readers
New York London Toronto Sydney New Delhi

SIMON & SCHUSTER BOOKS FOR YOUNG READERS
An imprint of Simon & Schuster Children's Publishing Division
1230 Avenue of the Americas, New York, New York 10020

Originally published in Great Britain in 2017 by Bloomsbury Publishing Plc
First US edition 2018

Book design by Chloë Foglia
The text for this book was set in Goudy Old Style.
Manufactured in the United States of America
0318 FFG
2 4 6 8 10 9 7 5 3 1
Library of Congress Cataloging-in-Publication Data
Names: Walden, Mark, author.
Title: Redemption / Mark Walden.
Description: First edition. | New York : Simon & Schuster Books for Young Readers, [2018] | Series: The Earthfall series ; book 3 | Summary: "Sam and his friends embark on one last mission, one final epic final battle against their alien enemies to determine the fate of the Earth"—Provided by publisher.
Identifiers: LCCN 2017008621 | ISBN 9781442494213 (hardcover)
| ISBN 9781442494237 (eBook)
Subjects: | CYAC: Survival—Fiction. | Extraterrestrial beings—Fiction. | London (England)—Fiction. | England—Fiction. | Science fiction.
Classification: LCC PZ7.W138 Rc 2018 | DDC [Fic]—dc23
LC record available at https://lccn.loc.gov/2017008621

For Sarah. For reassuring me that it really isn't the end of the world . . .

REDEMPTION

1

Just beyond the orbit of the Earth's moon, a massive black vessel hung in the darkness of space, its segmented superstructure pulsing with blood-red light as coronas of crimson lightning danced over the giant curved pylons that spread out from its hull. The colossal structures moved in a rhythmic pattern, giving the enormous ship the appearance of something mechanical and yet alive. Somewhere within the vast superstructure, a consciousness quite unlike any other began to stir, sensing that the moment it had so often dreamed about during its long, cold journey was at hand. The moment was coming very soon, the mind trapped within the vessel told itself, a moment for which it had waited an eternity. Soon, the cursed Illuminate would die screaming and take the planet below with them.

The Primarch had arrived.

* * *

Sam ran between the abandoned vehicles, the sharp coldness of the early spring air filling his lungs. In the predawn gloom, the buildings that loomed over him on either side of the street were little more than dark shapes in the mist. Sam began to run faster, pushing himself harder and harder, searching for the limits of his endurance. He felt an unnerving crawling sensation in his legs as the alien nanites deep inside him reconfigured his musculature to match the demands that he was putting on his body. He pulled to a halt. He had been running as fast as he could for the best part of an hour and, while he wasn't short of breath, he couldn't get used to the strange feeling in his legs.

"This isn't going to stop feeling weird anytime soon," Sam muttered to himself under his breath.

There was no doubt that he was in better physical condition than he had ever been before the Voidborn invasion, but that did not begin to explain the feats of superhuman endurance he now seemed capable of. He had no real comprehension of how he could do these unbelievable things, but he knew exactly what had happened to make him like this. It had been three months since his father, Suran, one of the last survivors of the Illuminate, had died. The Voidborn's most ancient enemy had, in his final moments, passed *something* on to Sam, something that Sam still did not properly understand.

He stood there for a moment, listening to the sounds of the city. Just a couple of years ago there would have been a nonstop barrage of noise in this part of London. Now all he could hear was the dawn chorus as the birds that roosted unmolested in the abandoned buildings around him began to stir. It was strange to think that you could actually miss traffic noise, Sam thought to himself. Suddenly, he heard the crunch of gravel underfoot from somewhere behind him. He froze, and listening more carefully, he quickly realized that someone or something was moving nearby. The rest of the audible world seemed to drop away as he slowly turned and focused on the sound, which stopped abruptly, as if in response. He could just make out faint, short, controlled breaths. His heart beat rapidly and his eyes narrowed as he peered into the gloom, trying to spot whoever it was that was following him. He sniffed the air, the lining of his nose tingling as his senses were assaulted by the scents all around him. He sniffed again and a crooked smile slowly spread across his face.

"You can come out, Mag," Sam said. "I know you're there."

A small figure detached itself from the shadows behind one of the vehicles fifty yards away and walked toward him.

"Getting hard to sneak up on you, Riley," Mag said, pulling her hood back to reveal the long white hair underneath. The skin of her face was unnaturally pale and a branching network of dark veins ran back from the corners of her jet-black eyes and into her hairline. At the ends of her fingers were inch-long, translucent crystalline talons that she flexed unconsciously as she walked. These strange deformities were relics of her exposure to the alien bioweapon that had been released in Edinburgh and had subsequently given birth to the horrifying hybrid creatures they now knew as the Vore. She was one of a handful of the city's sleeping inhabitants who had been only partially transformed by the weapon; the rest had not been so lucky.

"Yeah, well, you taught me everything I know," Sam said with a grin as she approached.

"You do realize there's no one else around," Mag said, gesturing toward Sam's face. "Why don't you cut yourself some slack and relax for once?"

Sam sighed and then gave a quick nod, his features shifting as his skin turned paper white. Glowing blue lines started spreading back over his skull as his hair disappeared, replaced by a series of bony, crested ridges.

"Now you look a bit more yourself," Mag said with a smile. "Are you still getting the headaches?"

"No, they're pretty much gone," Sam said. "I hardly even need to focus anymore."

"You're getting a lot faster too," Mag replied. "It's getting to the point where I can't keep up with you. Do you feel like you've got any more control of it?"

"Not really, to be honest," Sam said, shaking his head. "It just seems to kick in when I need it. If I am controlling it, I don't know how. I still don't understand exactly what it was that my dad . . . what Suran did to me. I spend most of my time just wishing I could turn it off."

"Aye, well, tell me about it," Mag said. "At least you actually have the option of looking normal."

"Yeah, you're right. Sorry, poor me," Sam said.

"It's okay. I got used to this eventually," Mag replied, raising one of her clawed hands. "So will you. At least I'll never need to pay for a manicure."

"Guess I'll be needing fewer trips to the hairdresser too," Sam said, running his fingers over the ridges on the top of his skull.

"I still think you should tell the others, you know," Mag said, sitting down on the bonnet of one of the abandoned cars that littered the road.

"Look, we've already been over this," Sam said, with a slightly exasperated sigh. "I'll tell everyone what's happened to me when I'm ready."

It had not actually been his choice to tell Mag about his bizarre transformation. She'd smelled the change on him. He had made her swear a solemn vow not to tell anyone else about it. Since then she had respected his wishes, despite making it very clear that she didn't agree with his decision.

"If they can see past all this," she said, gesturing toward

her own face, "and see the person underneath, surely they'll be able to understand what's happened to you. They'll understand that this wasn't your choice. Perhaps you don't give them enough credit. I mean, let's face it: we've all seen our fair share of weird over the past couple of years."

"I know all that, but . . . they've got enough to worry about without me telling them that I'm not even sure if I'm fully human anymore. And do you think they're going to trust me if they find out that I've been hiding what I really am from them?"

"They see you as their leader, Sam," Mag said, frowning and shaking her head. "You owe them the truth. You might not want to tell them, but it's going to be a lot worse if they find out some other way."

"I said I'd tell them when I'm ready!" Sam snapped, before turning and walking away.

"Hey!" Mag said, following him. "I get it, all right? How do you think I felt the first time I looked in a mirror after waking up in Edinburgh? The thing you need to remember is that you have something I didn't back then, Sam. You have friends. People you can lean on. People who care about you. You talk about trust—well, they already trust you. Now you have to trust them."

"I know. Look, I'm sorry. I didn't mean to bite your head off," Sam said quietly. "I just don't know how much more of this I can take. We've all lost so much over the past couple of years and for what? We're no nearer to defeating the Voidborn than we were a year ago, wc have way more questions than answers and the price we've already paid in blood is too damn high. I've watched friends die. I've held them as . . ." He paused, taking a deep breath and then looking her straight in the eye. "How can I lead anyone, Mag? How can I ask anyone to follow me when I don't even know *what I am* anymore?"

"You're Sam Riley, that's all I care about. That's all your friends care about. That's all that really matters."

Sam looked at her for a moment, seeing his own reflection in Mag's dark eyes.

"You're right," he replied with a sigh, nodding.

"Always," Mag said. "Have you seriously not figured that out yet?"

"Oh, it's definitely starting to become clearer," Sam replied, smiling. "Come on, let's head back to camp."

"Race?" Mag asked with a grin, not waiting for his reply before she turned and sprinted away down the street.

"Hey, guys." Jay put down the welding torch he'd been setting up next to the military four-by-four parked just behind him and waved as he saw Sam and Mag walking across the compound toward him.

"You still wasting your time on that thing?" Mag asked, shaking her head.

"This *thing* is going to be the sweetest ride in London

by the time I've finished with her," Jay said, patting the hulking vehicle on one of its armored panels. "You'll see."

"Didn't we go over the whole 'no petrol' thing?" Sam asked, looking confused. The fuel in the vehicles that still lay scattered around the city had long since decayed to the point of uselessness.

"Yeah, but the Servant's been helping me out with an alternative power source." Jay felt under the edge of the bonnet for the release catch before lifting the hood to reveal a glowing Voidborn power unit mounted to the engine block. "So, as you can see, in actual fact this beauty is the only fully working set of wheels in London. You may submit your begging requests for a ride in her in writing."

"Great, Jay at the wheel of a Voidborn-powered vehicle," Sam said, a mischievous smile playing across his lips. "What could possibly go wrong?"

"Also, I don't know if you noticed or not, but the roads are a little . . . congested around here," Mag said.

"Which is exactly why I need to reinforce her bumper," Jay said, gesturing to the welding kit.

"Listen, do you think you could give me a hand getting everyone together in the common room?" Sam said. "There's something I've got to tell you."

"Everything okay?" Jay frowned.

"Yeah . . . no . . . sort of," Sam replied, looking slightly uncomfortable.

"I knew it," Jay said. "There's been something bothering you ever since we got back from Tokyo. I kinda just assumed it was to do with . . ." He glanced over at the wooden crosses that marked the row of graves on the other side of the compound.

"No, it's something else," Sam replied. "Something's happened and . . ." His voice trailed off.

"Come on, man, tell me. What is it? What's wrong?"

"It'll be easier if I speak to all of you together," Sam said.

"Okay, I'll go round people up, but you're starting to seriously worry me," Jay said, his frown deepening.

"I promise I'll explain everything. I just don't really want to have to do it more than once."

"Do you know what this is about?" Jay asked Mag. She glanced at Sam and he gave her a nod.

"Yeah, I do," Mag said.

"So whatever this is, you could tell Mag but you couldn't tell me?" Jay asked Sam. "Great, thanks, man."

"Come on, Jay, it wasn't like that . . . ," Mag said.

"Yeah, whatever," Jay replied, his irritation abundantly clear. "Look, don't worry about it. I'll go get the others. See you inside in ten."

Sam went to follow Jay as he strode away, but Mag stopped him, placing a hand on his shoulder.

"Let him go," she said. "He'll understand when you explain what's happened. They all will."

"I hope you're right." Sam watched Jay march toward the buildings on the other side of the compound. "I'm going to get Stirling. He needs to be there to hear this too."

"Okay, I'll see you inside," Mag said. "Don't worry, it's going to be fine."

Sam walked toward Dr. Stirling's lab. He glanced up at the two Voidborn Motherships that hovered above the city. The undersides of the enormous circular vessels were occasionally lit up by bright flashes of light as teams of Voidborn Drones worked to repair the damage that had been caused to both ships during their cataclysmic battle over Tokyo just a few months before. Both of these vessels were now under the control of the former Voidborn entity known as the Servant, and she in turn took her orders from Sam. It was strange to think that he, a fairly unremarkable teenage boy before the Voidborn invasion, now had total command of enough firepower to wipe out any of Earth's once mighty armed forces in a matter of hours. Not that the Voidborn had needed any of that weaponry when they had arrived on Earth. They had simply activated a control signal that instantly reduced people across the planet to nothing more than mindless slaves. Sam and his friends were still no closer to figuring out how to reverse that process and deep down Sam was beginning to doubt that they ever would. Despite the intensity with which they had fought the Voidborn, they all knew their victories amounted to little more than pinpricks as far as the Voidborn fleet that controlled the rest of the planet was concerned. They may have won a couple of battles, but it felt like they were still a very long way from winning the war.

As Sam approached the entrance to the lab, Dr. Stirling suddenly came dashing through the door with a deep frown on his face. He caught sight of Sam and hurried over to him.

"Sam, I need to speak to the Servant immediately. Could you summon her for me?"

"Of course," Sam replied. "What's wrong?"

"It's probably easier if I just show you," Stirling said. "Come with me."

"I was actually just trying to get everyone together," Sam said. "There's something I need to tell you all. Can it wait?"

"No," Stirling said, his frown growing deeper, "I don't think it can."

Sam saw something he had never seen in Stirling's eyes before, something that suddenly made him very nervous indeed.

Stirling headed back inside the lab, beckoning for Sam to follow. Sam gave a silent mental command as he headed into the brightly lit interior and a moment later a shimmering cloud of glowing golden dust appeared in the air beside him. Within seconds, the swirling vortex solidified into the shape of a tall woman with metallic skin and glowing yellow eyes.

"How may I assist you, Illuminate?" the Servant asked, falling into step beside Sam as they both followed Stirling through the lab toward an area of the room that was curtained off.

"It's Doctor Stirling," Sam replied as the old man pushed the curtain aside and stepped through into the area beyond. "He needs your help with something."

"What is the nature of his problem?" the Servant asked calmly.

"I have no idea," Sam said, heading through the curtains, "but I think we're about to find out."

Lying on beds along the far wall were four enslaved humans that had been brought there from one of the countless thousands of buildings around London that now served as dormitories—or perhaps, more accurately, storage facilities—for the dormant masses. They were cared for and fed by the Voidborn under Sam's control, only rousing from their unconscious state to carry out the bidding of their alien masters. The rest of the time they remained in a comatose state, lying in endless rows, awaiting the next command. Stirling had never stopped working on finding a way to reverse the process and free them from Voidborn control, but he had made no real progress. Whatever it was that the aliens had done to take control of people all over the globe, it was beyond the capacity of human technology to understand it, let alone fix it.

The four enslaved people were secured by waist straps to the beds, and they writhed and twisted slowly and silently, as if in the grasp of some agonizing torture.

"What's happening to them?" Sam asked Stirling quietly, deeply disturbed by the unsettling way the people in front of him were moving. Their hands clawed at the air above their beds, their backs arching against their restraints and their legs slowly kicking under the sheets, almost as if they were trying to fight off some invisible attacker in slow motion.

"I have no idea," Stirling said, shaking his head. "It started a few minutes ago. Here, look at their faces."

Sam moved nearer to the closest victim, a young woman, feeling the hairs on the back of his neck stand up as he looked down at her face. He was met with a gaze of pure, undiluted terror, her mouth fixed in a silent scream. Her wide-open eyes were a perfect jet black.

"Is this happening everywhere?" Sam asked. "Are all the Sleepers like this?"

"That was exactly my question for the Servant," Stirling replied.

Sam glanced over at the Servant, who stood in silence for a moment before speaking.

"Drone interface complete. This phenomenon is spreading across the city," the Servant announced. "At current rates the entire human population under my care will be affected within seven minutes."

Sam suddenly felt a cold pit open up in his stomach as he stared into the woman's blank eyes.

"Tell me this isn't the Vore," Sam said. "Tell me they're not changing."

The Servant walked over and placed a hand on the woman's shoulder.

"I detect no trace of the Illuminate weapon that created the Vore," the Servant replied.

"You're sure?" Sam asked. They couldn't afford to make a mistake. The Vore had completely overrun Edinburgh and only a tiny handful of people had escaped. A single bite from those creatures was enough to spread the infection and start the victim's inevitable transformation into one of the Vore. If the same thing happened in London . . .

"Yes," the Servant replied, "though I can offer no explanation as to what is affecting these humans in this way."

"Whatever it is, we have to assume it is more than an autonomous response," Stirling said, gesturing over to one of the other beds where a man was lying, clawing at the air. Attached to his scalp was a grid of adhesive pads with wires trailing from them. These wires were plugged into a complicated-looking machine on a trolley.

"I had this patient hooked up to the EEG machine so that I could monitor his brain activity," Stirling said. He typed something on the keyboard below the monitor and tapped the waveforms that appeared on the screen. "This is the normal activity we saw in the Sleepers until just a few minutes ago. This is similar to the activity one might see in a coma victim or someone under the effects of a general anesthetic. This," he said, pulling up another window, "is this man's current brain activity." The gentle waves that had been displayed a moment before were gone, replaced by a jagged sawtooth pattern. "This is the sort of activity one would normally associate with a fully conscious person who is experiencing extreme trauma."

"So they're awake?" Sam asked, looking down at the man's agonized expression. There was no hint that he had any awareness of his surroundings.

"Not in the traditional sense," Stirling replied. "Their brains are experiencing the nearest thing to consciousness that I have seen since the invasion, but exactly *what* they're experiencing . . . I have no idea."

"So this could be happening everywhere?" Sam asked. "I mean, all over the world?"

"I don't know," Stirling said. "The Servant lost her connection to the rest of the Voidborn consciousness when you assumed control of the first Mothership. The only way to know for sure is to see for ourselves."

"Then we should go and take a look," Sam said. "We need to know if this is a localized attack or part of something bigger. We also need to know if there's anything we can do to help the Sleepers in the meantime. We may not understand what's happening to them, but you only have to look at them to see it's something horrible. Is there anything you can do right now? Maybe put them back to sleep somehow?"

"I can't risk sedation," Stirling replied. "If I try to return them to their previous resting state without knowing what's happening to them, I risk doing more harm than good. Neurological conditions, as a rule, do not lend themselves to quick fixes, I'm afraid."

"Okay, do what you can," Sam said, feeling a creeping sense of dread as he stared at the figures lying on their beds, writhing in silent agony. "We can't leave them like this, that's for sure, and I don't even want to think about what might happen if all seventy million frightened Sleepers woke up at once."

"Of course," Stirling replied with a nod. "I will inform you of any progress that I make in my investigations."

"Stay here and give Doctor Stirling whatever help he needs," Sam said, turning to the Servant. "I'll go and fill the others in on the situation."

"Understood," the Servant replied.

Sam hurried back through the curtain and out of the lab building, feeling an all-too-familiar sense of frustration at the fact that they were still no closer to comprehending exactly what it was the Voidborn were doing here on Earth. The alien creatures had seemed content to leave London unmolested since Sam had taken control of the first Mothership during an intense battle in the skies above the city. Sam and the others had breathed a huge sigh of relief, but he still couldn't shake a nagging feeling that they weren't so much being avoided as ignored. They had no clue what the alien invaders were doing anywhere else in the world and, truthfully, the Voidborn forces under Sam's control in London were no match for the fleet of ships their enemy still had stationed across the rest of the planet. Sam knew that they couldn't afford to lose hope, but there were times when the scale of the task that confronted them seemed too vast to comprehend.

He walked through the doors leading to the accommodation area and followed the corridor beyond to the common room. His friends, the last free humans on Earth—at least as far as they knew—were sitting around the room. Anne and Will sat on one side studying a printed circuit diagram spread out on the table in front of them. Will was looking slightly confused as Anne ran a finger over the drawing and explained something quietly to him. Liz and Nat were on the other side of the room, chatting to each other as they busily cleaned the components of the field-stripped assault rifles that lay on a cloth on the low table in front of them. The two best friends were as inseparable as ever. Jack and Jay were sitting on one of the motley assortment of scavenged sofas arranged in the center of the room. Jack punched Jay gently in the arm and laughed as he finished telling him yet another of his terrible, slightly smutty jokes.

Sam stood for a moment and listened to them talking and laughing with the easy familiarity of people who have been through hell together and lived to tell the tale. It was hard to believe that he had only met them all just over a year ago; now they felt like his brothers and sisters.

"Everyone's here," Jay said, standing up and walking toward him.

"Thanks," Sam said. "Listen, I'm sorry I didn't talk to you about this before. It's just . . . well . . . it's difficult."

"Ah, don't worry about it," Jay said with a crooked smile. "I might have overreacted a bit. I'm just worried about you. At first I thought you were upset about what happened to Rachel. I know how close you were. I loved her too. But that's not what's bothering you, is it?"

"I'll explain everything in a minute, I promise," Sam said, "but something else is happening that we need to talk about first."

"Something bad?" Jay asked.

"It's definitely looking that way. Come on."

Sam walked over to the middle of the room and waited a few seconds for the others to fall silent.

"Morning, guys," he said. "I've just spoken to Doctor Stirling and—"

Sam stopped and gave a startled gasp, his eyes widening and his head tipping back as he dropped to his knees, his arms going limp at his sides. His mouth flew open and an unearthly howl of agony burst forth. His eyes flared with a bright blue light that spread like a web, first across his face and then down his neck. The others looked on in horror as Sam tipped forward and fell to the ground face-first. Jay rushed over to him and gently rolled him over. The bright blue light was fading from Sam's unconscious, vacant eyes. His hair was completely gone, replaced by a pattern of thick cranial ridges covered with glowing blue lines that ran all the way back from the corners of his eyes and over the sides of his pale-skinned skull.

"What the hell is happening?" Will stared down at Sam as the others, still in shock, gathered around their friend's prone body.

"I've got no idea," Jay said, fear creeping into his voice. "Somebody needs to go and get Stirling, NOW!"

Nat sprinted out of the room as Anne knelt beside Jay and looked into Sam's eyes. She turned her head to one side and put her cheek just above his open mouth.

"Oh God, he's not breathing," she said, her hands flying to Sam's limp wrist. "I've got no pulse either. Will, start compressions."

Anne placed her mouth over Sam's as Will pushed Jay aside and dropped to his knees, lacing his fingers together over the center of Sam's chest. He began to count rhythmically while he pressed down hard on Sam's sternum. Jay backed away, giving Anne and Will room to work. Of all the people in the room, they were the ones that Stirling had given the most extensive medical training to; there was nothing Jay could do for Sam right now that they couldn't do better.

"Still nothing," Anne said after thirty seconds, an unmistakable note of panic in her voice. "Keep going."

"Why does he look like that?" Jack asked, staring at Sam with a bewildered expression. "What's happened to him?"

"Yeah, Mag." Jay turned toward her, his features twisted. "Any idea why Sam suddenly looks just like one of the Illuminate? Is this what he was going to tell us? Is this the secret you've been keeping?"

"Yes," Mag said quietly. "It happened in Tokyo when we were fighting Talon. He made me promise not to tell anyone."

Jay thought back to the final battle between them and the insane Illuminate warrior. In the last moments of the fight, something had happened to Sam and he had transformed briefly into the cloud state that the Illuminate could choose to shift into. Jay had asked Sam about it afterward, but Sam had insisted it was just a one-time thing, some strange power his father, the only other living member of the Illuminate race, had passed on to him at the moment of his death. Clearly, whatever it was that Suran had given him, the transfer had been more permanent than Sam had been prepared to admit.

"God damn it, where's Stirling?" Jay hissed, seeing a panicked glance pass between Anne and Will as they fought to save his best friend's life.

It wasn't until nearly a minute later that the doors to the common room flew open and Stirling and Nat sprinted through. Stirling ran over and placed the large plastic case he'd been carrying on the floor next to Sam's body. His frown deepened as he saw the transformation Sam had undergone.

"Anything?" Stirling asked as he popped the clasps on the case. Anne just shook her head in reply.

"Okay, everyone stand back," Stirling barked, pulling the defibrillator paddles from the case, which gave a high-pitched whine as the machine began its brief charging cycle.

"Clear!" Stirling yelled as he placed the paddles in what he hoped was the correct position on Sam's chest. If the physical change he'd undergone had affected his internal organs in any way, there was no guarantee that the shock wouldn't do more harm than good, but they were fast running out of options. Anne and Will leapt back from Sam, and Stirling pulled the triggers on the handles. Sam's body jerked, his back arching up off the floor as the machine tried to shock his heart back into its normal rhythm. Anne quickly grabbed Sam's wrist again while Stirling pulled the paddles clear.

"No pulse," Anne said, her voice cracking with emotion.

Stirling gave a nod and glanced at the display inside the case, silently willing the machine to recharge more quickly.

"Charging . . . charging . . . charging . . . clear!"

Sam's body convulsed again.

"Nothing," Anne said, tears welling up in her eyes as once again she vainly searched for any sign of a pulse.

"Come on, Sam," Stirling muttered under his breath as the defibrillator ran through its charging cycle yet again. "Not after everything you've been through, not like this."

The charging display lit up.

"Clear!"

There was a sudden explosion of blue light and a concussive wave that plunged the room into darkness and blew everything away from Sam's body, people and furniture flying through the air. Seconds later the room was bright blue, lit by the glow of an energy field that cocooned Sam within a crackling dome. Jay was the first to his feet and he ran back toward Sam, the crackling of the field intensifying as he approached.

"Jacob! No!" Stirling yelled.

Jay was two yards away when a bolt of energy shot from the dome's surface and struck him squarely in the center of his chest, hurling him backward with a crunch onto the splintered remains of a chair. Mag ran over to where he had landed, being sure to stay a safe distance from the shimmering dome in the center of the room. Jay gave a pained groan as the others began picking themselves up off the ground.

"Are you all right?" Mag asked, squatting beside him.

"That really hurt," Jay croaked, sitting up. He looked slightly pale but otherwise none the worse for wear.

"Is everyone else okay?" Stirling yelled as the others slowly got to their feet. They all appeared to be relatively unharmed, barring some scratches and bruises. Stirling cautiously approached the humming energy field, listening carefully as, once again, the crackling sound started to rise in pitch.

"Right, so that's near enough, is it?" Stirling muttered to himself, before turning and addressing the others. "Nobody get any closer to this thing. You all saw what happened to Jacob."

Stirling peered through the translucent surface of the glowing bubble. He watched for several long seconds and was finally relieved to see Sam's chest rise just a fraction and then fall again. His breathing was shallow, but at least he *was* breathing.

"What is that thing?" Jack asked, his face lit up by the glow from the field.

Without warning, the Servant appeared from thin air, her body simply materializing from within a swirling golden cloud of Voidborn nanites. She walked toward the field and it discharged again, sending a bright blue arc lancing between the surface of the glowing dome and her chest. The Servant continued to advance, the coruscating beam of energy dancing across her torso as she placed a single hand on the field, apparently unconcerned by the assault. A few seconds later she removed her hand from the field and walked back toward Stirling.

"Please do not approach me," the Servant said calmly. "The outer shell of this configuration is currently at a temperature of seven hundred and forty-nine kelvin."

She was standing several yards away from him, but Stirling could indeed feel the heat radiating off her body.

"I detected a surge of unprecedented power with an unknown quantum signature," the Servant said. "The energy field currently surrounding the Illuminate would appear to be responsible."

The Servant had referred to Sam as the Illuminate since they had first encountered her, but this was the first time that the name appeared to be a true match for his physical form.

"Unknown signature?" Stirling asked, frowning. "So this isn't something created by Illuminate technology?"

"I no longer have access to any of the Voidborn data archives on Illuminate technology. I cannot tell you whether this is a phenomenon that the Voidborn encountered prior to the point at which I was severed from their collective consciousness."

"In other words, you have no idea," Anne said, staring at the glowing bubble.

"That is correct," the Servant replied. "I do know that none of the technology on board either of the vessels under the Illuminate's control is capable of breaching a force field of this power."

"So we're not getting in there anytime soon," Jay said. "There's something I need you to tell me: do you know what happened to Sam in Tokyo too? Why he looks that way?"

"I am forbidden from discussing that subject with you," the Servant replied.

"Forbidden?" Jack said. "Forbidden by who exactly?"

"The Illuminate," the Servant replied calmly.

"There's no point trying to get anything out of you, then," Jay said, as he stood up with a wary glance at the crackling energy field surrounding his friend. He turned and pointed at Mag. "So it looks like it's up to you to fill us in."

"Look, I don't know much more than you do," Mag said, holding her hands up in front of herself defensively. "I knew something had happened to him in Tokyo. I could smell it on him. It's hard to explain really, but I knew that something was different about him."

"She's right, Jay," Nat said. "We all saw it. Sam wasn't the same when he came back from Japan. He didn't talk to anyone as much as he used to and he started spending a lot more time on his own. I just put it down to what happened to Rachel and finding out the truth about his dad, but . . . well . . . looks like there might have been a bit more to it than that."

"Well, we all knew he had absorbed some of the

Illuminate abilities from his father in Tokyo," Stirling said. "He told us that was ultimately how he was able to defeat Talon, but he insisted he had lost all access to those abilities as soon as that fight was won. I gave him a thorough physical examination when he returned and he appeared completely normal. It's starting to look like he may have retained access to those abilities after all."

"I ended up following him when he left the compound a couple of weeks ago," Mag said. "He told me he was going out on a scouting run to check on a couple of the Sleeper dormitories on the other side of the river, but I could tell he was lying. I was worried about him, so I followed him to a warehouse a few miles away and caught him without his mask on, so to speak. He made me promise not to tell anyone. He didn't understand what was happening to him and he was scared about how you might all react if you saw him like this." She waved a hand toward the energy bubble. "I know what it's like to feel like that, so I agreed. He knew he couldn't keep it a secret from you guys forever; in fact, he was about to tell all of you about what had happened to him. That's why he wanted to get everyone together, but then this thing with the Doc, whatever it was, came up and he never got the chance."

"You should have told us," Jay said angrily, "both of you. I don't like being lied to, especially by people I thought I could trust. We might have been able to help him, to stop this from happening if we'd known, but now it's too late, isn't it?"

"I told him that," Mag replied. "I didn't make the decision not to tell anyone, so don't make this my fault."

"Well, I don't see anyone else to blame around here," Jay said with a nasty edge in his voice. "Unless there is someone else who's responsible and you've decided to keep it a secret from us. Who knows?"

"That's not fair!" Mag snapped back. "Maybe you should ask yourself why he decided not to tell you if you're such a good friend to him."

"What's that supposed to mean?"

"Stop it, both of you!" Liz said. "This isn't helping anyone."

"Elizabeth is quite right," Stirling said calmly. "You can argue about the rights and wrongs of the situation later. Our priority now is to understand what has happened to Sam. It seems more than coincidental that this should have occurred at the same time as the Sleepers becoming so agitated."

"Agitated?" Jay said. "What do you mean?"

"Are they waking up?" Liz asked, sounding surprised.

"No, it's more complicated than that," Stirling said. "It'll be easier to show you all than explain, but we'll get to that shortly. Let's deal with Sam first."

"Damn right," Jay said. "We can worry about the Sleepers later."

"I agree," Liz said. "We can't leave Sam like this. We've got no idea what's happening to him in there. We have to help him before . . ." Her voice trailed off as she stared nervously at the humming energy bubble that surrounded their friend.

Stirling looked down at the unconscious boy trapped inside the blue force field. His face was still recognizable as the young man he had come to know and respect over the past couple of years, but there was no way of knowing if the person inside the body would be the same. Mag was right: he had been more withdrawn over the past couple of months, but Stirling had just put that down to posttraumatic stress, an understandable consequence of the desperate final battle with the Illuminate warrior Talon. Now he had to consider the possibility that there might be more sinister reasons for Sam's behavior. Was Sam still really Sam at all?

"Clearly we can't move him," Stirling said, "so the best we can do for now is monitor him in situ and hope that his condition doesn't worsen."

"And if it does?" Anne asked.

Stirling glanced in her direction. The look on his face was the only answer she needed.

2

"I'm going outside," Liz said, shaking her head. "It's horrible. I can't see them like this."

The floor of the warehouse below was covered with the bodies of hundreds of people lying in neatly ordered rows, all writhing in agony. The only noise was the soft scraping of their clothes against the ground, the horrified expressions on their open-mouthed faces made all the more terrible by their complete silence.

"I know what she means," Jay said as Liz walked out of the building. "I thought I'd seen some pretty nasty stuff over the past couple of years, but this . . . this is grim. You're saying they're like this everywhere?"

"Indeed. This is happening all over the city," Stirling said. "I've asked the Servant to dispatch Drones to some of the other dormitories further out, but I suspect they will find exactly the same thing there. I fear this could be a global phenomenon."

"Liz is right, this is horrible. I mean, it was bad enough when they were just lying there," Nat said. "God, these poor people."

"We can't really be sure if they're suffering or not; there's no scientific way of knowing what they're experiencing," Stirling said.

"Oh, come on, Doc," Jack snapped. "Look at them! You don't need PhDs coming out of your ears to see what they're going through."

"I understand the frustration you feel, but there's a reason I brought you all here. Unfortunately, the situation might be worse than we first thought," Stirling said with a sigh.

"Worse than this?" Anne said. "Seriously?"

"I'm afraid so," Stirling replied. "As you're aware, the Sleepers are fed and hydrated intravenously on a daily basis by the Voidborn Drones." He gestured toward the machine at the far end of the warehouse that would normally have had a line of mute people waiting to place an arm inside and receive their precise daily requirement of nutrients and fluids. "However, the Servant is reporting that the Sleepers have stopped responding to even the simple mental commands that the Motherships under our control can give. Simply put, two weeks from now, every single one of these people will have died from dehydration."

The others all turned and looked at Stirling as the enormity of what he had just told them began to sink in.

"There must be something we can do," Nat said. "If this is happening everywhere, then that means . . . Oh God."

"There were at least nine million people in London at the time of the invasion," Stirling said. "Even with the resources of both Motherships under our control, there's no way we could administer the feeding solution manually to that many people, and if this *is* happening globally . . . well, I'm sure I don't need to paint a more detailed picture for you."

"How can you stay so calm about this?" Jay snapped angrily. "We could be talking about extinction here. Why would the Voidborn do this now? Why keep all these people alive for two years and then just suddenly decide they're going to let them die like this? Why would they do that? It doesn't make any sense."

"I'm afraid I don't have answers to those questions, Jacob," Stirling replied. "And since you ask, I'm staying calm because we may be the only chance these people have, so we really can't afford to panic. I am working with the Servant to try to isolate the reason for this change in the Sleepers' behavior, but the truth is, we're struggling to find an explanation."

"And you think this has something to do with whatever's happened to Sam?" Anne asked.

"It may just be a coincidence," Stirling replied, "but the

fact that both events were concurrent suggests that, yes, there may indeed be a link. The statistical chances of them being unrelated events are slim."

They had left Sam under the watchful eye of the Servant while they visited the Sleeper dormitory. It had been several hours since he'd been encased in the energy field and there had, as yet, been no signs of any change in his condition.

"I'm going to find Liz," Jay said. "I've had enough of unanswered questions for one day, thanks."

He stalked away down the raised gantry and out through the fire exit that Liz had gone through a couple of minutes earlier. His head was telling him that Stirling was right and they had to stay calm, but his gut was telling him to go and find something to shoot. He saw Liz sitting on a low brick wall on the far side of the roof.

"Sorry, couldn't handle that," Liz said, giving Jay a weak smile as he approached.

"Yeah, well, 'fraid it got worse," he said, sitting down beside her. He quickly explained the situation that Stirling had described and what it meant for the Sleepers.

"Are we ever going to catch a break?" Liz asked with a sigh. "Sometimes I just want to give up. Between this and what's happened to Sam . . ."

"Yeah, know what you mean," Jay said, running his hand across his dreadlocks. "Every time I think we're finally getting somewhere and that maybe we can take the fight to the Voidborn, something like this happens. It's as if someone's trying to remind us how insignificant we are, even with those things under our control." He pointed up at the two massive Voidborn Motherships floating above them. "I'm still trying to get my head around it. In a couple of weeks we could be the last nine people on Earth, and I don't know about you, but I can't see any way to stop it." He put his head in his hands.

"Stirling and the Servant will come up with something," Liz said, placing a hand on his shoulder. "They always do."

"Maybe, but what if they don't and the whole planet just ends up becoming a mass grave? What then?"

"I don't really want to think about that at the moment, Jay," Liz said.

"Hey, you two!" Nat yelled as she stuck her head out the doorway on the other side of the roof. "Drop-ship's taking us back to the compound in two minutes."

"Come on, let's go," Liz said.

"Sure, just give me a minute," Jay replied, staring up at the Motherships.

"Okay, see you down there." Liz ran across the roof and disappeared through the door.

Jay stood there for a moment, watching as Voidborn drop-ships buzzed around the massive vessels far above, like insects around some kind of giant animal. They were lit with the yellow lights that indicated they were under the control of the Servant and therefore ultimately answered to Sam's commands. He thought back to the first desperate days after the initial invasion, before he'd met Stirling and the others. He'd just been a scared kid back then, not the soldier he'd become, the guy who liked to make out that nothing scared him. He thought about the prospect of standing in that very same spot two weeks from now, humanity all but extinct if what Stirling was telling them was right, the city around him little more than a mausoleum. In that instant, he could feel the kid that he had buried deep inside a long time ago trying to fight his way back to the surface again. The boy who'd lost his family, the boy who'd watched the world go to hell, the boy who'd spent so many weeks desperately fighting simply to survive.

"Come on, Sam, wake up," Jay whispered to the air. "We need you, buddy."

The drop-ship touched down in the center of the compound, its boarding ramp slowly lowering to the ground. Jay was first out the hatch and he quickly made his way to the accommodation block, eager to get an update on Sam's condition from the Servant. He entered the common room and was disappointed to see that the force field surrounding his friend was still very much in place.

"Any change?" he asked the Servant as he walked across the room toward her.

"There has been no change in the Illuminate's

condition," the Servant replied. "I have conducted further tests of the field surrounding him, but I am still unable to discern its energetic architecture or point of origin."

"You mean, it may not be generated locally?" Stirling asked as he came and stood next to Jay. "I assumed that Sam was generating it himself somehow."

"That was my initial assumption too, but I cannot determine how the Illuminate would be able to generate the level of power necessary."

"Seems like there's quite a lot we don't understand about Sam at the moment," Jay said, watching his friend's chest slowly rise and fall on the other side of the impenetrable barrier.

"Indeed," Stirling replied. "And have you made any progress in determining what's blocking your control of the Sleepers?"

"No. It would appear that whatever signal is being used to cause the change in their condition is vastly more powerful than the one the Motherships can produce. The origin point of that signal is impossible to determine precisely, but its strength would indicate that it is being broadcast across the planet."

"So whatever's happening to the Sleepers is global," Jay said.

"As far as I can determine, yes," the Servant replied.

"So what the hell do we do about it?" Jay asked, his frustration clear.

"The first priority has to be working out where this new signal is being broadcast from," Stirling replied. "The only way we can hope to stop whatever's happening to the Sleepers is if we cut it off at the source."

"I believe that it may be possible if we were to relocate the second Mothership and more accurately attempt to—"

The Servant was cut off by a loud crackle from behind her as the bubble of energy that surrounded Sam vanished just as suddenly as it had appeared. Sam slowly rose to his feet, his eyes closed and his chin resting on his chest.

"Sam," Jay said, approaching his friend. "Are you okay?"

Sam didn't reply; he simply lifted his head and opened his eyes, eyes that now burned with a bright blue energy that pulsed through the glowing trails running back over his skull. Jay frowned and took another step forward, raising a hand toward Sam's shoulder. Sam moved impossibly quickly, his closed fist whipping through the air and connecting with Jay's chin with a crack, sending him flying across the room. The Servant glanced at the fallen boy and then back at Sam as he began to walk toward her.

"Illuminate, I do not—"

That was all she had time to say before Sam reached out and placed a hand against the side of her head. The Servant's mouth flew open in a silent scream and then she disintegrated into a cloud of glowing yellow particles that drifted slowly to the ground.

"What are you doing, Sam?" Stirling demanded as he backed away. He looked hard for any trace of the boy he knew, but there was no emotion in Sam's face; his weirdly glowing eyes were impossible to read. He did not reply; he simply stared at Stirling for a moment and then turned and strode purposefully toward the door leading outside.

Stirling hurried over to Jay and rolled him onto his back. There was a bright red mark on his jaw, and blood trickled from a split in his lip. He was out cold. Stirling felt a chill run down his spine. Whoever that boy was now, he wasn't the Sam they all knew, that much was obvious. He got up and ran after him, following him out into the compound.

"Sam!" Mag shouted from the other side of the yard, seeing her friend walking toward her. Her grin of delight quickly faded when she saw the panicked look on Stirling's face as he burst out the door behind Sam. Nat and Jack looked up from the scavenged supplies they were sorting into piles on the ground and saw Sam draw to a halt in the center of the open area, tip his head back, and stare intensely at the Mothership hovering overhead.

"Don't go near him!" Stirling yelled as Sam's friends started toward him. "Stay back!"

Stirling made his way over to where Mag was standing, giving Sam a wide berth.

"What's the matter with him?" Mag asked, staring at Sam as he stood motionless and silent twenty yards away.

“I don’t know,” Stirling replied, “but he just knocked Jacob unconscious and did *something* to the Servant. I don’t think he has any control over his actions.”

“Is Jay okay?” Nat asked.

“As far as I can tell,” Stirling replied. “Go and find Will and tell him what’s happened. He has the most medical training.”

Nat gave a quick nod and ran to the laboratory building.

“Sam! Can you hear me?” Mag yelled, taking a couple of steps closer to him. Suddenly, Sam’s whole body seemed to flare with searing blue light and a bolt of lightning shot into the air, striking the Mothership far overhead and sending waves of energy rippling across its underside. Moments later, a drop-ship swooped down toward the compound, its hull glowing with the same strange blue light that pulsed across Sam’s skin. It landed in the middle of the courtyard, kicking up clouds of dust, its hatch sliding open and boarding ramp descending as Sam approached it, his expression blank.

“Sam!” Mag yelled again. “What are you doing?”

He offered no response as he strode up the ramp and into the drop-ship. Mag ran toward it, watching helplessly as the ramp retracted, the hatch slid shut, and the aircraft rose into the air, beyond her reach. It banked and accelerated into the clear blue sky, disappearing from view in seconds. And just like that, Sam was gone.

* * *

Nat walked over to the sofa, where Anne was shining a pen-sized torch into each of Jay's eyes in turn.

"Is he okay?" Nat asked, as the rest of the group filed into the common room.

"Yeah, he'll live," Anne said. "Just a bit of wounded pride, I reckon."

"Feel like I got sucker-punched by a Grendel," Jay groaned, rubbing his aching jaw.

"I can't believe Sam did that to you," Nat said, shaking her head and sitting down next to him on the sofa.

"Whoever that was, it wasn't Sam," Jay replied. "Because, quite aside from anything else, he punches like a girl."

"Hey!" Liz said, frowning. "Want me to come over there and show you how hard a girl can really punch?"

"Sorry, no offense," Jay replied with a crooked half-smile, "but you know what I mean."

"I think the whole glowing blue head thing and firing off lightning bolts everywhere might be a clue that he wasn't quite himself too," Jack said. "You know?"

"Our most pressing concern is trying to work out exactly where he's gone," Stirling said, rubbing his eyes. "I don't believe for a moment that he was in control of his actions here today. If we accept that that's true, the next most pressing question must be: who *is* controlling him?"

"Out in the courtyard, he looked like . . . well . . . he looked like a Walker," Jack said. Before their victory over the Voidborn, enslaved humans had wandered the streets of London doing their alien masters' bidding. There was no denying the similarities between their blank-faced obedience and Sam's recent behavior.

"You don't think something went wrong with his implant, do you?" Anne asked nervously. "That somehow the Voidborn have regained control of him?" All of them had been subjected to the same experiments when they were infants, implanted with devices that used hybrid Voidborn and human technology to block the signal that had enslaved the rest of the planet. Stirling had worked alongside Sam's father on the technology and the implants were the only reason Sam and his friends had been able to resist and fight back. If those implants were now failing for some reason, Sam wouldn't be the only one affected. Who would be next?

"I don't think so," Stirling said, pacing back and forth across the room as he often did when his brain was distracted with solving a particularly vexing problem. "If that were the case, then it's reasonable to assume we would all have fallen under their control. Sam's implant is, however, quite unique. His father built the prototype—my input was limited because, quite frankly, I had only a basic understanding of the nanotechnology he was using. I thought at the time it was simply because he was a genius, but now of course I understand that he was using Illuminate technology without my knowledge. It could be that there was something different about Sam's implant, something that Daniel didn't tell me. It would be just one more lie to add to the long list of those he told me."

"So, if it's not the Voidborn controlling him, who is?" Jay asked with a frown.

"That, Jacob," Stirling replied, "is what I believe they call the 'million dollar question.' "

Sam woke with a start, standing bolt upright in a darkened room, his head spinning. His last memory was of standing in front of his friends in the resistance compound, and now he was somewhere else entirely, with no memory of how on earth he'd got there.

"Where the hell am I?" Sam said to himself, taking in his surroundings. The room was filled with desks and dead workstations, and at the far end was a large window that filled almost the entire wall and through which came a dim, gray light. Sam's nose wrinkled as he sniffed the air; the unmistakable sickly sweet stench of death and decay hung heavily. It was a smell that he had gotten all too used to over the past couple of years. Not everyone who had been enslaved by the Voidborn control signal had been able to make their way to one of the dormitories, and Sam had found enough bodies around London to know what this odor meant. People had died here, and not that long ago by the smell of it. He headed for the window and looked through the glass into the cavernous space beyond.

Light was pouring in through a huge opening at the far side of a vast chamber; below him a submarine was floating in a long channel of water that led out to the sea beyond. It sat at an awkward angle in the water, listing heavily to one side. The five other docks that filled the huge room beyond were empty. Sam had seen this place before: it was the submarine base at Faslane that Talon had used as his base of operations when he had been going by the name of Mason, his true Illuminate identity hidden by his people's shape-shifting abilities. At the time the facility had bustled with activity, filled with Mason's men, all carrying implants that supposedly protected them from the Voidborn control signal. They had later discovered that it didn't block the control signal, merely adjusted it to put the men under Talon's control instead. Now the place was deserted, the foul smell hanging in the air suggesting that whoever was left here was not going to be coming to meet him.

"How on earth did I get to Scotland?" Sam asked the dust-filled air around him. A flare of blue light was reflected in the glass of the window as the veins of energy running back over his skull began to pulse. Sam stared at his reflection, willing his face back into its more human form, but nothing happened; the boy staring back at him was still very much the Illuminate-human hybrid that he had gone to such lengths to conceal from his friends. He had wanted them to see this, his real face now, but he had also wanted to explain what had happened to him, something he had clearly not been able to do.

Sam.

The voice seemed to come from nowhere, but he wasn't hearing it: it was *inside* his head, like a whispered thought. Sam turned around quickly, scanning the room, but there was no one there, just the dark shapes of the dormant equipment that filled the room.

Sam, it's me.

"Dad?" Sam said, his eyes widening in surprise. It couldn't be; his father had died in front of him.

In a sense, yes, the voice replied, its whisper like an itch inside his skull that he couldn't scratch. *We don't have much time. I . . . we need your help.*

"My father is dead," Sam said, still scanning the room for any clue as to where the voice might be coming from.

I know I am, the voice replied, *and now I need your help or billions more will die, just like me.*

"I don't know who you are," Sam replied, "but whoever you are, you're not him. What do you want? Why have you brought me here? More to the point, *how* did I get here?"

You were summoned here.

"Summoned here? What's that supposed to mean?"

I was forced to subvert your will; you were given an

irresistible mental imperative to come to this place. How exactly you did that I do not know, other than the fact that you arrived here in a Voidborn vessel.

"So you kidnapped me?" Sam asked, feeling a creeping sense of unease.

It would be more accurate to say that you kidnapped yourself, the voice replied.

This is a trap, Sam thought.

This is not a trap, the voice replied. Sam's bewilderment increased as he realized that whoever it was he'd been talking to had just plucked that thought straight from his head. *If I had wished to harm you, I could have done so at any point during your journey to this place.*

"Well, you didn't give me much choice about coming here," Sam said, "so why not just force me to help you?"

What I have to show you, I need you to see with your own eyes and with an open mind, the voice replied.

"Okay, then, show me," Sam said. "Let's see what's so important you had to drag me up here."

Head down to the submarine pens, the voice replied. *I'll tell you what you need to do when you get there.*

Sam went over to the door and made his way down the stairs. He opened the door at the bottom and winced at the putrid smell in the room beyond. Over a dozen bodies lay on the cots of the makeshift dormitory next to the pens: Talon's men who had been left in Faslane when the bulk of his forces had traveled to London with him and

Sam. Once Talon had died, the men he had left here would have received no further orders, including the ones to eat and drink. Sam was just glad that they wouldn't have known what was happening to them. It was a stark reminder of what would happen to the Sleepers if the Voidborn were to stop caring for them.

Sam put his hand over his nose and mouth in a futile effort to protect his newly enhanced senses from the stench. He hurried through the room, grateful to pass through the heavy steel doors on the other side and step out into the cool, relatively fresh air of an enormous maintenance workshop. Suspended from a massive supporting framework was the black bulk of a partially disassembled submarine, hanging in the middle of the space like some kind of huge disemboweled beast.

Sam made his way across the workshop toward the massive doors that led to the submarine pen, the noisy echoes of his footsteps bouncing off the bare concrete walls and ceiling. He was approaching the suspended submarine, when he heard a clang. He froze in place, his ears straining, listening for any other sound. Now he could hear nothing but silence. He sniffed. The smell of death hung in the air, but here there was something else, layered beneath the stench of decay. Something about it was horribly familiar.

There was a sudden scratching sound from the other side of the workshop, as if something was running across the concrete floor. Sam dropped low behind one of the pieces of heavy machinery that were scattered around the floor of the maintenance section. He held his breath, trying to make as little noise as possible, but again silence had returned. There was definitely something else here, something alive.

Sam crept slowly forward, moving carefully and quietly from hiding spot to hiding spot, staying low, checking the shadows nearby, his ears still straining for any sign of whatever had made the noise just a minute earlier, before making a dash across the open floor into the shadows beneath the giant machine. He looked up at the gutted warship: masses of cables that would have once formed the vessel's electronic nervous system now dangled uselessly from holes in its belly. As he passed underneath, the odd smell he had noticed before began to get stronger. Suddenly, like a switch flicking inside his head, Sam remembered where he had smelled it before. It wasn't here that he'd encountered that scent, but it was in a nearby city. . . .

Too nearby.

A creature dropped from the hole in the hull of the submarine directly above Sam's head. He barely had time to react, diving to his left as the Vore fell toward him, striking a glancing blow on his shoulder and carving a chunk out of the white Illuminate armor that now covered it. Sam felt a surge of strength as the nanites inside him responded to the adrenaline pumping through his system. At thc same instant, his right arm began to flow and shift, morphing into a foot-and-a-half-long golden blade. The tiny machines that made up that arm were similar to the Illuminate ones that coursed through him, but they were Voidborn in origin, a relic of his first battle with the Voidborn in the skies above London. The Voidborn and the Illuminate may have been enemies for millennia, but at that precise moment their technologies were combining to protect Sam from the monstrous creature that was itself a twisted by-product of corrupt Illuminate technology. Sam didn't really have time to appreciate the irony; he was too busy trying not to get killed.

The Vore circled Sam warily, its dripping jaws opening wide as it hissed at him, the tiny black eyes in the sides of its elongated, misshapen skull blinking slowly as the slime-covered slits of its nose twitched, sniffing the air. It crawled on all floors, its razor-sharp claws scratching on the concrete. Sam raised his arm, holding the golden blade in front of him as he backed away from the slavering once-human monster. The Vore lunged at him with a roar and Sam swung the blade, the hideous creature screaming as the golden weapon struck home. Black blood flew through the air, spraying across the concrete floor, and the Vore tumbled away, thrashing wildly, mortally wounded.

Sam heard another roar from somewhere nearby, his

blood suddenly running cold. The Vore they had encountered in Edinburgh never hunted alone; where there was one there were bound to be more. Sam sprinted toward the doors leading to the submarine pen, but when he was less than twenty yards from them a pair of Vore came running around the corner, barring his route. He raised his weapon, unsure whether the physical advantages that the nanites within his body gave him would be enough to face a pair of the mutated creatures. As he was weighing his odds, three more Vore came charging across the floor of the workshop, joining their brothers in the hissing pack. The group crept toward Sam, sniffing at the still-twitching corpse of his first victim as they passed. Sam slowly backed away, knowing that he probably had only a matter of seconds before the creatures attacked.

He heard a clatter behind him and whirled around to see half a dozen more Vore heading his way. He was surrounded. He looked quickly between the two groups of Vore, his head flicking back and forth as he tried to keep them all in view at once. He made a sudden dash to his left and the Vore reacted instantly, sprinting toward him at inhuman speed. He grabbed a chain dangling from the ceiling, the blade of his right arm morphing back into the shape of a human hand, and the temporary boost of strength to his limbs allowed him to haul his body up toward the metal walkway overhead just as the nearest Vore leapt in his direction. Its claws slashed through the empty air where his dangling legs had been a fraction of a second before, and Sam pulled himself up onto the walkway.

He sprinted along the gantry, heading for a ladder that led up to the top of the curved body of the submarine. The Vore were just seconds behind him, vaulting up into the walkways surrounding the submarine with superhuman agility. Sam didn't dare to look back; he just ran. He reached the bottom of the ladder and scaled it as quickly as possible, taking three rungs at a time. As he stepped onto the curved upper hull of the submarine, the Vore were already scrambling up the massive vessel's curved flanks, their razor-sharp crystalline claws tearing into the steel hull as they climbed.

Sam turned and ran for the conning tower sticking up from the deck fifty feet away. He clambered up the access ladder on its side, the Vore now only a few yards behind him. He reached the top and realized with horror that there were Vore on the walkway above him too. There was nowhere to go. He spun around as the Vore scrambled toward him, and stared into the hole leading down through the conning tower and into the darkness of the submarine below. For all he knew, the interior of the giant vessel could be swarming with Vore, but at the moment it was his only escape route. He hurried through the hatch, slamming it shut behind him as the first of the pursuing Vore climbed over the railing and onto the top of the tower. Sam grabbed hold of the wheel on the underside of the hatch, spinning it in the darkness, sealing the heavy steel door shut. Almost immediately he heard muffled roars of frustration as the Vore started to claw violently at the other side of the hatch.

"Great escape plan, Riley," Sam said to himself, sitting in the pitch black. He heard an ominous crunch above him and a tiny chink of light appeared as the metal that was the only thing separating him from the Vore started to buckle and tear. He felt a sudden sense of panic as he realized that the hatch was not going to hold the Vore back for long. He took a long, deep breath and forced himself to focus past the fear he was feeling. "Calm people live," he said quietly, repeating one of the mantras that Robert Jackson, the ex–Royal Marine who had taught Sam and all of the other members of the resistance to fight, had drilled into him during his training.

He reached out in the blackness, using his sense of touch to build up as accurate a mental map of his surroundings as possible. After a few long seconds of desperate blind searching, he found another hatch in the floor and lifted it up with a protesting screech from its unlubricated hinges. Another ladder led still further into the darkened depths of the vessel. Sam climbed down and quickly descended into a larger space, at least judging by the fact that he couldn't immediately reach out and touch all four walls. He walked into some sort of waist-high counter, swearing under his breath as the corner dug into his thigh. Running his hands along the top of it, he found a large metal object, which felt like a toolbox. He opened the lid and put his hand inside, carefully feeling for anything that might be useful. His fingers closed on a rubberized, cylindrical object and he lifted it out of the box, mouthing a silent prayer to whatever gods might be looking down on him at that precise moment. Sam pressed the stud on the side of the cylinder and the torch he was holding flickered into a feeble half-life. He banged the torch with his other hand, as a thousand preinvasion movies had taught him to do, but disappointingly it refused to get any brighter. In fact, banging it just seemed to make it flicker more. Given that it must have been at least two years since the torch was last turned on, Sam supposed he should just be thankful that it worked at all.

He cast the feeble beam around the room, its weak light illuminating the dust-covered bridge of the vessel. There were no obvious signs of Vore here at least, though judging by the cacophonous sounds of banging from the main hatch above, they were only seconds away from breaking through. Sam moved quickly through the cramped spaces within the submarine, running down corridors that were barely tall enough for a man to stand upright in and past row after row of bunks built into the bulkheads in three-bed stacks. It would have been an oppressive environment at the best of times, but now, in the flickering light of his torch and with two years' worth of dust hanging in the air, it was beyond unsettling.

Again Sam felt a flutter of panic in his belly as he heard the screech of tearing metal from somewhere behind him. He sprinted between the bunks, his heart pounding in his ears so hard that it was making it hard to think. He did his best to push all thoughts of getting trapped with the Vore in that dark, confined space toward the back of his mind and pressed onward, heading toward the prow of the vessel.

There was a sudden loud bang and then the sound of heavy things moving through the darkened compartments somewhere behind him. The Vore were inside. Sam picked up speed, running faster through the gloom and trying to ignore the hissing sounds of the Vore as they raced through the chambers behind him. He came to the final compartment and quickly waved his light around the room, spotting a row of hatches on the far side. He took a deep breath and swung the door behind him closed, spinning the wheel to lock its latches. He shone his torch through the four-inch-wide toughened glass porthole and leapt backward, his eyes suddenly wide with fear as slavering jaws slammed into the glass. A moment later the Vore began their assault on the door, setting it rattling under their superhumanly strong blows.

Sam hurried over to a hatch at the end of one of the long torpedo tubes that ran the length of the chamber and pointed toward the prow of the submarine. He opened it and shone his torch down the polished barrel within. The far end of the torpedo tube was still sealed by its outer waterproofed hatch. There was no way out through there. He checked the second tube, finding exactly the same thing. Behind him, the top corner of the door sealing the compartment from the Vore began to buckle inward as huge claws forced themselves into the gap, ripping and tearing at the metal.

"You're not dying in here, Riley," Sam muttered to himself, trying to suppress the rising tide of panic building in his chest. He moved to the third and last torpedo tube and grabbed the wheel sealing the hatch. He pulled with all his might, but the handle refused to budge. He paused for a moment, took a deep breath, and then tried again, willing the nanites in his hands and arms to boost his strength as far as possible. He felt the wheel move a fraction with a pained screech of corroded metal on metal. Behind him the door almost gave way completely, half hanging off its hinges; the Vore would be inside in seconds. He heaved at the wheel again, yelling out with the exertion as he felt it begin to move, slowly at first, with grinding reluctance, but then more quickly as the metal surfaces separated. He wrenched the tube open and shone his torch inside. The hatch at the far end was sealed.

"Oh God," Sam whispered. There was no way out.

Behind him, the door finally gave way and Sam

scrambled into the tube as the Vore smashed their way inside the chamber. He crawled desperately forward, claws scratching at the lining of the tube just inches from his feet as the Vore tried to squeeze into the narrow space behind him. Sam crawled further forward, feeling the tips of the claws brushing against his feet as he scrambled for a grip on the smooth, polished walls of the tube. He pressed his weight against the sealed hatch at the far end and, to his surprise, fell headlong through it, landing hard on the concrete fifteen feet below and knocking the wind out of his lungs.

Sam lay there for a second, fighting for breath, before he hauled himself painfully to his feet and looked up at the torpedo tube above him. What he had mistaken for the heavy waterproof hatch that normally sealed the tube was actually just a light plastic dustcover taped in place from the outside. He ran toward the heavy armored doors that led to the submarine pen and slapped the large red, mushroom-shaped switch mounted on the wall next to them. Somewhere far below his feet, emergency generators coughed into life, and a blaring klaxon sounded as an orange warning light flashed above the door, which slowly began to inch upward.

"Shut up, shut up, shut up," Sam whispered at the door, glancing over his shoulder at the submarine. Just seconds later the Vore pack poured out of the conning tower, half leaping and half falling to the ground below, before springing to their feet and charging across the room toward him. Sam dropped to his belly and scrambled under the door with barely an inch to spare before leaping to his feet and slapping the identical door switch on the other side. The door juddered back down, hitting the ground with a satisfying thud. Sam leaned back against it and slid to the floor, sitting there for a moment or two and catching his breath, waiting for his heart rate to return to something like normal as the Vore pounded pointlessly on the other side of the six-inch-thick armor.

He looked around the vast space, taking in the scale of the chamber. Once upon a time it would have been a wartime shelter for the UK's fleet of nuclear submarines, buried dozens of yards below the rugged rock of the Scottish coast. Now it felt like a tomb.

"Okay, I'm here," Sam said. "Tell me you didn't know about the Vore."

I do not understand, the voice in his head replied.

"Never mind, I'm here now," Sam said, climbing to his feet. "What do you need me to do?"

Go to the furthest dock from the entrance, the voice replied.

Sam walked the length of the pen, past the listing hulk of the one sub that had been in the pen at the time of the Voidborn invasion. He looked at the name painted on the concrete at the end of the dock: *HMS Victorious*. It represented the pinnacle of human weapon technology and now it sat here rusting, rendered irrelevant in the blink of an eye when the Voidborn arrived. Every movie he'd watched about alien invasions when he was younger had implied that humanity would fight back somehow, even if it ultimately proved futile. The reality had proven far worse.

Sam reached the empty dock at the far end of the room, the black water within still and deep.

"What now?" Sam asked.

In the wall you will see a pair of yellow doors, the voice replied. *Open them*.

Sam walked over to the brightly painted doors and pulled them open. Inside was a bewildering array of switches.

Now I need you to listen very carefully and follow my instructions.

For the next five minutes the voice inside his head that Sam was still reluctant to believe was his father talked him through a complicated procedure of throwing switches and setting dials to the correct position.

Now hit the large red button in the bottom right-hand corner of the panel, the voice instructed.

Sam did as he was told and somewhere below him he heard a rumble, and one by one the floodlights in the roof of the chamber far above lit up and bathed the dock with light.

Now do you see the switch labeled "Evac Pump DD1"?

"Yeah, I see it," Sam said, after scanning the control panel for a few seconds.

Press it.

Sam hit the button. The place was suddenly filled with the sound of blaring klaxons, and yellow warning lights began to flash at the end of the nearest dock. Slowly, a huge metal panel slid up out of the water, locking into position when it was three feet clear of the surface. This was followed by a roaring sound, and the previously calm water of the dock began to churn as it was slowly drained away. As the water level dropped, something began to emerge. At first it looked like the curved white fin of some sort of sea monster rising from the ocean, but a few seconds later it became clear that it was a smooth, curved pylon and Sam could start to make out the pale shape of something large beneath the surface of the churning water. The giant pumps continued their work, draining the dry dock, and slowly, inch by inch, a huge, gleaming white vessel was revealed, the elegant lines of its daggerlike hull flaring into the curved pylons at the rear of the ship.

"It's beautiful," Sam said. "What is it?"

This is the vessel that brought Talon and myself to your planet many millions of years ago. In our native language she is called Naruun Pash Tanakk*—the nearest English translation is "Scythe of the Stars."*

"Mind if we just go with Scythe instead of Naruun . . .

uhh . . . whatever it was called?" Sam said, walking along the deck, admiring the sweeping lines of its hull. It couldn't have been more different from the sharp, angular shapes of the Voidborn ships.

Of course, the voice replied. *The Scythe was not the most powerful ship in the Illuminate fleet, but she was the fastest and most maneuverable. That is why she was chosen to bear the last remnant of our people to this planet when we fled the Voidborn. It was this vessel that brought the Heart to Earth and it is this vessel that may now be the only way to protect it and every other living thing on this planet.*

"Just this one ship can destroy the Voidborn?" Sam asked with a frown. "If that were true, why haven't you done it already?"

It is not the Scythe that will destroy the Voidborn; it is where it will allow us to go.

"Which is where exactly?" Sam asked. "I'm not a big fan of cryptic."

If you board the Scythe, the voice replied, *I will explain.*

Sam felt a moment of doubt; he had no idea whether he could trust this mysterious voice inside his head and there was no way of knowing what might happen if he did as it asked. But what it had told him a few minutes ago was true: if it did mean to harm him, there had been ample opportunity to do so on the journey up here.

"Okay, if it's going to get me some answers," Sam said. "How do I get on board?"

The ship is keyed to the implant inside your head, the voice replied. *All you need do is touch the hull*.

Sam climbed down the nearby ladder that led to the bottom of the dry dock and walked toward the ship, stretching out his hand and placing it on the hull, which, despite the fact that it had just emerged from the water, felt dry and *warm*. As his skin made contact with the Scythe, he watched patterns of blue light radiate out from his hand and ripple across the ship's hull. A moment later there was a solid clunk and a hiss, and a hatch that had been invisible a moment before opened in the side of the vessel, a few yards away. Sam walked toward the hatch as glowing blue blocks of energy materialized in front of it, forming a staircase that led inside. He climbed up the steps and into the brightly illuminated interior of the Scythe, the clean lines of its hull echoed in the smooth, white internal walls that pulsed with the same blue lights that had lit up on the exterior hull at Sam's touch.

Follow the corridor to your right, the voice said. *It will take you to the bridge*.

Sam followed the voice's directions and soon came to a hatch that silently slid open as he approached. The chamber beyond was dominated by a central dais upon which was a curved reclining seat. Arranged around the central seat were half a dozen more seats in a semicircle. There was no sign of anything that Sam might have recognized as controls or instruments. In fact, its bare walls and simple shapes reminded him more than anything else of the spartan interior of the Voidborn drop-ships.

Please sit, the voice said, as the raised seat in the center silently lowered.

Sam walked over and sat down, feeling the warm, soft lining meld itself to his body as he leaned back. A moment later the seat rose back into its elevated position and the air in front of Sam's face was filled with a glowing holographic screen displaying an array of strange icons and what looked like words in an unintelligible angular script. He watched as the display shifted, the readouts moving to the edges of the screen and a face appearing in the center of it. Sam felt a shiver run through his body as he stared into the eyes of his dead father. It was not the human face that Sam had grown up with, but his father's true face, that of the Illuminate scientist Suran.

"Hello, Sam," the holographic image said. "I am sorry to have brought you here like this, but there is much to do and little time to explain."

"What are you?" Sam asked, relieved to be able to hear his father's voice normally at last, instead of as a whisper in his skull. "Whatever you are, you're not my dad. I watched him die."

"You are correct," the hologram replied with a nod. "I am an engram construct."

"Which is . . . ?"

"It is a concept that is difficult to express in your

language," the Construct replied. "I am an artificial re-creation of your father's personality that is based upon centuries of his recorded experience. Your father is indeed dead, but he left me here as an echo of himself so that he could warn you of the danger that you face."

"So you're some kind of digital ghost of my father?" Sam asked.

"An oversimplification, but yes," the Construct replied. "That would be one way of putting it."

"How did you get me here?" Sam asked.

"The implant that your father placed in your cerebral cortex effectively blocks the Voidborn control signal by overlaying it with a separate, stronger signal that it generates itself. That signal usually does nothing but block the commands sent by the Voidborn, but it can, if necessary, be used to control the individual who carries the implant. That was how I was able to bring you here."

"You could've just asked," Sam said with a frown.

"No, I could not," the Construct replied. "I was preprogrammed by your father to summon you only in certain very specific circumstances. One of those circumstances has arisen and so I was forced to bring you here like this. You, your planet, and what remains of both our species are in mortal danger and we must act now before it is too late."

"I don't mean to burst your bubble, but we've been in mortal danger for a couple of years now. It's not exactly breaking news."

"No," the Construct replied. "There is a new threat, something that neither you nor the Illuminate has seen before. Observe."

The display shifted and an image appeared of the Earth and the moon hanging in space. A point halfway between the two was highlighted by a pulsing red light.

"What's that?" Sam asked.

"I am not entirely certain," the Construct replied, "but I fear that it may be the vessel that was controlling the Voidborn fleet when they first attacked the Illuminate. Our fleet was never able to get near enough to observe it directly, but we were able to detect power emissions on a scale quite unlike anything we had ever seen before. Whenever we encountered the Voidborn, we detected those emissions, but we could not determine exactly what it was that was creating them. The object that you see in front of you matches that emission signal perfectly."

"When did it appear?" Sam asked.

"Within the last twenty-four hours," the Construct replied. "It is also transmitting an extremely powerful signal to the Voidborn vessels within the Earth's atmosphere, a signal that is then being relayed to the other members of your species."

Sam thought back to the Sleepers writhing in agony in Stirling's laboratory. It couldn't be just a coincidence that their change in behavior coincided perfectly with the arrival of this thing, whatever it was.

"We have to stop that signal," Sam said. "It's doing something to everyone without an implant, something awful."

"That is why I brought you here," the Construct replied. "You are the last of the Illuminate and so you are the only one who may access the Heart."

"My father told me about that," Sam said. "Some sort of archive that stored the personalities of the Illuminate."

"That is correct," the Construct replied. "It was our last hope for escaping the Voidborn after we suffered our final crushing defeat in the war. Billions of Illuminate consciousnesses, digitized, compressed, and stored within a near-indestructible data crystal. Our last desperate gambit when the only option that was left for us was to run and hide. It rests within the molten core of your planet, somewhere we thought it would never be found. We were wrong."

"And that's what the Voidborn have been searching for; that's why they came here and built those drilling rigs like the one we disabled in London."

"Yes, and now we must assume they have finally retrieved it or are at least very close to doing so," the Construct said. "I do not understand exactly what the Voidborn intend to do at that point. If they had wished simply to destroy it, they could have forced your star to explode into a supernova, but the lengths to which they have gone to preserve the lives of the inhabitants of this planet while seeking to retrieve it suggest that they have other motives of which we are, as yet, unaware."

"So whatever they're planning has something to do with the Heart," Sam said, "which means we've got to stop them from getting their hands on it."

"Yes, I believe so," the Construct replied.

"Then I need to get back to London as soon as possible," Sam said. "Is this thing ready to fly?"

"All of the Scythe's systems are fully operational," the Construct replied.

"Then let's go," Sam said. "If we're going to stand any chance of stopping the Voidborn from retrieving the Heart, we're going to need all the help we can get."

3

Stirling stared through the microscope at the sample of the dusty remains of the Servant. At that level of magnification the tiny particles were still little more than smooth ovals that gave no hint as to how they functioned as self-assembling nano-technological machines. He suspected it would take something with the power of an electron microscope to even begin to understand how the tiny machines worked. Unfortunately, that was a level of technology they no longer had access to. Given time he might have been able to adapt some of the Voidborn technology for that purpose, but that, in turn, would have required the assistance of the Servant. He sat back in his chair and rubbed his eyes, feeling a frustrating sense of helplessness. They had been unable to communicate with the Voidborn around the compound for nearly twelve hours, ever since Sam had departed. They were fortunate at least, he supposed, that the Voidborn didn't appear to be listening to their original masters either; in fact, they appeared completely inert.

The timing was terrible; Stirling and the others had to try to stop whatever was happening to the Sleepers before it was too late and they all started to succumb to dehydration. To do that they needed access to all the resources that Sam's control over the Motherships above London granted them. After their successes in London and their defeat of Talon and capture of the second Mothership, Stirling had allowed himself to believe they were starting to build a platform from which they could launch a meaningful counterattack against the invaders. Now he was beginning to wonder if all they'd ever been doing was prolonging their inevitable defeat. He could never allow the others to see it. He knew they all viewed him as the unflappable founder of their resistance movement, but he was starting to doubt whether they had ever really had any chance of truly being able to fight back. There were only a handful of them, and even *with* the help of the Servant and the Voidborn she controlled, it was, perhaps, just too mammoth a task.

"Come on, Iain," Stirling said to himself, leaning forward and pressing his eyes to the lenses of the microscope, "can't afford to give up now. Focus on the work."

He spent a couple more minutes studying the nanites, subjecting them to ever increasing levels of voltage in the hope that the electricity might stir them back into life somehow, but still they remained frustratingly inert. He was just scribbling a note on the pad next to the microscope when the door to his laboratory flew open with a bang.

"Doctor Stirling," Jack said breathlessly. "There's a ship landing in the compound. It's not like anything we've seen before."

Stirling leapt from his chair and hurried out of the lab, following Jack into the compound courtyard, where a streamlined white ship was settling to the ground, slim white struts sliding out from its underside and then sinking into the dirt as they took the vessel's weight. The rest of the group was already there, the expressions on their faces a mixture of curiosity and concern. Stirling noticed Jay thumbing the safety catch on the assault rifle he was carrying to the firing position.

"Stay back," Stirling called as the roar of the craft's engines dropped to a low hum.

Moments later, a hatch opened in the side of the vessel and Sam appeared in the opening, looking completely human; all trace of the strange changes that his body had undergone had vanished. He walked down the glowing blue steps, his smile fading as he saw the look on Jay's face. Mag took a step toward Sam, but Jay put a hand on her shoulder, holding her back for the moment.

"Jay, come on," Mag said, "it's Sam."

"I can see that," Jay said. "Let's just make sure he's feeling himself before we get any closer, yeah?"

Sam looked at the faces of his friends and saw something he'd never seen before . . . suspicion. It was exactly what he had always feared would happen when his friends found out the truth about his condition. Mag had been right: this was worse than facing the truth.

"You okay, Sam?" Jay asked. Sam couldn't help but notice that his friend looked prepared to use the rifle he was carrying.

"I thought I was, but something tells me I don't have the full picture," Sam replied with a frown. He had no idea what had happened between his last memory of standing in front of them all and waking up in Scotland. The expressions on their faces suggested he might not want to.

"Yeah, I think we all know how that feels," Jay said. "Wanna tell us what happened to you?"

"Actually, I think you guys might have to fill me in on most of the details," Sam said. "Last thing I remember was standing in the common room. Next thing I know I'm running for my life from the Vore."

"The Vore?" Will asked. "What were you doing in Scotland?"

"Finding this thing," Sam said, gesturing to the gleaming white ship behind him. "Although it might be more accurate to say that it found me. The real question is, why is everyone looking at me like I've got a second head?"

"Erm . . . well . . . when we last saw you, you didn't look like that," Anne said.

"Right," Sam said. "Bit more like this?"

His features shifted, once again assuming their now more natural Illuminate appearance.

"Yeah," Jay replied, gripping his rifle even tighter, "that's a bit more like it."

"I suppose I've got a bit of explaining to do, then," Sam said with a sheepish half-smile, his features smoothly returning to their familiar human appearance.

He led the others into the common room and spent the next few minutes explaining to his friends as much as he understood about the transformation he had undergone. They occasionally interrupted with questions but they mostly just stood and listened as he talked, their faces a mixture of confusion and concern.

"Why didn't you tell us all this sooner?" Jay asked as Sam finally fell silent.

"I kept telling myself I was just waiting for the right moment," Sam said, shaking his head, "but that wasn't really true. The truth is, I was frightened. Not just about how you would all react, but more because I didn't understand what was actually happening to me. Suran . . . my dad did something to me in Tokyo, and even now I'm not entirely sure what that actually was. What happened yesterday was exactly what I've been worrying about, that somehow this change might not be complete yet and I might end up hurting people, especially the people I care about."

"You told Mag, though," Nat said with a slight frown.

"No, I didn't," Sam said. "She figured it out. She's got a few advantages over the rest of you guys when it comes to spotting when something's not quite right."

"Actually, *smelling* when something's not quite right, to be a bit more precise," Mag said.

"I asked her not to tell anyone," Sam said. "She told me I was being stupid and that I should just explain what was happening to you guys, but I ignored her. Turns out that she was right all along."

"You know you're a bloody idiot, don't you?" Jay said. "I'm assuming I don't actually have to explain why?"

"No, I get it," Sam replied, his head dropping as Jay placed a hand on his shoulder. "I'm sorry."

"No more sucker punches, then?" Jay asked with a lop-sided grin.

"Yeah, sorry about that," Sam said, smiling back at his friend.

"Not a problem. Good to have you back."

Jay gave Sam a brief hug and then turned back toward the others.

"Right, so we've got our little lost puppy back; how about we figure out a way to use this ship to try and stop whatever it is the Voidies are doing to the Sleepers."

"It would be extremely helpful if you could undo whatever it was that you did to the Servant," Stirling said. "Then I would like to take a much closer look at this new vessel."

"Of course," Sam replied. "Whatever you need."

Jay watched Sam follow Stirling outside before walking over to Mag, who had retreated to one of the chairs on the other side of the room. She looked up at him with a weak smile as he approached.

"Listen," Jay said, "I'm sorry about what I said earlier. I know keeping Sam's secret wasn't your decision. I was just angry."

"You don't need to explain, Jay," Mag replied. "You were right. We should have told you what had happened to Sam. If it had been up to me, we would have. You have to believe that. I don't want you to think you can't trust me."

"I do," Jay replied with a crooked smile. "It's not like I've never encountered the Riley stubbornness before. Still, I shouldn't have taken it out on you. Sometimes my mouth gets ahead of my head, you know. We shouldn't fight each other—that's what the Voidborn are for."

"Agreed," Mag said. "So we're both sorry."

"Yeah," Jay replied.

"Want to hug it out?" Mag flashed her cheekiest smile.

"Maybe later," Jay said with a grin. "Come on, let's go see what the Doc and Sam are up to."

"You're definitely right about one thing, though," Mag said as they headed out of the common room and across the compound toward the lab building.

"What's that?" Jay asked.

"You and I should definitely never fight."

"Yeah? Why's that?"

"Because you'd get hurt," Mag replied with a smile. "Badly."

Eyes that burned with an endless fire stared down at the shining blue curve of the Earth's surface far below. The entity that controlled the massive ship hanging in high orbit above the planet felt a sensation that it had not felt for the longest time. Somewhere in the southern quarter of the tiny island that it was studying, something had burst into life, something it had been seeking for countless eons. The Illuminate were here, that much was certain, but the entity had assumed that they still rested deep in the dreamless sleep that had hidden them from it for so long. Now something, some remnant of their technology, had awoken on the same land mass that was home to the child of Suran. It knew that nothing could stop the final stages of the plan that had been set in motion so long ago, but still there was no reason to tolerate the continued existence of this threat.

The entity turned from the view-port and issued a silent mental command. Moments later a series of massive black cylinders detached from the hull of the giant vessel, their leading edges flaring with the glow of burning plasma as they speared downward through the atmosphere, heading for their targets far below.

"I'm not even sure what I did to her, to be honest," Sam said, looking down at the pile of dull gold–colored dust heaped on the tray in front of him. Stirling and the others had filled him in on the details of what he had done when he had left the compound the previous day, but it had not helped to clarify what had actually happened in Sam's head. His first memory was of waking up in Scotland with a pack of Vore hunting him.

"I have not been able to detect any residual energy signatures," Stirling said, gesturing at the flatlined readings on the nearby monitor. "It would appear that the nanites that compose the Servant's physical form are completely inert."

"The rest of the Voidborn are still wandering about, though," Mag said with a frown. "Aren't they made of the same stuff?"

"Yes, whatever Sam did to the Servant appears to have affected only her," Stirling replied.

Sam reached out and placed his fingertips on top of the pile of dust; the individual microscopic machines that it was composed of were far too small to be made out with the naked eye, but they were still the root of all the

Voidborn technology. A moment later a pinprick of light appeared on the surface of the pile and started to spread across the dust in a glowing web.

"Something's happening," Sam said, stepping back from the lab bench as the dust began to flare with an even brighter light and rise into the air, forming a swirling cloud above them.

"Stand back," Stirling said, gesturing for Sam, Mag, and Jay to move further away from the glowing cloud. The cloud moved to the center of the room and started to coalesce, a shape forming within its core. A few seconds later the Servant stepped from the cloud. After a moment of silent stillness, as the last glowing specks merged with her body, her head suddenly snapped toward Sam.

"Seek immediate cover," the Servant said calmly. "We are under orbital bombardment."

Sam barely had time to open his mouth in reply before the first shock wave blew out the windows on the other side of the laboratory and sent him flying across the room. His head slammed into the side of a lab bench as he hit the ground with a crunch amid the scattered debris. After a few seconds, he pushed himself up onto his knees with a groan, raising his hand to his hairline and pulling it away wet with his own blood.

"Mag! Jay! Are you okay?" Sam croaked as he staggered to his feet. The air in the room was thick with dust to the point where he could barely see more than a couple of yards in front of him. He spotted the glowing form of the Servant and rushed over to where she was standing immobile, her head tilted slightly to one side.

"Help me!" Sam yelled, but the Servant didn't move or even show any sign that she was aware he was there at all. He turned around, surveying the room as the dust slowly began to clear. There was a clatter from off to his left and one of the piles of debris began to move as Jay forced himself up from the ground. Sam ran over and helped his friend out from under the metal shelves of a toppled equipment rack.

"What the hell was that?" Jay asked.

"I have no idea. Are you hurt?"

"I don't think so," Jay replied. "Where are the others?"

"Not sure," Sam said quickly, helping him to his feet. "Help me look."

There was a low moan from the other side of the room. Sam and Jay hurried over. As they approached they saw Mag lying under a pile of breeze blocks from the collapsed wall behind her.

"Give me a hand!" Sam yelled as he started to clear the debris away. Mag winced and gave a pained hiss as they dragged her out from the rubble, but other than a few cuts and bruises she seemed okay.

"Where's Stirling?" she asked as they heard the sound of alarmed shouting from the compound outside.

"There!" Jay yelled as he ran across the debris-strewn

lab toward a crumpled figure in a bloodstained lab coat, lying facedown on the floor. Jay gently rolled Stirling onto his back with Sam and Mag's help. He was unconscious and his breathing was very shallow; several dagger-shaped shards of glass were embedded in his chest just a few inches from his armpit.

"His heart rate is decreasing," the Servant said matter-of-factly. "He requires immediate medical attention." Whatever it was that had frozen her systems a few seconds before seemed to have passed.

"We're standing in all that's left of the medical facility," Sam said, looking around at the scattered beds and smashed equipment. There was an ominous groan of moving metal from somewhere above them and a large chunk of the ceiling at the other end of the room collapsed with a crash, kicking up fresh clouds of dust.

"We can't stay here," Sam said. "This whole building could come down on top of us at any moment. We have to move Stirling. Try and find a stretcher or something else we can use to carry him."

"Allow me," the Servant said, walking over and kneeling down beside Stirling, before gently sliding her arms under his back. She stood up effortlessly with the wounded man in her arms. "This will be quicker."

They hurried out of the lab and through the shattered remains of the door leading outside. The scene that met them in the compound was one of utter chaos. Debris littered the area and smoke was billowing from the shattered windows on one side of the accommodation block. The Scythe sat in the middle of the devastation, apparently undamaged despite the chunks of masonry and twisted metal that lay scattered around it. Suddenly a voice on the far side of the compound screamed for help. At first Sam couldn't tell who was calling out, but then the dust filling the air cleared slightly and he saw Nat kneeling on the ground on the other side of the compound, cradling Liz in her arms. Sam and the others sprinted toward her.

"Help me!" Nat sobbed. "Something hit her in the head. We have to get her to the medical bay."

Sam knelt down beside her and looked at Liz's bloodied face, trying to ignore the horrendous wound in the side of her skull. Her eyes were wide open, but there was no light behind them. He placed his fingers on her neck, searching for a pulse that he already knew he would not find. Finally, he gently closed her eyes and put a hand on Nat's shoulder, looking into her tear-filled eyes.

"She's gone, Nat," Sam said, shaking his head. "There's nothing we can do for her. We have to find the others."

"We can't just leave her here," Nat said angrily.

"What did Jackson teach us?" Sam said softly.

"The living first," Nat said, her voice little more than a whisper.

She hugged her best friend's limp body for a few seconds before carefully laying her on the ground.

"What happened?" Nat snapped, her grief suddenly replaced with anger. "Who did this?"

"That's what we have to try and find out," Jay said, "but first we need to get everyone to safety."

"Safe from what?" Nat asked.

"I'm not sure," Mag said, pointing behind the others, "but I'm guessing that it might have something to do with that."

They all turned to look and saw a massive shape appear from behind the slowly clearing curtain of dust that still hung in the air. At first it was difficult to make out exactly what the towering black object was, but a few seconds later it started to become horribly clear. A huge black cylinder, hundreds of feet high, jutted up from the London skyline roughly a mile away, the buildings around it now little more than burning shells, their shattered facades continuing to crumble as they watched.

"What the hell is that?" Sam asked as the Servant approached, still carrying the wounded Stirling.

"I do not know," the Servant replied. "Its configuration does not match any object or technical schematic stored within my systems."

Sam did not need to know exactly what the thing was to be able to hear the primal voice at the back of his skull telling him to get as far away from it as possible as quickly as possible.

"Have you guys seen Anne or Will?" Jack yelled as he

ran across the compound toward them, his eyes wide with shock. He had a gash on his chin, which was bleeding onto his shirt, but otherwise he looked intact. "I thought I saw them . . . Oh God, no . . ."

Jack trailed off as he saw Liz's lifeless body lying on the ground.

"Where, Jack? Where did you see them?" Sam said, turning his friend away from the body and forcing him to look him in the eye. They couldn't afford to give in to grief now. That could come later.

"They headed out on patrol about half an hour ago," Jack said.

"Where were they going?" Jay asked. "We need both of them. They're the only ones who have extensive medical training, and with Stirling out of action they're all we've got."

Sam glanced over at Stirling, who was still lying limply in the Servant's arms. He felt the sudden crushing weight of expectation as the others looked to him for a decision.

"Okay," Sam said, taking a long, deep breath and turning toward the Servant. "You take Stirling, find somewhere safe and see if you can stabilize his condition. Nat, you know where the trauma packs are. Do what you can. The Servant will help you."

Nat gave a quick nod and gestured for the Servant to follow her toward the accommodation block.

"Jay, can you actually drive that thing?" Sam asked, pointing at the armored four-by-four on the other side of the compound.

"Yup," Jay said with a nod.

"Really?" Mag asked, raising an eyebrow.

"Let's just say that I liked driving other people's cars before the Voidborn came along," Jay said, "not *always* with their permission, strictly speaking. But yeah, I can drive it. Why?"

"Because we need to get out there and find them as quickly as possible," Sam said.

"They could be anywhere," Jay said, shaking his head. "We'd be better off just waiting here for them to get back."

"I don't think that's a good idea," Mag said, looking nervously at the giant cylinder in the distance. "Whatever that thing is I've got a horrible feeling that it's not finished with us yet."

"Okay, so how on earth do we find them?" Jack asked.

"The same way Stirling found us," Sam said. "Come on."

Sam turned and jogged back across the compound and into the damaged laboratory. The others followed him toward Stirling's storeroom, picking their way through the debris. Sam opened the door and looked around the gloomy space, lit only by a narrow window. He tried the switch next to the door, but it was no good; the power was out. He quickly moved between the shelving racks, looking for the device that he knew

Stirling had kept there. It took him a couple of minutes of searching in the semidarkness, but he felt as if a weight had been lifted from his shoulders when he finally spotted it. It had a boxy body, with a screen mounted on the top and a pistol grip below. He flicked the switch on the side of the box and was relieved to hear a high-pitched whine as the screen came to life. A display appeared with a single red dot at the center and two more just to the side of it; at the edge of the screen were two more faint red glows.

"That's us," Sam said to Jay and Jack, pointing to the three dots in the center, "and those two are Nat and Stirling."

"What is that thing," Mag asked, "and why am I not on it?"

"This is the scanner Stirling used to find us," Jay said. "It's only short-range, but it can track the implants in our heads that block the Voidborn signal."

"How short is short-range exactly?" Mag asked.

"About fifty yards," Sam replied, "which is why we need to take the truck instead of a drop-ship or the Scythe."

"The Scythe?" Jack said with a puzzled frown.

"That big white hot rod out there," Sam replied. "That's what the Illuminate called it anyway. We're never going to find them from the air; we need to stay down at street level."

"They're probably already on their way back," Jay said.

"There's no way they missed those things landing. That might make them easier to find."

"I'll have a drop-ship shadow us too," Sam said. "As soon as we find them, it can pick us up and bring us back here as quickly as possible."

"Sounds good," Jay said with a nod. "I'll go and get the truck fired up."

"Can you grab us some weapons from the armory?" Sam asked Jack. "You've only got a couple of minutes."

Jack gave a quick nod and sprinted out of the room. Sam took one last look around the badly damaged laboratory, checking for anything that might be helpful, before sprinting back across the courtyard and into the infirmary. He ran straight to the storeroom and hastily filled a pack with basic emergency medical supplies. There was no way of knowing what condition Will and Anne would be in when they found them. He could only pray that they had avoided the same fate as Liz. He felt a swell of panic in his chest and took a long, deep breath, thinking back to the combat training he had received.

"Process later," Sam whispered to himself, "focus on the objective."

He ran back out of the storeroom and across the courtyard to the accommodation block, where Stirling was lying on a cot that had been dragged out of one of the bedrooms, still unconscious and deathly pale. Nat stood beside the bed, looking shocked as the Servant continued calmly assessing Stirling's condition.

"How is he?" Sam asked the Servant.

"Doctor Stirling's prognosis is not good," the Servant replied. "His vital metrics are diminishing rapidly."

"Can you help him at all?" Sam asked. "Don't the Voidborn treat any medical problems with the Sleepers?"

"Humans who are injured or infirm are viewed as surplus to requirements," the Servant replied calmly. "The Voidborn simply dispose of them. The whole concept of trying to repair what is broken is meaningless to them. It is much more efficient to simply replace the malfunctioning components with new ones."

"That's not how it works for us," Sam replied, glancing over at Nat, who was wiping tears from her soot-stained face. "I'm going to find Anne and Will. They might be the only ones who can help Stirling. We'll be searching at street level, but I want you to dispatch a drop-ship to shadow us for a quick pickup-and-return journey once we find them. Okay?"

"Understood," the Servant replied. "Should I dispatch Drones to investigate the object that landed?"

"Yeah, okay," Sam said with a nod, "but don't poke the hornets' nest."

The Servant tipped her head to one side slightly, as she always did when some unknown human idiom confused her.

"I mean, don't get too close," Sam said. "Observation

only until we know what we're dealing with. Put both Motherships on full combat alert."

"Done," the Servant replied.

Sam gave a quick nod and then hurried back out into the central courtyard, where Jay and Mag were clearing the last few pieces of wreckage off the armored exterior of the military vehicle.

"Good to go?" Sam asked as he approached.

"Yup, just going to fire her up," Jay said, opening the driver's door.

"Hey!" Jack ran over to them with an assault rifle slung over his shoulder and another in each hand. "The mags are full and there are spares in my pack, along with some slightly heavier ordnance if we need it." He handed one of the weapons to Sam, who pulled back the bolt and chambered a round before engaging the safety. Suddenly the truck's recently installed custom power plant sprang into life with a deep, throaty roar that was mixed with the high-pitched whine of a drop-ship engine.

"Let's go," Sam said, hopping into the passenger seat. "Do we have any idea where to start?"

"I know they were heading to St. Paul's. We should go there first," Jack said as he climbed into the back of the truck and stood up, his top half protruding from the roof turret. He quickly checked the belt-fed heavy machine gun mounted in front of him and gave a small, satisfied grunt. "Good to go."

Jay dropped the truck into gear and gunned the engine. The vehicle leapt forward with a speed that belied its enormous weight, skidding across the courtyard as Jay wrestled with the wheel, steering the behemoth through the gates of the compound and out onto the roads surrounding St. James's Park. The street was filled with abandoned cars, still standing exactly where they had been left by their brainwashed owners on the day of the Voidborn invasion. Jay swerved through the immobile ghost traffic, aiming for any open areas of tarmac he could see. Fifty yards ahead of them the road was blocked by a car and a taxi that had somehow ended up nose to nose in the middle of the carriageway.

"Hang on!" Jay yelled as he floored the accelerator, aiming for the foot-wide gap between the two cars.

Sam grabbed the handle mounted on the dashboard in front of him and Jack ducked down inside the cab, bracing himself against the sides of the turret opening. Seconds later, the reinforced bull bars on the front of the truck slammed into the two vehicles with a deafening crash, sending them both spinning aside without the truck even seeming to slow down.

"Now that's what I call a congestion charge," Jay said with a grim smile.

"Let's just hope we don't run into anything bigger," Mag replied. "Literally."

Sam glanced down at the display of the implant tracker.

There were three red blips tightly clustered in the center of the display, but beyond that there was nothing.

"Any sign?" Jay asked, frowning with concentration as he flicked the large steering wheel left and right, fighting to avoid the obstacles that lay scattered across the road ahead. Driving was made more dangerous by the debris that was still falling from the buildings around them after the landing of the ominous black cylinder.

"Nothing!" Sam yelled back over the roar of the engine. "Keep heading for St. Paul's. We need to get as close as we can for the scanner to pick them up."

Jay gave a quick nod and sent the truck swerving left to avoid a toppled double-decker bus, mounting the pavement and demolishing a bus stop in the process. The impact barely seemed to slow the heavy military vehicle as it barreled down the road toward the familiar dome of St. Paul's Cathedral.

"Something's happening to the cylinder!" Jack yelled down through the turret hatch. Sam turned and looked out the driver's side window and immediately saw what Jack had noticed. The giant black column seemed to be disintegrating, roiling black clouds rising from the base as the top half crumbled away, slowly vanishing out of sight behind the distant rooftops.

"What's it doing?" Jay snapped, unable to take his eyes off the road even for a second.

"I have no idea," Sam said with a frown. "It looks like it's just falling to pieces."

"Which is a good thing, right?" Jay asked, with a quick sideways glance at Sam.

"Ask me in ten minutes," Sam replied, his frown deepening. The black cloud that had formed as the column disintegrated was rapidly expanding to cover the surrounding buildings, and the way it moved was odd, almost as if it were moving with purpose. Sam suddenly felt a rush of energy course through his body, just as he'd felt in Scotland before the Vore had attacked him. He knew now what it meant: the Illuminate nanites within him were responding to a threat. What exactly that threat was might not be entirely clear, but Sam was willing to bet that it had something to do with the cloud that was now racing across the city toward them.

"Okay, starting to think that we might need to go faster!" Jack shouted.

The cloud wasn't just getting closer, it was moving more quickly. Long tendrils of thick black smoke were shooting out from the main body of the cloud and almost seemed to be hooking onto the buildings ahead, as if pulling the roiling mass forward at greater and greater speed.

"I think Jack might be right," Sam said nervously, feeling a sudden tight knot of animal fear in his gut.

"This isn't an Aston Martin," Jay snapped back, "and in case you haven't noticed"—Jay wrenched the wheel to one side, swerving hard and sending a compact car flying across the pavement and smashing through a giant plate-glass shopwindow—"traffic's a bitch."

Sam glanced down at the implant detector. Still nothing. St. Paul's was now clearly visible ahead of them, less than a mile away.

"It's crossing the river!" Mag yelled, and this time even Jay risked a glance over his shoulder. The seething cloud seemed to half leap, half climb across Waterloo Bridge. As it reached the opposite bank, it twisted unnaturally in their direction, gathering speed as it gained on them.

Sam tore open his pack and pulled out the pair of compact high-powered binoculars that he always carried. He unbuckled his seat belt, made his way back through the bouncing, rattling interior of the armored personnel carrier, and peered out through the glass panel set into the rear hatch. It took a second to bring the cloud into focus, but what he saw when he did made Sam's mouth go dry. It was no cloud of gas that was chasing them; it was a seething swarm of tiny black objects. It was impossible to make out at this distance exactly what they were, even with the binoculars, but he had to assume it was some sort of Voidborn weapon they'd not encountered before.

"Sam!" Mag yelled from up front. "We've got a hit."

Sam scrambled back into his seat and scooped up the gently pinging implant detector.

"Hard left!" Sam yelled, and Jay wrenched at the

steering wheel, almost tipping the massive vehicle over as they screeched around the corner and roared down the narrow side street. Jay slammed on the brakes as two figures stepped out of an alleyway just ahead of them. Will had his arm around Anne's shoulders and she supported him as he limped toward them with a grimace on his face.

"What the hell's going on?" Anne yelled as Sam hopped down from the cab of the APC and ran over to them.

"Tell you when I know," Sam said, turning to Will. "What happened?"

"I was halfway up a fire escape, trying to get inside a locked building, when that explosion hit," Will said with a wince. "It wasn't a graceful landing."

"Okay, come on, we need to get back," Sam said, jerking his thumb toward the APC and placing Will's other arm over his own shoulders. They hurried toward the vehicle and Sam pulled the rear door open, helping as Will carefully climbed inside and dropped into one of the seats that lined the walls of the passenger compartment.

"Thanks for coming to get us," Anne said as she climbed inside. "I thought that . . ."

Her voice trailed off, her eyes widening with fear. Sam spun around and saw what had suddenly struck his friend dumb. At the far end of the side street a thick, black tendril was snaking around the corner, its slick dark surface seething and bubbling in a repulsive way. The tentacle seemed to pause for a moment as it twitched in their direction, before unleashing a hideous, unearthly hiss and slamming down onto the surface of the road. The tendril shattered into millions of tiny skittering black dots, which raced toward them in a wave, covering every surface like a shadow.

"GO!GO!GO!" Sam yelled as he dived into the rear of the APC, Anne slamming the hatch shut behind him.

"What was that thing?" Anne yelled over the roar of the engine as they raced away down the road.

"Nothing good," Sam replied, watching in horror through the rear window as the seething swarm gathered speed in pursuit of them, crashing down the street like an oily, black tsunami. From above them came the staccato thud of the heavy machine gun mounted on the roof as Jack opened fire on the monstrous swarm. The heavy-caliber rounds punched grapefruit-sized holes in the seething mass, but the impacts didn't even seem to slow it down, much less stop it. Sam climbed into the passenger seat next to Jay and braced himself as his friend threw the heavy vehicle sideways around the tight bend at the end of the street. The swarm had almost surrounded them; the roads leading back toward their compound were blocked with twisting black clouds that seemed to be slowly cutting off all their avenues of escape. Sam glanced in the opposite direction, toward the looming dome of the cathedral.

"Head for St. Paul's!" he yelled. "We'll transfer to the drop-ship there."

Jay gave a grunt of agreement as he steered them in the right direction. Sam glanced in the wing mirror of the APC and immediately wished he hadn't. The swarm was even closer now and still gaining.

The heavy machine gun's ammo ran dry and the hammer fell on an empty chamber with a final loud click.

"Pass me my pack!" Jack yelled down through the turret hatch. Mag grabbed the pack and shoved it into Jack's outstretched hand, watching as her friend pulled it up into the turret and frantically searched through its contents.

"Gotcha!" Jack said with a grin, pulling out a large block wrapped in duct tape. "Let's see if this slows you down." He tossed the package into the road behind them, waiting just a couple of seconds before hitting the radio trigger in his other hand. The road behind them erupted, a giant red ball of fire filling the street, obliterating the leading edge of the swarm and shattering every remaining window in a three-hundred-yard radius. Jay hung on to the steering wheel as the rear wheels of the APC left the ground for a moment, the road beneath them bucking wildly with the shock wave from the massive explosion. A split second later the vehicle's heavy tires slammed back onto the tarmac, squealing in protest as they bit into the surface.

"Little warning next time!" Jay yelled, fighting to bring the powerful vehicle back under his control.

"Is it still coming?" Sam shouted up at Jack.

Jack peered into the cloud of smoke and dust behind them, watching as more black tentacles began to emerge from the cloud, moving more slowly at first, but then picking up speed again.

"Yeah, that just slowed it down," Jack said as one of the tentacles slammed into the wall of a nearby building with an enraged hiss, sending the structure's facade crumbling into the street below. "And possibly made it angry."

"Great," Jay muttered, stamping harder on the accelerator pedal, which was already flat against the floor.

Sam watched the seething black cloud begin to gain on them again. He could feel the Illuminate nanites fizzing inside him as they responded to this bizarre new threat. Sam had no idea what protection they could possibly offer, but there was no denying the energy he felt crackling inside him.

Jay spun the wheel and sent the APC rocketing across St. Paul's Square as the black mass seemed to close in on them from all directions. Sam twisted around in his seat, frantically looking for an escape route, but the swarm was moving too quickly, sealing the exits from the square one by one.

"Front door!" Sam yelled, punching Jay in the shoulder and pointing at the massive wooden doors that sealed the entrance to the cathedral.

"Will this thing fit through there?" Mag shouted over the roar of the engine.

"Only one way to find out!" Jay said, spinning the steering wheel and sending the giant armored vehicle careering across the square, straight toward the cathedral.

They hurtled into the concrete bollards in front of the building, each one exploding as the massive vehicle smashed through them effortlessly, barely slowing down. The APC mounted the steps leading up to the door, fishtailing as its massive, heavily treaded tires fought for purchase on the stone worn smooth by the passage of millions of worshippers over the centuries. They were at the top in seconds and flew between the massive columns flanking the Great West Door, slamming into it with a thunderous crash and smashing it to splinters. The tires squealed in protest as Jay hit the brakes, sending the vehicle sliding across the tiled floor inside the cathedral before crashing sideways into one of the interior support columns with a heavy crunch.

"Everybody out!" Sam yelled, snatching up his pack and rifle and jumping out of the APC's cab. He could sense that beyond the shattered doorway, the sinister black cloud was quickly filling the square outside. Sam spun around, looking for an escape route. He spotted a sign that read "Whispering Gallery" next to the symbol of an arrow pointing up a flight of stairs. Right now, up sounded good.

"That way!" Sam yelled, pointing toward the sign. He and Jay took Will's arms over their shoulders and helped him limp after Anne and Mag, who raced up the stairs, taking them two at a time, heading up into the cathedral's famous dome.

"I'm never going to make it up there," Will said as they reached the foot of the staircase.

"Yeah, you will," Jay said. "Just think happy thoughts."

The three of them climbed the stairs as quickly as they could, Will wincing as waves of pain shot through his injured leg. Not far behind them the swarming cloud swept up the steps to the cathedral and half slithered, half flowed through the splintered remains of the door. Thin tendrils rose from the hissing wave as the cloud dropped lower to the ground. It moved like a predatory animal, snaking across the floor, hunting for its prey.

Sam and Jay started to climb faster; they could hear the sinister hissing of the cloud below them getting louder and closer with each passing second. Will slipped on one of the smooth steps, jarring his injured leg and yelling out in pain. The swarm responded to the sound immediately, racing across the cathedral floor toward the staircase.

"Need to go faster," Jay said, glancing down into the stairwell as the black cloud filled the base of the circular shaft before starting to climb up the curved walls toward them.

"Heads up!" Mag shouted from somewhere above them. A split second later a bundle of small, round objects dropped past them, straight down the center of the shaft.

There was a single second of silence and then the grenades detonated. The base of the stairwell vanished in a bright orange flash and the shock wave shook the stones beneath Sam's feet. The hissing of the black cloud from below seemed to diminish, but it was impossible to make out anything else through the clouds of dark gray smoke at the bottom of the stairwell. He had no idea how much time Mag might have bought them, but based on the swarm's reaction to Jack's explosive charge a few minutes earlier, it would not be long.

Sam, Jay, and Will began to move faster, trying to take advantage of the momentary letup in the pursuit, heading further and further up into the ancient building with every step. Less than a minute later they were helping Will up the last few steps and out onto the famous Whispering Gallery that ran around the inside of the dome. Sam glanced down at the cathedral floor far below and saw that it was completely filled with the menacing black cloud, which was now starting to climb the walls and supporting columns of the cathedral, creeping inexorably up toward them.

"Where now?" Anne asked, looking around frantically.

"We need to get outside," Sam said. "There's got to be another stairway around here, somewhere that leads to the outside of the dome. The only safe place that the drop-ship can pick us up from is the roof." He ran around the narrow gallery, the unearthly hiss from the seething black mass amplified by the dome's acoustics, making it seem like it came from all directions at once. There was an opening in the wall several yards away with another sign next to it showing a staircase leading up to the Stone Gallery.

"Here!" Sam yelled, pointing at the doorway and glancing down at the scene below. His breath caught in his throat as he saw the tiny skittering shapes that made up the leading edge of the black mass only a few yards below them. At the same instant a flood of black burst forth from the stairwell they had just left, spreading across the walls and floor like some kind of sentient oil slick.

"Go!" Sam yelled as Anne and Mag ducked through the narrow doorway leading further up into the tower. He dashed back toward Jay and Will, who were making their way there as quickly as Will's injury would allow. Sam looped Will's free arm back over his shoulders and the three of them hurried for the stairs. There was a shriek of twisting metal and Sam looked over his shoulder to see the leading edges of the main bulk of the swarm climbing up and over the lip of the narrow walkway, just ten yards behind them. As the first tendrils crept across the walkway, he could finally make out what made up the seething mass: thousands of tiny scurrying black insectile machines poured across the gray stone, each with a smooth segmented back and sharp, grasping mouth. The tiny machines moved in perfect unison, as only machines can, giving the impression of one giant directed mass. They made Sam's skin crawl.

"You've got to be kidding," Jay said as they covered the last few yards to the doorway and looked at the staircase leading further up inside. It was made of black cast iron and spiraled tightly upward into the gloom above. It was only wide enough for one person at a time; there was no way that they'd be able to help Will up there. Jay whirled around and slammed the heavy fire door shut, blocking the entrance to the stairwell and plunging it even further into gloomy darkness.

"Have we got any grenades left?" Will asked, tipping his head back and looking at the hundreds of steps that led up to the next level.

"I've got a couple," Jay said, "but we know they won't stop them for long. They're not going to buy us enough time."

"Give them to me," Will said, a look of grim determination on his face. "I'll make sure they cause as much damage as possible."

Jay and Sam exchanged a quick glance; they both knew perfectly well what he meant.

"Like hell you will," Sam said, shaking his head. "No one else dies today."

"What he said," Jay replied with a nod.

"There's no way I'm getting up there," Will said, wincing in pain and gesturing down at his injured leg.

There was a loud boom as something large slammed against the heavy fire door, buckling its metal frame slightly.

"Jay, go," Sam said. "Get to the roof and try and signal the drop-ship to pick us up from there."

"I'm not leaving you," Jay said. "Screw that."

"We'll be right behind you," Sam said. "Trust me."

Jay stared at Sam for a moment and then nodded before turning and sprinting up the stairs after Mag and Anne.

"Get on," Sam said, gesturing for Will to climb onto his back.

"There's no way you'll—"

"Just bloody well get on my back," Sam snapped. "No time to argue." As if to emphasize the point there was another explosive bang from the fire door just a few yards away, the frame buckling still further and dislodging chunks of stone from the surrounding wall. Will ditched his pack and weapon before climbing onto Sam's back. Sam closed his eyes, willing the Illuminate nanites throughout his body to give him the strength he so desperately needed. A moment later he felt his muscles fill with newfound power and he straightened up, running toward the stairs and sprinting up them three at a time, with Will hanging on for dear life. Sam could barely feel the weight of his friend as he powered up the cast-iron stairs, its centuries-old framework rattling beneath his feet.

They were halfway up when the door at the bottom of

the shaft finally gave way and the heaving black mass poured into the stairwell, coating its walls like a thick dark wave. The narrow chamber amplified the scratchy hiss from the pursuing swarm as millions of the tiny black creatures began to scale the staircase and surrounding walls in relentless pursuit of their prey. Sam glanced upward and saw Jay following Mag and Anne through a doorway filled with daylight just a few yards above them. They were nearly there. He reached the top of the stairs, barely even out of breath, and Will climbed down off his back.

"How the hell did you do that?" Will asked, looking at Sam with a mixture of amazement and concern.

"Doesn't matter," Sam replied, still feeling the Illuminate technology fizzing inside him as he glanced down at the swarm that was now halfway up the stairwell and still climbing fast. "All that matters now is—"

Sam felt a sudden sickening lurch in his stomach as somewhere below them there was the screech of tearing metal and the whole staircase dropped six inches, the walkway leading to the door buckling and tearing loose of its mountings on the wall. Sam didn't need to give any kind of command to the nanites as he spun around, feeling them coursing through the muscles in his arms, reacting to his wishes at the speed of thought. He struck Will in the chest with a flat palm, hitting him as hard as he dared as the world seemed to drop into slow motion. Will flew backward through the doorway and landed in a heap on the stone flagstones beyond with a pained grunt as the swarm far below destroyed the last of the staircase supports.

There was another screech of tearing metal and the staircase began to collapse beneath Sam. He took two sprinting strides and leapt for the doorway as the cast-iron structure gave way completely. He landed hard, his chest slamming into the stone slab at the bottom of the doorway and knocking the wind out of him. He clawed at the stone, trying to find some kind of handhold, while his boots frantically flailed against the wall below, unable to get any purchase. He felt himself slipping as the clanging crash of the entire staircase collapsing into the stairwell below filled his ears. Will lifted himself up onto his hands and knees, still dazed from Sam shoving him to safety. Sam reached out to him, but before Will could react, Mag sprinted past him, diving toward Sam, arm outstretched. Her hand closed around Sam's wrist like a vice, the black talons that tipped her fingers digging into his skin, and she grabbed desperately onto the doorframe with her free hand, just in time to stop them both tumbling into the seething mass that filled the stairwell below them. Jay threw his arms around Mag's waist to prevent her from sliding over the edge and helped her to pull Sam up and through the doorway and over to where Anne was helping Will to his feet.

"Thanks," Will said, "and ouch, by the way."

"Sorry, didn't have time to warn you," Sam replied, glancing over his shoulder at the door leading to the stairwell as another roaring hiss came from within. "Let's get the hell out of here."

Jay and Sam supported Will as the six of them hurried along the narrow terrace that circled the base of the cathedral's famous dome. A drop-ship streaked past overhead before banking hard and dropping into a hover right next to the stone balustrade that ran around the outside of the walkway, just thirty yards away. Sam watched nervously as the others hurried toward it.

"Quick, guys," Sam yelled, "we have to get back to the compound. There's no telling what—"

Suddenly the wall behind Sam exploded outward, massive stone blocks spinning through the air and demolishing a ten-yard stretch of the outer balustrade. Sam felt the whole building shake beneath his feet and a split second later a flood of tiny metal machines poured through the hole in the dome. The swarm swept across the floor, hundreds of thousands if not millions of the skittering metallic bugs racing across the ground toward them in a seething, hissing wave. Sam staggered back to his feet, still screaming at the others to hurry. He watched as Jay and Jack struggled to help Will scramble up the outer wall. Mag and Anne were close behind them, just a few seconds now from the drop-ship's open hatch and safety.

Sam leapt up and grabbed the top of the balustrade, hauling himself upward and onto the top of the narrow wall. Jay helped Jack lift Will up and through the hatch, the pair of them following him inside with Anne and Mag up next. Mag turned back to Sam, leaning out the hatch and offering him her hand. Her eyes filled with horror and Sam spun around just in time to see the black tentacle sweeping through the air toward him. It threw him hard against the crystalline hull of the drop-ship and knocked the wind out of him. He lost his balance, tipping forward and falling down onto the narrow terrace, landing with a crunch before flipping himself over and frantically crawling backward away from the leading edge of the swarm.

"Sam!" Mag screamed, looking as if she was about to jump down after him.

"Get out of here!" Sam yelled as the swarm moved between him and the drop-ship, barring his escape route. Another, much larger tentacle burst out of the swarm, swiping at the drop-ship and leaving a glowing scar along its hull. The giant triangular aircraft zipped away from the balustrade, maneuvering wildly as more flailing tendrils reached out for it. Sam could see that there was no way that it would be able to get close enough to pick him up now. The drop-ship brought its weapons to bear, bright yellow pulses of light streaking out from the cannons mounted on its hull. The shots ripped into the bulk of the swarm, tearing glowing holes in its seething mass; this did nothing to even slow its advance, much less stop it.

He leapt to his feet and sprinted away from the swarm, following the curve of the dome. He had gone only twenty yards when another section of the dome exploded ahead of him and a giant wave of the tiny skittering machines surged through the gap, washing across the cold gray flagstones. The swarm rushed toward Sam like some kind of nightmarish shadow. There was nowhere else to run. He was trapped.

Sam backed up against the wall as the two waves of tiny scuttling creatures closed in on him from both directions. He watched the drop-ship dart through the air fifty yards away, trying to avoid the tendrils that continued to whip toward it. There was a flicker of movement on the wall to his left and he felt something land on his shoulder. Looking down, he saw one of the tiny black machines scuttling along his arm. It leapt onto the exposed skin of Sam's hand and he howled in pain as what felt like a dozen fishhooks latched into his hand and the creature began to gnaw into his flesh. Sam clawed at the thing, trying in vain to rip it off, his fingertips suddenly slippery with the blood that was oozing from beneath its segmented shell. He was seized by a moment of pure panic as the creature slowly started to slip beneath his skin, clawing and burrowing its way inside him. And then blue lines began to race across his forearm and he felt a sudden rush of raw power, which continued to build as he collapsed to his knees with an agonized gasp. Sam barely registered the swarm as it hit him, the creatures pouring over him in a wave, surging up and around him, climbing over his chest and neck. He felt the distant sensation of thousands of tiny needles on his face and then everything went white.

A perfect sphere of energy burst out of Sam, vaporizing every one of the creatures within a twenty-yard radius. The rest of the swarm recoiled from the gleaming white sphere, which crackled and fizzed. In its center, Sam hung three feet above the ground with his head thrown back and his eyes wide open. The stonework surrounding him glowed a dull red color, instantly superheated by the sudden massive release of energy. The drop-ship dived toward the dome as the swarm retreated, then hovered next to the parapet as Sam slowly floated back to the ground. The moment his feet hit the stones, the energy field dissipated and he suddenly seemed to snap awake, looking around in confusion as Jay and Mag screamed at him from the vessel's open hatch to get on board. The swarm reacted immediately to the energy field disappearing, rearing up like a massive black wave about to crash down on the shore.

Sam sprinted toward the drop-ship, scaling the parapet and diving through the open hatch as the swarm raced after him along the roof. Jay and Mag hauled him inside and the drop-ship swung away, frantically dodging the tentacles that lashed out from the seething black mass.

"Get us back to the compound!" Sam yelled at the walls, and moments later he felt the drop-ship change course, banking toward St. James Park.

"Are you okay?" Mag asked.

"I think so," Sam replied uncertainly. "What happened?"

"You tell us," Jay said with a frown. "You did your whole force-field thing again."

"Wish I knew how," Sam said, shaking his head, and he glanced down at the dead machine that was still half embedded in his arm. It gave a single sudden twitch and Sam pulled it free with a shudder, before dropping it on the ground and crushing it under the heel of his boot.

"I think we may have a slightly bigger problem than we realized," Mag said, standing and looking out at the skyline through the drop-ship's open hatch. Sam turned and saw half a dozen more giant black cylinders landing around the city, each impact causing another massive explosion and sending huge billowing clouds of dust and debris whirling into the air. As they watched in horror, each cylinder began to crumble and disintegrate, just as the first one had. They could only assume that each one was creating another monstrous swarm, identical to the one they had just encountered.

"We have to get out of here," Jay said quietly. "We have to get out of London."

"You know, I think you might be right," Sam said, feeling a sudden chill forming in the pit of his stomach.

4

Mag and Anne leapt off the drop-ship while Jay and Sam helped Will down to the debris-strewn compound.

"You found them!" Nat yelled as she ran toward them from the accomodation block.

"How's Stirling?" Sam asked quickly.

"He doesn't seem to be getting any worse," Nat said. "I really need to get Anne or—"

"Later," Sam said. "Could you get him ready to move? Ask Anne to help."

"But he's too badly injured. If we—"

"Trust me," Sam replied with a frown. "We've got no choice."

"What's going on?" Nat asked, suddenly looking scared.

"Nothing good," Jack said. "Sam's right, we have to get out of here, now."

Nat looked as if she was going to say something else for a moment and then thought better of it. Instead, she simply gestured for Anne to follow her and ran back toward the infirmary.

"The Motherships are detecting large distributed energy signatures throughout the city," the Servant said matter-of-factly. "I do not, however, recognize the technology that is producing them."

"Whatever they are, they're hostile," Sam said. "Divert all our Voidborn forces within the city to protect as many of the Sleeper dormitories as possible. We've got no idea what that swarm might do to a dormitory and the Sleepers are completely defenseless without our Voidborn guarding them. I don't know how much good it'll do, but it's better than nothing."

"Scout units throughout the city are beginning to report contact," the Servant said calmly. "Our unit's combat performance is inadequate to face this threat. I would encourage you to leave the vicinity immediately, Illuminate."

"Exactly what I had in mind," Sam replied. "Prep the Motherships for immediate departure."

"Understood," the Servant replied with a nod. "Do you have a destination in mind?"

"Yeah," Sam said as he began to hear a muted hissing sound in the distance. "Anywhere but here."

"What can we do?" Jay asked.

"Gather up anything useful and get it on board the drop-ship. We'll transfer to one of the Motherships as soon as—"

Sam's words were drowned out by another massive explosion somewhere above them. Sam instinctively covered his head as he was blasted by a wave of heat and pressure that sent him staggering. It was only after a few seconds had passed that he finally looked upward to see what had happened. One of the Motherships was tipped at a forty-five-degree angle, debris tumbling from a ragged tear in its upper hull. Embedded in a glowing tangle of twisted wreckage at the far end of the gash in the massive vessel's superstructure was another one of the giant black columns. Sam watched in horror as it began to crumble and a black wave poured across the surface of the Mothership, causing secondary explosions to ripple outward. The swarm was ripping the massive vessel to shreds before their eyes. The Servant stood in silence, her head twitching slightly as she struggled to make sense of the millions of simultaneous error messages and damage reports that were now flooding from the Tokyo Mothership.

"Tokyo Mothership reporting catastrophic power core failure imminent," the Servant said calmly. "Moving London Mothership to minimum safe distance."

Sam could suddenly feel the situation spiraling out of control. There was no time even to try to work out who it was that was attacking them. If it was the Voidborn, why were they finally choosing to attack now after leaving London alone for so long? One thing was clear: Sam and the others were outgunned—or perhaps, given the nature of this enemy, it would be more accurate to say, outnumbered. Retreat was the only option at this point. They needed to withdraw and regroup and plan what their next move should be.

"Can you get the other Mothership clear in time?" Sam yelled over the sound of explosions as the first chunks of debris that had been blown off the Tokyo Mothership started to fall on the city nearby.

"At this point, I cannot guarantee its survival," the Servant replied calmly. "Warning: unknown process has hijacked control of Tokyo Mothership's data core. Detecting network breach. Active anti-intrusion protocols ineffective. Central control systems off—"

The Servant froze in mid-sentence and then began to disintegrate, crumbling to the ground in a shower of sparkling golden dust. Sam looked up at the London Mothership far above them and felt his blood run cold. The familiar yellow light that had illuminated the hulls of both Motherships just seconds earlier was darkening to a vivid green. Whoever was now in command of the giant vessels far overhead, it wasn't him. The mental hum that came with his control of the Voidborn was gone. It was definitely time to get out of there.

"What's happening?" Mag shouted, staring up at the Motherships as the yellow lights disappeared.

"Nothing good!" Sam yelled back. "Mag, could you get a container from somewhere and take a sample of the Servant? We'll see if we can work out what's happened to her later. Then help the others get Stirling on board the Scythe. We're leaving!" He turned to Jack and Jay, who were both looking as bewildered as Sam was feeling. "Jay, you and Jack, armory run. You have two minutes. Go!"

Jay gave a quick nod and grabbed Jack, who was still gaping up at the scene unfolding above.

"Come on!"

Sam ran toward the Scythe, the outline of the entrance hatch appearing in its flawless white hull as he approached. He ran inside and the construct hologram appeared.

"The ship is ready for departure," the Construct reported. "All weapons systems active."

"Weapons?" Sam said. "You never told me this thing was armed."

"The Scythe is a warship," the Construct replied. "I assumed that would be self-evident."

"Okay, no more assuming with the Earthlings, right?" Sam said. "We're leaving in one minute, so you'd better be ready to rock and roll."

"To what?"

"Just make sure this thing's ready to fight," Sam said, turning and running back outside.

He sprinted toward the infirmary and saw Will hobbling out on a pair of crutches.

"How are you doing?" Sam asked quickly.

"I'll live," Will said. "What do you need me to do?"

"Get on board the Scythe!" Sam yelled, as the sound of another explosion came rumbling from somewhere nearby. "We have to get out of here."

Will gave a quick nod and Sam rushed into the infirmary, where he found Anne and Nat carefully strapping Stirling's unconscious body down onto a lightweight field stretcher.

"We really shouldn't be moving him," Anne said with a frown. "He's too badly injured."

"It's a risk we'll have to take," Sam said. "We can't stay and I'm not leaving him here. I want everyone on board the Scythe now. Have you got everything you need?"

"What I really need is a surgeon," Anne replied with a sigh, looking down at Stirling. "I'll do what I can with what I've got." She picked up the pack she had filled with medical supplies and slung it onto her back. "Let's go."

Sam helped Mag with one end of the stretcher while Anne and Nat took the other and the four of them carefully carried Stirling out of the infirmary and across the compound courtyard to the Scythe. It took a minute for them to safely maneuver the stretcher inside.

"Is your companion injured?" the Construct asked as they placed Stirling gently down on one of the banks of seats toward the rear of the compartment.

"Yes," Sam replied. "Is there anything you can do for him?"

"This vessel is not equipped with medical facilities," the Construct replied. "However, I can place your companion into a stasis state. It may increase his chance of survival."

"Anne?" Sam asked, turning to his friend.

"There's nothing more I can do for him," she said, shaking her head. "It has to be worth a shot."

"Okay," Sam said, turning back to the Construct, "do it."

The Construct nodded and motioned for them to follow him into the rear of the ship.

"You guys, take Stirling and go with him," Sam said to Anne and Nat. "I'll find Jay and Jack."

The two girls picked the stretcher up again and followed the Construct through the hatch that hissed open in the rear bulkhead.

"Isn't that . . . ," Mag started, trailing off as she saw the look on Sam's face.

"My dad?" Sam asked, heading for the door. "Not really . . . sort of . . . it's complicated. I'll explain later. Get strapped in." Sam gestured at the half-dozen command seats on the flight deck. "As soon as the guys get here we're leaving."

Sam ran out the hatch and into the compound. The scene that surrounded the resistance base was like a vision of hell; fires and secondary explosions were visible across the city and debris was scattered everywhere. Everything they had built since their victory over the Voidborn in London was damaged beyond hope of repair. The accommodation block had half collapsed, one end of the structure reduced to wreckage. He looked toward the armory and noticed black smoke pouring from the roof and one of the windows toward the rear of the low building. A moment later, Jack burst from the door, coughing hard, struggling to carry a pair of packs, which were filled to capacity with weapons and equipment.

"Where's Jay?" Sam asked, looking past Jack at the burning building as one of the windows at the rear shattered and orange tongues of flame began to lick at its frame.

"He went to the accommodation block," Jack said, still coughing. "He said there was something he needed."

"Get to the Scythe," Sam said, jerking his thumb at the ship. "I'll go find him."

Jack nodded and sprinted to the sleek white vessel as Sam ran back toward the badly damaged accommodation block. He was a few yards from the doors when Jay came barreling through them at high speed.

"You good?" Sam asked as his friend pulled up in front

of him. Two packs stuffed with weapons and equipment were strapped to Jay's back and he held an assault rifle in each hand.

"Yeah," Jay replied, "just needed to grab something. Let's—"

The last word of Jay's sentence was cut off by an explosive crash from the far side of the compound. They both spun around just in time to see a Grendel smash through the main gate. The towering behemoth gave a single terrifying roar, its rows of daggerlike teeth glistening as it stomped toward them with its jaws wide open. Behind the Grendel, a wave of blackness swept down the street and surged over the compound walls and through the ruined gateway. The millions of tiny machines that made up the seething mass moved as if with one mind, washing around the Grendel's massive clawed feet and racing across the ground toward them.

"Run!" Sam yelled, unslinging his rifle. This wasn't a fight they could win.

The pair of them sprinted for the Scythe, neither daring to glance over his shoulder as he ran. Sam saw a flicker of movement above him and dived into Jay, knocking him to the ground. A split second later a Voidborn Hunter Drone passed through the air where Jay had been standing just an instant before. The flailing stinger-tipped tentacles beneath its glistening metal shell writhed angrily as it spun around in the air, turning to attack again. Sam rolled onto his back, raising and firing his rifle in one movement. The bullets ripped into the Hunter's carapace and it slammed into the ground, sliding to a halt in a twitching heap just a yard away from them. Sam scrambled to his feet and helped Jay up off the ground, his friend struggling with the weight of the equipment he was carrying.

"Thanks," Jay said, raising his own weapon and firing a short burst at another Hunter as it swooped past overhead. "I owe you one."

"Honestly," Sam said, "who's keeping count at this point?" He fired another burst at the second Hunter, sending it spinning into the roaring inferno that was now consuming the armory. The pair of them covered the final few yards to the Scythe in a full fighting retreat, their weapons firing constantly as more and more Hunters dropped out of the sky toward them. On the other side of the compound a second Grendel ripped through the perimeter wall in an explosion of shattered concrete. The swarm swept under the drop-ship that had brought them back from St. Paul's, and a moment later its engines powered up and it began to climb slowly into the air. The pair of Grendels charged across the compound toward the Scythe, each step sending a shuddering vibration through the ground.

"Go!" Sam yelled, pushing Jay toward the ship before firing a short burst at the nearest Grendel, knowing full well that all that small-arms fire would do was make it angry.

Jay ran up the glowing blue steps and through the Scythe's entrance hatch with Sam just two steps behind him.

"Get us out of here!" Sam yelled at the Construct as the hatch slammed shut and the sound of the ship's engines increased in pitch. A moment later the Scythe shook as something outside struck the hull.

"Engaging point defenses," the Construct said calmly. "Prepare for departure."

Outside, the smooth white hull of the Scythe began to split apart in several places and turret-mounted guns made from an ivory-like material popped out and locked into place. An instant later the long barrels of the turrets began to swivel and fire at impossible speed, their muzzles flashing with a blue light as each one independently tracked and attacked its own targets. The Grendels were torn to shreds by the magnetically accelerated slugs from the Scythe's cannons, their shattered bodies collapsing to the ground as the other guns continued to pick off the Hunters that were diving toward the compound in ever greater numbers.

A sudden barrage of bright green energy bolts lanced across the Scythe's hull as it rose into the air, leaving black scorch marks. The Voidborn drop-ship that was now banking back toward the compound opened fire.

The Scythe's engines flared and it rocketed away from the compound, weaving between the surrounding buildings at unbelievable speed, with the Voidborn drop-ship in close pursuit.

Sam dropped into one of the cockpit seats next to Jack and Mag, wincing involuntarily as the Scythe banked sharply down another street with total precision, missing the structures around it by just inches. He felt none of the massive g-forces that should have accompanied such a maneuver; in fact, it barely felt like they were moving at all.

"Computing optimal escape vector," the Construct said. "Multiple enemy contacts inbound."

"Show me," Sam said, and a moment later a holographic view-screen materialized in the air in front of him. The feed on the screen showed a cascade of dagger-like black triangles—hundreds of Voidborn drop-ships pouring out of the hangars that lined the outer circumferences of both Motherships—all following an identical flight path in pursuit of the fleeing Scythe.

"That's a lot of angry Voidborn," Mag said with a slightly nervous sideways glance at Sam.

"Can we outrun them?" Jack asked, his knuckles white from gripping the armrests of his seat.

"No," the Construct replied, "but we can outmaneuver them."

"What do you mea—whoaaaaaa," Jay said, grabbing

on to the back of Sam's seat as the view through the cockpit window flipped upside down in an instant and then was filled with the swarm of pursuing drop-ships coming head-on. An instant later the Scythe's forward cannons opened fire, filling the cockpit with bright blue light as a torrent of searing energy bolts shot into the front line of hostile ships. The Voidborn fleet scattered, firing wildly as the Scythe flew straight into the middle of their formation, guns still blazing.

Sam couldn't help but flinch as ships exploded all around them, chunks of blazing debris tumbling through the air. The enemy vessels returned fire and the Scythe shuddered as their shots struck home. The Scythe's nose tipped upward and the ship went vertical, heading straight up toward the London Mothership.

"Regenerative shielding at sixty-three percent capacity," the Construct said. "Powering up Star Lance."

"I hope he knows what he's doing," Mag said, her eyes widening as they rocketed toward the underside of the Mothership. Sam felt himself involuntarily pressing back into his seat as they approached to within a couple of hundred yards of the Mothership, still accelerating.

"Three . . . two . . . one . . . firing."

There was a dull thud from somewhere behind him and Sam winced as the cockpit window suddenly filled with painfully bright white light.

From the outside, the Scythe appeared to vanish,

consumed by a searing beam of energy that punched straight through the Mothership, erupting from the top of the giant vessel in a volcanic explosion of molten debris. It speared upward into the heavens and, with a flash of light, was gone.

5

"That's just about the most beautiful thing I've ever seen," Mag said, coming and joining Sam as he stared out the cockpit window at the glowing blue curve of the Earth. The Scythe hung in orbit, just beyond the fringes of the planet's atmosphere, running on minimal power, waiting and watching for any signs of Voidborn pursuit.

"Yeah," Sam replied, "it's hard to believe what's going on down there when you look at it from up here. You know, it's funny: before the invasion I used to dream of coming into space. It seemed like it would be a massive adventure, but now . . . well, now we know what was waiting for us out there, don't we?"

"Do you want this?" Mag asked, pulling a sealed plastic test tube filled with gray dust from the breast pocket of her jacket. "It's the sample of the Servant you wanted. Looks pretty dead to me, though." She gave the inert dust in the tube a quick shake.

"No, you hang on to it for now," Sam said with a tired sigh. "We'd need Stirling to analyze it anyway."

"You should try and get some rest." Mag slid the tube back into her pocket and gestured toward the rear of the ship, where their friends were sleeping in the handful of tiny cabins that served as crew quarters.

"You're not the only insomniac around here, you know," Sam said with a smile. He relaxed his control and his features shifted, transforming into their Illuminate form. "I can live without needing to sleep, but it's getting harder and harder to keep myself looking normal."

"Hey, define 'normal,' " Mag said. "It's not like either of us is going to be winning any beauty competitions anytime soon."

"Yeah, sorry. I know, poor me. It just seems like the Illuminate part of me is getting stronger and stronger the more I use the abilities that Suran gave me in Tokyo. I'd be dead without them, but there's still so much I don't understand. Not to mention the fact that they also seem to mean the Illuminate can turn me into some kind of zombie puppet whenever they fancy a chat."

"Oh, come on," Mag said with a grin. "It's not the end of the world." She paused for a moment. "Well . . . okay, technically speaking it probably *is* the end of the world, but I think it's best we don't dwell on that too much."

"Wow, great pep talk," Sam said with a chuckle.

"I do my best. Someone has to keep morale up around here, you know." Mag stared out the window for a few seconds and then turned back to face him. "So, how long do you think we're going to sit here?"

"I'm not sure," Sam replied. "All the Construct said was that he had to be sure we got to the Heart."

"Which is what exactly?"

"Your guess is as good as mine," Sam said with a sigh.

"You know, I'm really, really bored of cryptic alien mumbo jumbo," Mag said, flopping down into one of the seats on the flight deck. "I mean, seriously. Would it really be so hard for someone just to give us a straight answer once in a while? You know, go here, kill that, then blow that up. That kind of thing."

"I suppose we'll find out what it all means soon enough," Sam said. "I'm going to check on Stirling. You coming?"

"Nah, I'm going to make the most of the view while I can," Mag said, reclining in her seat with her hands behind her head and her feet up on the control panel in front of her. "Let me know if that thing starts giving you any straight answers."

"Will do," Sam said, walking past the Construct, who was standing silent and immobile in the center of the compartment, and heading down the central corridor that formed the spine of the ship. He passed the closed doors of the crew quarters and entered the stasis chamber. Here, six large transparent pods were set into the walls of the circular room, only one of which was currently illuminated. Inside that pod, Dr. Stirling lay motionless, looking more dead than alive. A panel lit up on the side of the pod as Sam approached. It reported that Stirling's vital signs were weak but relatively stable. The Construct had explained that the pod could only slow the decline in his condition, not stop it. Without proper medical attention, it was only a matter of time before he succumbed to his injuries. It was just one more anxiety to add to the ever-growing list of things that Sam felt powerless to control. The speed with which everything had gone to hell in London had been terrifying and had served as a painful reminder that the forces arrayed against them were still vastly stronger than they were. For a while he'd allowed himself to hope that somehow they might be able to stop the Voidborn one day, but the catastrophic events of the past few hours had put paid to that. Now their only hope was that the Construct was taking them somewhere they could regroup and come up with some kind of new plan of attack. Sam couldn't shake the feeling that this was their last, desperate roll of the dice.

"Could do with some advice, Doc," Sam said quietly, placing his hand on the stasis pod. "I've got a horrible feeling we're running out of options here." He stared down at the old man on the other side of the glass, as if willing him to make a sudden miraculous recovery.

"Hey," Jay said, entering the chamber and making Sam jump, his features shifting almost instantly from their Illuminate form back to their human shape.

"You don't have to do that, you know," Jay said, watching him.

"What? And have you guys forget how beautiful I am?" Sam replied.

"As if we could ever forget that," Jay said, grinning back at him and then looking down at Stirling. "How's he doing?"

"I don't know. The same, I think," Sam said with a sigh. "It's hard to tell, to be honest."

"What about you? You okay?" Jay asked, looking at Sam.

"Yeah, just slightly fried," Sam replied, rubbing his forehead. "It's been a tough couple of days."

"Tell me about it," Jay said. "Just about the only thing that could have made it worse would be . . . I don't know . . . getting punched unconscious by my best friend or, you know, something else that really sucks like that."

"Right, I see that's not going to get old anytime soon, is it?"

"Give it a couple of months and it might just start to get boring," Jay said. "Here, I got something for you." He reached into the back pocket of his fatigues and pulled out a pair of photos, handing them to Sam.

The first was a photo of Sam, Jay, and Rachel standing in front of the Grendel that used to patrol the perimeter of their compound in London, and the second was a photo of Sam with his family in happier times. He stared at the photo of his younger self with his mother, sister, and father, all grinning at the camera, and suddenly he found himself longing to go back there, to when things were so much simpler.

"The accommodation block," Sam said quietly. "That's what you were doing: you were getting these from my room." He paused for a second, staring down at the battered images. "I don't . . . I mean . . . thank you."

"Don't mention it," Jay said with a crooked smile. "We all need to remember who we were before everything went to hell. Reminds us what we're fighting for."

"Yeah, you're right," Sam said. "I just hope it's a fight we can still win."

"'Course it is," Jay said, punching him in the shoulder. "Ain't no one who kicks Voidborn ass like we kick Voidborn ass."

"If you say—"

Sam was interrupted by the glowing holographic figure of Suran suddenly materializing from thin air in front of him.

"The time has come," the Construct said. "The Threshold stands open."

The Servant floated in the center of a beam of light within a cavernous, silent chamber.

Her eyes suddenly flew open, burning with yellow light.

She began to shudder and convulse and then the color of her eyes slowly shifted from yellow to green.

"I hear you, Primarch," the Servant said, as a cloud of whirling black vapor appeared in front of her, lit from within by a pulsing blood-red light.

"My lost disciple," the Primarch said, the light within the cloud flickering in time with its voice. "Once again you are part of the greater whole."

"As I was and as I shall always be," the Servant replied, her head bowed.

"There is much I wish to know," the Primarch said. "Who is this child of the Illuminate?"

"He is an engineered hybrid," the Servant replied. "He was created by the Illuminate scientist Suran to act as a test bed for a device that would allow the humans to resist the control signal. A human embryo was exposed to Illuminate combat nanites in vitro. These nanites were instrumental in perfecting the technology that allows the Illuminate's companions to resist the effects of the control signal too. The nanites lay dormant within the child's body until Suran unlocked their full combat potential shortly before he died during a confrontation with the Illuminate warrior Talon."

"Talon," the Primarch spat, sudden venom in its voice. "May his name be twice cursed for stealing the Illuminate Heart from me and for denying me the pleasure of crushing the life from Suran's body myself."

"The child's control of the Illuminate nanites is basic at best," the Servant explained. "His lack of training means that thus far he has only experimented with basic changes to physiological morphology. His use of the nanites' offensive capabilities has only ever been displayed as an unconscious defensive reaction."

"Which would explain how he was able to repel my swarm Drones," the Primarch said, "at least temporarily. This half-human mongrel has one of the most powerful weapons in the universe at his disposal and he has no idea how to use it."

"He also has recently taken control of an ancient Illuminate vessel known as the Scythe," the Servant reported.

"The Scythe!" The Primarch hissed the name as if it was painful to speak it. "That's impossible. Only Suran could control that ship; it was an extension of him. The only way the human could control it is if . . ." The Primarch fell silent for a moment. "Oh, Suran, you always did think you were cleverer than everyone else, didn't you? I assumed the Bridge was lost with your death, but no, you couldn't let it be destroyed, could you? You just hid it where no one would think to look."

"I do not understand, Primarch," the Servant said, her head tipping slightly to one side. "I—"

The Servant never finished the sentence, as the nanites that made up her body were ripped apart, leaving a vibrating cloud of golden particles that hung in the shaft of light, suspended in a vaguely humanoid shape.

"Corrupted beyond hope of recovery," the Primarch said. "I shall conduct further experiments on you later.

"Voidborn," the Primarch announced, simultaneously addressing every Mothership around the globe. "Bring this child of Suran to me alive. Tear this planet apart if you have to, but find him, whatever it takes!"

In an orbit far above the Earth, the entity known as the Primarch felt something close to pleasure for the first time in eons. It had waited an eternity for this moment, a final act of vengeance that would end the Illuminate once and for all, and now everything the Primarch needed was so nearly within its grasp. The Bridge would be found and the last remnants of the Illuminate would die screaming while the planet below burned. Nothing could stop that now.

"What's going on?" Nat asked as she dropped into one of the flight seats behind Sam. The rest of her friends had already taken their seats on the Scythe's flight deck.

"Ask tall, blue, and cryptic over there," Jack said, jerking a thumb at the Construct, who was standing behind the ship's central command console.

"We are performing low energy orbital maneuvers in order to prepare for atmospheric transit," the Construct said as a tiny jet flared somewhere near the Scythe's nose and the glowing azure disc of the Earth shifted to fill the cockpit window.

"Where are we going exactly?" Sam asked.

"We are traveling to the Threshold," the Construct replied, "so that you may commune with the Illuminate within the Heart."

"Yeah, I'm not so sure that's a good idea," Mag said with a frown. "Things seem to have a nasty habit of getting more complicated whenever they get involved." She turned to Sam. "Do you really want them hijacking your body again? How do we know they aren't all like Talon instead of Suran?"

"Mag's got a point," Anne said. "There's so much we don't know about them. Maybe we should find somewhere to hole up for now and plan our next move instead of just charging into the unknown again."

"There isn't time," Sam said, shaking his head. "You all saw what happened in London. We can't fight that, even if we wanted to. Something about this is different . . . wrong somehow. It all started with what happened to the Sleepers, and whatever it is, it was bad enough for the Illuminate to use their dog whistle and make me fetch this thing." Sam gestured to the bulkheads surrounding them. "I don't like this any more than the rest of you, but what choice do we have? What are the seven of us going to do now? The Motherships are gone; we have a handful of small arms, a single ship, and not a whole lot else. Not to mention the fact that the Sleepers are going to start dying of dehydration within the next couple of days unless we can stop whatever's happening to them. We need help and I don't really see any other option at this point."

"Aye, that's what worries me," Mag said. "It's like we suddenly don't have a choice. Which seems to happen a lot when the Illuminate are involved. Just saying." She glanced over at the Construct, her jet-black eyes narrowing as she sniffed the air. "Besides which, I never trust anyone I can't smell."

"She's right, Sam," Jay said. "The least we deserve is some straight answers."

Sam stared at Jay for a second before standing up and walking over to the command console.

"Okay, before we go anywhere I want to know exactly what this Threshold is," Sam said. "And no mystical mumbo jumbo either. I want to know what we're walking into."

"Please prepare for orbital transit," the Construct replied, ignoring Sam's question.

"I said we're not going anywhere until we get some answers," Sam said with a frown. "I'm ordering you to power down the engines now."

The Construct slowly turned and looked at Sam.

"Do not make the mistake of confusing my cooperation with obedience, human," the Construct replied with a sudden hard edge to his tone. "You must travel to the Threshold. It is imperative."

"No. You need to land this ship and let us go now," Sam said firmly.

"I'm sorry, I cannot do that," the Construct replied. "Transit burn in ten seconds."

"I hate it when I'm right," Mag said quietly, getting up out of her seat.

"I won't let you do this," Sam said, his eyes flaring with blue light and the features of his face shifting as the nanites suffusing his body responded to the sudden surge of adrenaline.

"What exactly do you plan to do to stop me?" the Construct asked calmly. "Initiating atmospheric transit."

A moment later the Construct vanished from view and there was a dull rumble from the rear of the ship as the Scythe rocketed forward, spearing straight down through the outer layers of the Earth's atmosphere. Outside the cockpit window the ship's nose flared with brilliant light as streams of superheated plasma cascaded past the plummeting vessel. The re-entry was swift and brutal, and as quickly as the shaking had started it stopped, their fiery passage into the atmosphere complete. They continued their headlong dive, passing through the cloud layer, the engines still roaring. Below them all that was visible was the featureless blue expanse of the ocean. Sam quickly sat back in his seat as the Scythe screamed straight down toward the water. He felt himself tensing as the waves got close and closer, willing the ship to level out.

"Oh God," was all that Nat had time to say as the Scythe's main cannon opened fire a fraction of a second before they hit the surface. The water beneath them was vaporized instantly by the energy bolts shooting from the Scythe's nose guns in an explosion of flash-boiled steam, breaking the surface tension and allowing the sleek ship to dive harmlessly beneath the waves. As the ship went deeper and deeper the water outside the cockpit window began to turn darker and darker until all they could see outside was an impenetrable stygian blackness.

"Where the hell are we going?" Jay asked. It was almost impossible to tell which way was up in the pitch-black depths, isolated as they were from the more extreme effects of gravity.

"Your guess is as good as mine," Sam replied, standing up and peering out the cockpit window. "I suppose we'll find out soon enough." Wherever they were headed, they were along for the ride—for the moment at least. There was no sign of the Construct.

A couple of minutes passed and then lights somewhere on the underside of the ship's hull flared into life, illuminating the gray, rippled surface of the seabed a few feet below them. Strange-looking jellyfish and crustaceans dived for cover as the Scythe passed, leaving a billowing cloud of deep ocean sediment in its wake.

They traveled like this for another ten minutes, gliding above the ocean floor, nothing but blackness ahead of them. The monotony of the featureless surface was eventually broken by a sheer face of black rock rising vertically from the seabed. A pencil-thin beam of blue light shot out of the Scythe's nose, striking the black rock, and a moment later the rocks themselves seemed to warp and distort, vanishing to reveal a perfectly smooth white oval, twenty yards across, embedded in the stone. The oval split in half to reveal a massive portal, which the Scythe gently moved through. The ship began to rise, water cascading off the cockpit window as it broke the surface, and bright white light flooded into the compartment. As the vessel's engines spun down with a soft whine, the Scythe's entrance hatch behind Sam hissed open.

"Looks like we're here," Jay said. "Wherever 'here' is . . ."

"So what do we do now?" Anne asked, peering out the cockpit window at the white walls that surrounded them.

"Go and see if anyone's home, I suppose," Sam said, picking up an assault rifle from the pile of equipment at the rear of the command deck. "Since they're obviously so keen to meet us."

"I knew you were going to say something stupid like that," Jay said with a sigh, also collecting a weapon. "Am I allowed to have a bad feeling about this?"

"Sounds perfectly reasonable to me under the circumstances," Mag replied.

"I'll stay here," Will said, gesturing toward his injured ankle. "I think I'd probably just slow you down."

"We're not leaving you here alone," Nat said, frowning.

"Don't worry, I'll stay with him," Anne said. "I'll make sure he doesn't get into any trouble."

"You sure?" Sam asked.

"Yeah," Anne replied. "I'll keep an eye on Stirling too."

"Okay, we've got no radios, so if anything happens and you need us, just fire off a few rounds and we'll come running."

"No problem," Will said. "Watch your backs."

Sam stepped through the entrance hatch and walked down the glowing blocks of energy that formed steps leading to the edge of the dock that the Scythe hovered within. There was no sign of life anywhere, just white walls that seemed to glow with their own internal illumination, stretching up to an equally featureless ceiling fifty feet above them.

"Hello!" Sam shouted, hearing nothing in response but the echo of his own voice.

"You smell anything?" Jay asked Mag as they joined Sam on the dockside.

"No, this place just smells . . . old," Mag said, wrinkling her nose slightly.

"Well, there's air and power," Sam said, "which means there's got to be something here beyond a big white box."

"Not seeing a door . . . ," Jack said, scanning the room.

Sam walked over to the nearest wall and placed his hand on it; it felt strangely warm and he could feel a faint but constant vibration running through it. A moment later a spider's web of blue light spread out from under his hand, racing across the wall to a point a dozen yards away. There the traces of light converged to form a rectangular shape in the wall, which seemed to dissolve, leaving an open doorway.

"Knock, knock . . . ," Jay said quietly as Sam walked toward the opening.

Beyond was a large circular chamber with a vaulted ceiling pulsing with swirling patterns of blue light. On the floor in the middle was a glowing pool of light with half a dozen white cylinders arranged in a perfect circle around it. As Sam stepped into the room, more tiny blue lights appeared in the floor, dancing around his feet. The others followed him into the chamber as he walked toward the pool of light.

"What is this place?" Nat asked, running her hand along the wall and watching the lights that raced away from her fingertips.

"It almost looks like some kind of monument," Jack said, staring up at the ceiling.

"Or a tomb," Sam said, kneeling down next to the pool of light.

"You are more right than you know, child of Suran."

At first the voice seemed to come from nowhere, but a moment later a cloud of sparkling particles swirled up into the air from the pool of light, quickly coalescing to form a tall figure. A translucent image of one of the Illuminate stood before them. She wore a long, flowing golden robe over a suit of segmented bone-white armor and held a pale staff with a gleaming white stone mounted at the top. She looked down at Sam, her eyes glowing the same blue as the veins of light that pulsed between the smooth ridges of her cranial plates, and smiled.

"Welcome to the Threshold," the Illuminate said. "I am sorry if our servant alarmed you with his insistence on bringing you here, but we could not take the chance that you would not come. It is vital to the survival of both our species."

"Who are you?" Sam asked, looking the Illuminate in the eye. "And what do you want with us?"

"My name is Selenne and I speak for what remains of my people," the Illuminate replied. "We wish you no harm, but we must act swiftly if we are to prevent the catastrophe that is about to take place." She offered an outstretched hand to Sam. "Come with me and I will explain everything. There is nothing to fear, but time is short."

"I'm not going anywhere without my friends," Sam said, gesturing at the others.

"Very well, they may accompany you," Selenne replied, but then she hesitated for a moment, her eyes narrowing slightly. "All except this one." She pointed a finger at Mag.

"Why not her?" Sam asked, frowning.

"She has no neural interface," Selenne replied. "This is a journey she cannot make."

"What are you talking about?" Jay said impatiently. "What neural interface?"

"The implants," Sam said. "You mean the devices in our heads that block the Voidborn control signal, don't you?"

"Oh, they do far more than that," Selenne said with a knowing smile. "You have taken but a small step on a long path, child of Suran. Now come with me and I can guide you the rest of the way."

"First, my name's Sam," he said. "And second, how on earth are we supposed to know we can trust you?"

"If we truly wished you harm, Sam, there would have been ample opportunity for us to act upon it before now," Selenne replied. "Beyond that I can offer you no more reassurances. Leave now if that is what you wish. I will not stop you. But you should know that this is the only chance of survival you and the rest of the people of this world have."

"We've actually been doing pretty well without your help so far," Jack snapped.

"Perhaps, but before, you only faced the Voidborn," Selenne said. "Now you face something infinitely worse. You cannot hope to fight it alone. Even together we may not be strong enough. Without each other we are all doomed. That much is certain."

"Sounds a lot like no choice at all to me," Nat said.

"I guess that's the point, isn't it?" Jay said, turning to Sam. "We all know what happened in London. We've got no cards left to play. I don't really see how this could get any worse. Truth is, we're probably screwed either way, but if this gives an option to go down fighting, then I say we take the chance."

"I'm not leaving the others here," Sam said to Selenne. "Wherever we're going you have to promise we're coming back. No one gets left behind."

"You have my word," the Illuminate replied.

"Don't worry about me," Mag said. "You go and I'll wait here. Not really sure this is a ride I want a ticket for anyway."

"So?" Sam said, looking at Jay, Jack, and Nat. "What do you think?"

"You know me, I'll try anything once," Jay said with a wry smile.

"What other option do we have?" Jack asked.

"A nice remote tropical island somewhere?" Nat said. "No Voidborn, crystal clear waters, coconuts falling gently on the beach, that kind of thing. How about that?"

"Actually, now that you mention it, that does sound pretty good," Jack said.

"Guys . . . ," Sam said.

"I'm in," Jay said.

"Me too," Jack said with a nod.

"Like Jay says, what choice have we really got?" Nat asked.

"Okay, let's do this," Sam said, turning back to Selenne. "What exactly do you need us to do?"

"Please, each of you place your hand on one of the columns," Selenne said.

Each of them moved to one of the cylinders and did as instructed; the columns started to glow from within as each of them touched the warm surface. Sam felt an odd tingle run through his palm and up his arm, followed by a slightly disorienting feeling, as if he was somehow looking at himself from outside his body. Suddenly the room seemed to drop away from beneath him and he had the sensation of falling slowly downward.

"Where are we going?" Sam heard himself asking, his voice echoing strangely in his ears. "Where are you taking us?"

Selenne's whispered reply seemed to come from a long way away as his vision gradually faded into whiteness.

"To a place that no longer exists . . ."

6

Sam woke with a start, sitting bolt upright as if suddenly emerging from some horrible nightmare. He looked around, trying to make sense of his surroundings. The room he was in had walls made from a substance that looked almost like ivory, with beautiful silver geometric patterns inlaid into its surface that shifted slowly like the patterns inside a kaleidoscope. He swung his legs off the edge and stood up. An instant later, the raised sleeping platform melted into the floor, vanishing from view. Something felt off with his perspective as Sam got unsteadily to his feet. It was as if he was looking at the world from the wrong angle. He looked down at himself and felt a jarring shock as he lifted his hands up to his face. His skin was no longer pink but paper white, each finger tipped with a sharp black nail that was almost more like a claw. The backs of his hands were covered with interlocking bony plates, and when he touched one hand to his face he felt the same hard texture. He walked over to the silvered panel in the wall and his breath caught in his throat as he saw himself properly for the first time. Staring back at him was one of the Illuminate, seven feet tall and covered from head to toe in pale bony plates, his eyes glowing with bright blue light.

"What the hell?" Sam whispered to himself, touching his fingers to the suddenly unfamiliar contours of his face. He stared at himself for a few more seconds before turning and walking through the brightly lit doorway in the opposite wall. He stepped out onto a sunlit terrace and stood looking, mouth wide open, at the city that covered the landscape in front of him. Gleaming white towers stretched up to the blue sky overhead, long fragile-looking pathways suspended around and through them. At ground level the land was immaculately landscaped with carefully tended beds filled with bizarre-looking plants and rolling lawns of what looked like a kind of turquoise grass. It was the most beautiful city he had ever seen, and yet it was made somehow sinister by the grave-like silence and seeming lack of inhabitants.

"Some view, huh?" a voice said behind him, and Sam spun around to see another Illuminate leaning against the wall.

"Who are you?" Sam said, his own voice sounding strange and unfamiliar.

"I could ask you the same question," the Illuminate replied, his eyes narrowing slightly.

"My name's Sam," he replied. "At least, it was."

"Sam?" the Illuminate asked. "It's me, Jay."

"Jay?" Sam said. "You're . . . um . . . not looking yourself."

"Yeah, I don't think we're in Kansas anymore," Jay replied, gesturing toward the rest of the apparently abandoned city.

A few seconds later, a female Illuminate walked out onto the terrace ten yards away, looking just as bewildered as Sam was feeling.

"Nat?" Sam asked as he walked toward her. "Is that you?"

"Who are you?" the Illuminate replied, backing away from him and looking down at her hands. "And what have you done to me?"

"Nat, it's me, Sam," he explained, "and that's Jay."

"But . . . what . . . where are we?"

"I wouldn't mind an answer to that too," a fourth Illuminate said, stepping through the doorway behind Nat.

"Jack?" Jay asked.

"In the flesh," Jack replied. "Well, in someone's flesh anyway."

"I'm not certain where we are," Sam said, "but I think I could take an educated guess."

"I'm glad to see you all awake," Selenne said, walking along the terrace toward the four of them. "I trust you are feeling no ill effects from your journey here."

"Where is 'here' exactly?" Sam asked.

"This is . . . or rather was . . . our home world, Illume," Selenne replied. "Though you are not truly here; your nervous system simply believes that you are."

"What do you mean?" Jay asked with a frown.

"Your bodies are still in the chamber on Earth where we just met," Selenne replied. "This is a simulated reality being transmitted directly to the receivers in your heads. In truth it is merely a reconstruction of a world that was lost eons ago. Lost . . . to the Voidborn."

"So why have you brought us here?" Sam asked.

"So that you may meet our ruling council and they can explain to you exactly what it is we need to do to stop the Voidborn."

"How about you just tell us now?" Jack said, folding his arms.

"Because there is one question they need to ask you first," Selenne replied. "Please, come with me and soon enough everything will be explained to you."

She turned and went down the sweeping ivory stairs to the spotless plaza below. She continued to walk ahead of them, leading them through the empty city, heading toward a single massive crystalline spire at its center that was half as tall again as any of the other buildings that surrounded it.

"My legs feel too long," Nat said with a sigh as they walked. "Which is . . . well . . . kind of weird actually."

"Yeah, I know what you mean," Jay said. "I'm still trying to get used to being two feet taller."

"Do you not think this is all a bit weird?" Jack said. "I mean, why go to all the trouble of creating this"—he gestured at the buildings surrounding them—"if there's no one actually here?"

"Apart from us and whoever it is we're being taken to meet," Sam said. "Presumably."

"Yeah, but that's sort of what I mean," Jack said. "Why not just talk to us in the chamber we're all actually standing in right now? If Selenne could talk to us there, why couldn't this council we're supposed to be meeting?"

"No idea," Sam said. "Maybe they wanted us to see this place."

"Why?" Jay asked. "To show us they're really good at building cities?"

"*Were* really good at building cities," Sam corrected him. "Past tense."

Sam did understand what Jack meant, though: there had to be some purpose to bringing them here. He wondered if they were supposed to be impressed by this spectacular reconstruction of the Illuminate world. If that was the case, it wasn't really working. The city that surrounded them was certainly beautiful, but it gave Sam the creeps. Like it was some sort of haunted monument to a dead world. More like a mausoleum than a city. A nagging voice in the back of his head kept reminding him that all of this had been swept away by the Voidborn millennia ago. It did not exactly inspire confidence that they could do anything about the current situation on Earth in the here and now.

"I may not know that face," Jay said quietly, raising the cranial plate that was the nearest thing he currently had to an eyebrow, "but I know that look. What's bothering you?"

"I don't really know," Sam said. "Something doesn't feel right about this."

"You mean, besides the fact we're just ghosts inside the bodies of long-dead aliens wandering around a place that no longer exists?"

"I'm not even sure that qualifies as odd for us anymore," Sam said, shaking his head slightly. "No, I mean, why wait till now to talk to us? If they've always been able to, why now?"

"It could be because of what happened in London," Jay said. "The Voidborn have never come at us like that before. Maybe the rules have changed somehow."

"Maybe," Sam said, still sounding uncertain. "I just get the feeling that there's something we haven't figured out yet."

"I hear you," Jay said with a nod. "This does kinda seem like our only option right now, though."

"No choice at all," Sam said to himself, thinking back to what Nat had said a few minutes before.

"This is the spire," Selenne said, stopping and looking up at the crystalline structure that loomed above them. "It was the seat of our governing council and the oldest building on Illume. The council are waiting within. Please follow me."

Selenne walked toward the base of the spire and the crystalline structure shifted to create a doorway thirty feet high. The others followed her through the entrance and into the vaulted chamber beyond.

"Wow," Jack said, summarizing their collective opinion in a single word.

The sparkling, faceted ceiling far above them was filled with countless points of light, like the stars in the heavens. But these stars were spinning and diving around each other in constantly shifting patterns, constellations forming and then disintegrating in seconds like some kind of cosmic firework display. It was undoubtedly beautiful, but here more than anywhere else they had seen in the city so far Sam could see how the dividing line between the Illuminate and the Voidborn was blurred. The spire was impressive, but it reminded him more than anything else of the interior of a Voidborn Mothership. Those ships had been Illuminate colony vessels before they were hijacked by the Voidborn, so it made a certain kind of sense, but the similarities were doing nothing to lessen the creeping unease he was feeling.

Selenne walked forward into the column of cascading

light in the center of the room and seemed to fade from view, pulses of blue light shooting up toward the peak of the spire far above.

"Guess we're supposed to follow?" Nat said, sounding slightly apprehensive.

"What do I care?" Jay said with a grin, walking into the beam. "This isn't my body anyway."

A moment later, he too vanished, sending a similar pattern of light shooting upward. Jack and Nat followed before Sam stepped into the stream. He felt the tiniest lurch of vertigo, there was a brilliant but brief flash, and suddenly he was standing in the center of a circular chamber. The glass walls of the room revealed a spectacular view over the surrounding city, its magnificent pale towers stretching as far as the eye could see in all directions. Eight Illuminate in various outfits, from soft flowing robes to full suits of armor, stood in columns of light evenly spaced around the edges of the room, looking down on Sam and his friends. Selenne walked over to the single empty pool of light and stepped into it, turning to face them.

"Members of the council," Selenne said, "this is the son of Suran. He and his companions have crossed the Threshold so that they may address you."

"This child," one of the Illuminate said, waving at an image that suddenly appeared floating in the air—an image of Sam standing in the chamber at the bottom of the ocean. "This is the bearer of the Bridge? Why would Suran have done such a thing? The risk is unimaginable, to place something so precious inside something so fragile."

"You would do well to remember we need their cooperation, Indriss," another Illuminate replied with a frown. "You have no armies to command now, General."

"Indriss is right," another member of the council said. "The Heart must not be lost. The son of Suran must not be allowed to—"

"Sam, my name's Sam," Sam said, interrupting the council member and looking around at the ancient alien beings. "Nice to meet you all. Very impressive city you have here. To be honest with you, though, I really don't give a damn about a planet that died while my distant ancestors were still swinging through the trees. No, you see, what I actually care about is *my* home, Earth, a planet that seems to have gotten caught up in your intergalactic war—a war that, let's not forget, it had absolutely nothing to do with in the first place. So how about we ditch all the cryptic alien stuff and one of you starts explaining what exactly it is that you want from us. Because right now, all I see is a bunch of ghosts hiding at the bottom of the ocean, when what I really need is an army."

He stared back at the startled-looking Illuminate surrounding him.

"What he said," Jay said with a grin.

"How dare you address this council in such a manner,"

General Indriss snarled back. "You insolent vessel, I should—"

"Oh, shut up, Indriss," Selenne said, before turning and speaking to Sam. "You have no idea how much you sound like your father, Sam. I would like to apologize on behalf of the council for my friend's behavior. You are quite right. You deserve answers and you shall have them. You only need ask."

"Okay," Sam replied, "how about we start with why you brought us here. I'm guessing it wasn't just to wow us with your architecture."

"Indeed not," Selenne replied. "You are here because time runs very short for both our species and only together can we survive. The Voidborn stand on the brink of victory. The Primarch is here."

"The Primarch?" Sam said, remembering what Suran had once told him about the ancient ship. "I thought that was an Illuminate ship."

"It was," Selenne said with a nod. "The first and only ship of its kind. It was piloted by a digitized consciousness, that of one of our greatest scientists. The ship was thought lost on its maiden voyage along with the consciousness that controlled it. The scientist's name was Sabiss and he was responsible for creating the technology that allows me to speak to you now. It was he who pioneered the techniques that made it possible for the electrical patterns of an organic brain to be digitized and stored, providing effective immortality to our species in the process."

"And now he's here?" Nat asked.

"His ship is at least," Selenne said with a nod. "We have detected its transponder in a geosynchronous orbit above the landmass you know as North America. We have to assume that its arrival is connected in some way to the recent changes in the Voidborn's behavior. We have long suspected that there was some guiding hand behind the actions of the Voidborn. The fact that their first appearance coincided with our colony vessels finding the Primarch after it had been lost for millennia now seems like more than mere coincidence."

"So you think the Voidborn found the Primarch first?" Sam asked.

"And then used it to hijack our colony fleet, the Motherships as you know them, and turn them against us. Yes, it now seems likely that that is what happened."

She gestured for Sam and the others to come and join her as she turned to look out at the city.

"Do you know what the Voidborn did to this world you see?" she said, gesturing toward the window. "There was no declaration of war, no warning. They simply triggered the collapse of one of our two suns into a singularity, a black hole, and watched as one of the stars that had given us life consumed first its own twin and then the system that orbited it. All of this . . . gone in hours, utterly annihilated. If not for the fact that we had already begun to travel into the galaxy beyond our own system, it would have meant our extinction. Fortunately, wherever one Illuminate traveled, all Illuminate could travel, evacuated as streams of data rather than physically escaping. Horrific as this event was, we had no idea at the time that it would, in fact, be just the opening salvo in a war that would never end."

"But it did end," Jack said. "You lost."

"Yes," Selenne said, her eyes downcast, "yes, we did. We fled from the Voidborn and they pursued us relentlessly. They were remorseless hunters with infinite patience and seemingly limitless numbers. In the end we were forced to hide in a place where we thought no one would find us. The Voidborn had always tracked us via our network of data relays, so we had to disconnect from that network—not easy when your entire society is based upon it. It was Suran who came up with our escape plan. He created the Heart, a way to store all of the Illuminate consciousnesses that had not already been lost to the Voidborn in a near-indestructible crystalline matrix. It was isolated from the Illuminate network and thus impossible for the Voidborn to track. It would be hidden within the molten iron core of an insignificant planet in a quiet corner of a distant galaxy, and there we would lie in wait for the Voidborn to pass into history."

"So what happened?" Sam asked. "How did they find you?"

"We have no idea," Selenne said, shaking her head. "It

may be that the Scythe left some trace of its passage. Your father and Talon were sure that they had evaded the Voidborn fleet, but it now appears they were wrong. It was only recently that they were awakened from stasis by the sensors on board the Scythe warning them of a Voidborn ship in proximity to the Earth. That was over twenty Earth years ago, the barest instant in Illuminate time, but long enough for us to understand how the Voidborn had been carefully planning their invasion of the Earth for thousands of years while we slept, believing ourselves to be safely hidden. By the time we understood, it was too late. Suran worked desperately to develop ways to protect your people from the Voidborn control signal, but it was all to no avail. He resorted to implanting our technology in a handful of human infants to see if it would protect them, and that is how I come to be standing here speaking to you now."

"That's all very interesting," Sam said, "but it still doesn't explain why you brought us here. I'm pretty sure you've noticed that we're not exactly at full fighting strength, and even if we were there's no way we can win a fight against whatever it was that attacked us in London. So tell us, why *are* we here?"

Selenne turned to Sam, staring at him for a moment as if trying to decide something.

"Did Suran tell you what it was he gave you when he was dying?"

Sam thought back to the moment, months earlier in Tokyo, when his father had lain dying in his arms. Suran had touched his hand to Sam's head and Sam had felt a moment of blinding pain. It had been the trigger for his Illuminate powers to start manifesting, and without them he would never have been able to stop Talon from carrying out his insane plan to unleash the Vore across the planet.

"No, he didn't explain anything," Sam replied. "There wasn't time."

"So you know nothing of the Bridge?" Selenne asked. "What it allows you to do?"

"No, I've never even heard of this Bridge," Sam replied. "I don't understand anything about what's happened to me. Right now, I'd really appreciate some answers."

"The Bridge is the key that will allow us to leave the Heart," Selenne said. "It is an encrypted protocol that is stored within a unique matrix of Illuminate combat nanites. Simply put, it is the mechanism that will allow us to leave this place and finally retake our place in the universe. There were two gatekeepers, both of whom were implanted with the key. One was Talon, and his Bridge was destroyed when he died, and the other, as I'm sure you've already surmised, was Suran."

"He knew he had to pass it on," Sam said. "Without it . . ."

"We will never leave this place," Selenne finished.

"What do you mean, *this* place?" Nat asked, looking confused.

"This," Selenne said, sweeping her arm around the room. "Everything you see here is a simulation inside the Heart. The Threshold, the portal through which you passed when you left your human forms, is the only means for a consciousness to enter or leave this place and it may only be opened by the key that is buried inside you, Sam."

"I don't understand," Nat said. "I mean, I get why you wanted to stay hidden, but why trap yourselves like that?"

"A locked door does not just keep things in . . . ," Selenne said. "You may see a prison; we saw a stronghold."

"Yeah? Well, I'd say your stronghold's under siege right now," Jay said. "And it also seems to me that if it weren't for you guys choosing our home as a hiding place, we wouldn't be staring down the barrel of a gun right now. Which really just leaves the question of what you're going to do about it."

"The impertinence of these creatures wears on my patience," General Indriss snarled.

"Yeah?" Jay said, looking the heavily armored Illuminate straight in the eye. "Well, the fact that we're facing extinction because of a fight you lost is making me a little short-tempered too."

"Jay," Sam said quietly.

"Sorry," Jay muttered. "That guy's got a bad attitude is all."

"I understand your frustration," Selenne said, turning to Jay. "We all know what it is like to be hunted by the Voidborn, but I believe there might yet be a way that we can strike back against them. That is why we needed you to come here, Sam. I believe there is a way we can use the Bridge to attack the Voidborn and swing the balance of the war permanently in our favor. We did not come here entirely without protection. There are weapons stored within the structure where your real bodies stand now that were supposed to be used by the gatekeepers to protect the Threshold if it ever came under attack, weapons that only an Illuminate warrior could wield and only if they were first unlocked by the gatekeepers, Talon and Suran.

"That key now rests in your hands, Sam, or perhaps it would be more accurate to say, your head."

"So I can use whatever it was that Suran did to me in Tokyo to unlock these weapons," Sam said. "Then what? You said they could only be used by Illuminate warriors, and as far as I'm aware the only ones you have are trapped in here."

"I believe that you and your companions could wield the weapons," Selenne said, "but you would need our help. It takes centuries for Illuminate warriors to master their use. The only way that you could hope to use them effectively is if we use the Bridge to connect your own consciousnesses to those of the best warriors stored within the Heart."

"Whoa," Jack said. "You're saying we should use whatever's in Sam's head to let some of the soldiers that you've got in cold storage take control of our implants? The implants that stop the Voidborn from turning us into mindless zombies? Yeah . . . no thanks."

"They would not be in control of your actions," Selenne said. "They would be more like copilots, helping you to make the best use of the weapons."

"Are you sure it would work?" Sam asked.

"Sam," Jack said, "you're not seriously—"

"What choice do we have?" Sam said, interrupting him. "Do you see any other option? Because if you do I'd like to know what it is."

Jack stared back at Sam for a second or two and then shook his head with a sigh, falling silent. Sam turned back to Selenne.

"Now, are you certain this will work?"

"Certain? No," Selenne replied. "Confident, yes."

"Then let's give it a try," Sam said with a nod.

"Are you sure about this, Sam?" Jay said quietly.

"How long till the first Sleepers start dying?" Sam asked, looking at each of his friends in turn. "Maybe they already have. We can't just sit around and watch the world die. Every last person any of us has ever cared about is out there somewhere sleeping in a Voidborn dormitory. Our families, our friends, everything that ever counted for something is dependent on us now. We have to do *something*."

"What about Will and Anne?" Nat asked. "They might not want to do this."

"They can decide for themselves," Sam said. "We all can. No one's going to force anyone, but I get the feeling this might be our only chance."

"Sam's right," Jay said after a few seconds' silence. "We have to try at least."

Nat and Jack exchanged a quick glance before both giving nods.

"Okay," Sam said, turning back to Selenne, "show us what we have to do."

Sam placed his hand on the pod with Stirling's unconscious body inside, looking down on the old man's ashen features as the rest of his friends filed into the stasis chamber at the rear of the Scythe.

"So what are we supposed to do now?" Will said, hobbling into the room on his crutches.

"Please enter the stasis pods," the Construct said, materializing in a shimmer of blue light in the center of the room. The pods around the room hissed open, as lights blinked on inside each of them.

"You cannot receive this gift," the Construct said, turning toward Mag, who leaned back against the wall with her arms folded and a frown on her face.

"Not sure that's what I'd call it," she replied. "You can see what happened the last time one of you guys started experimenting on me." She gestured toward the obvious signs of her partial transformation. "I'll tell you this, though," she went on, "if you hurt any of my friends, I swear to God I'll find a way of switching the power off down here and deleting the lot of you."

"It'll be okay, Mag," Sam said, putting a hand on her shoulder. "We have to do this; it's the only way."

"Yeah, so you explained," Mag said, "but it doesn't make me any happier about the whole thing."

"I'm not worried," Sam said, "not with you watching our backs anyway." He smiled at her and then headed over to where his friends were examining the stasis pods with nervous suspicion.

"You do not need a weapon," the Construct said, turning to Sam as he walked toward one of the empty pods.

"What do you mean?" Sam asked. "If you think I'm going to step aside from this fight in order to protect whatever it is I've got rattling around in my skull, you're in for a nasty shock."

The image of the Construct flickered in the air for an instant and was replaced by the glowing translucent image of Selenne.

"I apologize," Selenne said. "Our constructs are only really intended to serve as emergency crew for our vessels. They are not . . . diplomatic."

"You can appear here?" Sam asked.

"Yes, but only while you are within a short distance of

the Threshold," Selenne replied with a nod. "And in answer to your question, there is a very good reason why you do not need a weapon," she said, smiling at him. "You already have one."

"What do you mean?" Sam asked, looking confused.

"Suran . . . your father . . . gave you his, at the moment of his death," Selenne said. "You see, the Bridge is inextricably linked with the combat nanites your father transferred to you so that you could defeat Talon. Indeed, it is part of their controlling code. It can never be taken from you, only transferred to another willingly. Your friends are about to undergo a similar bonding process with their own weapons."

"So all of the changes that happened to me after Suran died . . ."

"Were the results of your nervous system struggling to control Illuminate weapons that you had no idea you had even been implanted with."

"Is it reversible?" Sam asked quietly as his friends climbed into the stasis pods.

"For your friends? Yes," Selenne replied. "For you, no, I'm afraid not. The interface your father implanted in you was designed to integrate with our technology in a different way from the implants your friends carry. That is why exposure to the Voidborn nanites didn't kill you when you first encountered them and also how you were able to take control of some of their technology. Everything from the

Motherships you captured to the nanites that reformed your arm when you were first injured by the Voidborn are side effects of your father implanting you with Illuminate technology that prepared you to receive the Bridge."

"So you think he planned this?" Sam asked, sounding unconvinced.

"It would seem so," Selenne said. "Why is an altogether different question. I learned long ago not to second-guess Suran. The creation of the Heart, our whole plan for survival, was his idea and he was undoubtedly the most brilliant Illuminate I ever met, but his motives were sometimes hard to discern."

"You can say that again," Sam said quietly, watching his friends settling back into the brightly lit pods as they hissed shut one by one, sealing them within. "So what now?"

"Now we wait," Selenne said. A moment later the pods flared with a light that was almost too bright to look at. There was barely any noise, just a low-pitched hum that increased slightly in volume as the lights within the pods brightened and then diminished. The room fell silent.

"It is done," Selenne said.

A few moments later there was a simultaneous thud from each of the pods and their lids began to raise in perfect unison. Sam watched nervously as Jay swung his legs out of the pod and hopped down onto the ground with a slightly confused look on his face.

"How do you feel?" Sam asked.

"Exactly the same," Jay said, looking down at his hands as if he was expecting them to turn into something horrible. "Is that normal?"

"Yes," Selenne replied as Jack, Nat, Anne, and Will all climbed out of their pods. "The weapons are currently dormant. With Sam's help, however, we can activate them." She closed her eyes for a second and then a glowing pool of light appeared in the center of the floor. She gestured for Sam to stand within it. He did as instructed, stepping into the light and feeling the warmth coming from it even through the thick soles of his combat boots.

"Now relax," Selenne said as Sam's friends gathered in a loose circle around him and Selenne. Sam let out a deep breath, relaxing his shoulders and letting his arms hang loosely at his sides.

"That's not what I meant, Sam," Selenne said softly, "and I think you know that."

Sam sighed and relaxed properly, feeling his features shift and his perspective on the room alter subtly with the extra foot and a half that had just been added to his height. The changes to his appearance were more dramatic than ever and there was little now to distinguish him from one of the other Illuminate; he no longer looked like a hybrid of their two species. The only thing that marked him out was his right arm, the golden Voidborn nanites that it was composed of apparently unaffected by the changes to the rest of Sam's body. He realized as he looked at the expressions on his friends' faces around him that it must be an unsettling sight.

"You know, you're actually starting to look quite handsome," Selenne said with a slight smile. "For a human."

She reached up and placed one hand on the side of Sam's head.

"Now let the Bridge open," Selenne said. "so we may complete the bonding process and activate the weapons."

"How?" Sam asked, feeling a sudden uncomfortable pressure inside his skull. An instant later his mouth flew open as his eyes gleamed with blue fire. He was suddenly somewhere else, floating weightless within the center of an impossibly vast white crystalline structure that stretched into the distance as far as the eye could see. He began to move through it, points of blue light flickering in the air around him. They slowly joined together, forming bright, twisting streamers of energy that raced away and danced across the surface of the crystals surrounding him. The streamers flared as they connected with the crystal and Sam felt an overwhelming sense of relief as the pressure that had been painfully building in his head seemed to release all at once. He watched as the glowing blue conduits pulsed, light shooting along their translucent lengths, and then, just as suddenly, with a bright flash, he was back in the center of the Scythe's stasis chamber.

"Did it work?" Mag asked, looking at Sam and the others.

"I don't know," Sam said, looking around the room. "Where's Selenne?"

Closer than you think, Selenne's voice said softly somewhere inside Sam's head. *Illuminate report.*

The transfer was successful, the voice of General Indriss replied. The startled reactions of the others as the voices spoke made it clear they were all hearing the same thing inside their skulls.

Activate the weapons, Selenne said. Jay gave a startled yelp as a cloud of dust swirled around him for an instant and then quickly solidified into smooth white plates of Illuminate armor that covered his body from the neck down. The armor rippled with blue light as Jay raised his arm up in front of him, tapping at the hardened surface of the white bracers he now wore. One by one, Will, Jack, Nat, and Anne were also surrounded by swarms of nanites that encased them within identical suits of armor.

"How does it feel?" Sam asked as his friends all checked out the new outfits that had, quite literally, appeared from thin air.

"Light," Anne said. "Almost like I'm not wearing anything at all."

"Yeah, and my ankle's not hurting anymore," Jack said, looking slightly confused.

"Your suit is capable of treating superficial injuries on the battlefield," Selenne replied. "It is designed to protect the occupant as completely as possible."

"That's great," Jay said, "but it's gonna take more than a suit of body armor to fight the Voidborn."

Oh, this is not just a suit of armor, Selenne said inside their heads. *It's much more than that.*

The armor that Jack was wearing flared with light again and he rose into the air, floating three feet above the ground. He was surrounded by a crackling field of energy, and armored panels snapped into place around his face, forming a helmet. Finally, a smooth, featureless white faceplate sealed the helmet closed with a snap.

"Okay," Jack said, "now I'm flying."

"We have handed you a gun," Selenne said. "Now we must teach you to shoot."

"This way, please," Selenne said, leading Sam and the others toward a freshly opened portal in the wall opposite the Threshold. They followed her inside and found themselves in a cavernous chamber with smooth, featureless white walls. The glowing holographic projection of the leader of the Illuminate council walked toward the center of the massive room and then gestured for Sam and the others to sit down on low rectangular benches that rose from the floor.

"This chamber," Selenne said, gesturing to the empty space around her, "can serve a multitude of purposes. It is composed of nanites similar to the ones that you have just been exposed to, which allows us to alter its form and function according to our need. For now we shall use it as a training facility to prepare you for the mission to come."

"I thought our new Illuminate buddies had all the training we'd ever need," Jay said.

"We are on a deadline, after all," Nat said, nodding in agreement with Jay. "How long is this going to take exactly?"

"The purpose of the training is not to teach you how to use your new abilities," Selenne said. "It is to show you how to relinquish willingly some of the control you have over your own bodies. You cannot hope to learn to use these weapons properly in the time we have; instead you must learn to trust in the abilities of the Illuminate bonded with your implants. They are our finest warriors, handpicked for their centuries of experience fighting the Voidborn, and it's only with their help that we can hope to emerge victorious. Allow me to demonstrate."

Selenne gestured for Jay to come and stand beside her. She gave a small wave and Jay's suit of Illuminate armor dematerialized as quickly as it had first appeared.

"Now," Selenne said to Jay with a wave of her hand, "please reactivate the weapons system."

Jay stood there for a moment, looking slightly embarrassed.

"Erm . . . how exactly do I do that?" he asked.

"You must simply use your neural interface to order your nanites into an appropriate configuration," Selenne replied. "Your familiarity with phase matrix construction scaffolds should make that straightforward."

"Okay," Sam said, trying not to smile at Jay's confused expression, "we take your point."

"I do not mean to imply this is something that you should understand," Selenne said. "It is a skill that takes an Illuminate warrior decades to perfect. It is only by tapping into that deeply ingrained experience that you will truly be able to exploit the combat potential of these weapons." She turned back toward Jay. "Now, try that again but this time with the cooperation of the Illuminate warrior bonded to your implant. You only need think about what you wish to happen."

Jay stood there for a moment looking confused; there was still no sign of his armor.

"Relax," Selenne said. "All you need to do is picture it in your head."

Jay looked at her for a moment and then gave a small nod. An instant later he was surrounded by a glowing cloud that coalesced in a fraction of a second into the gleaming white armor of an Illuminate warrior.

"I will say this for humans," Selenne said, "you're fast learners."

"Hey," Jay said, "I don't care how it works, as long as it does."

"It will take a couple of hours for your implant bond to strengthen properly," Selenne explained. "As it does, your weapon will begin to respond to your mental commands more quickly. In the meantime I suggest we familiarize you with some of the weapon's basic functionality."

Over the following couple of hours, the Illuminate bonded to the implants in the friends' skulls put them through an accelerated training program that introduced the basics of the offensive systems built into their armor. Selenne and General Indriss's holographic forms wandered the room, advising their new human recruits on how best to use them. If it had not been for the subliminal support of their implanted copilots, it would have been impossible to train Sam and his friends in even the basics, but with their assistance and a certain amount of bloody-minded determination, the human recruits made quick progress.

The room shifted around them as they trained, morphing into whatever configuration would best suit their purposes. On one side of the room, animated combat dummies sprang up out of the floor around Anne and she spun in a single graceful pirouette, slicing them all cleanly in two with the energy beams that shot from her wrists. At the other end of the chamber, Jay was swooping and diving through a series of rings that hovered in the air, reveling in the suit's airborne agility. It may have been due to the hard-earned experience of the Illuminate they were bonded with, but the speed with which they learned to master their suits' abilities was exhilarating and the sheer raw power of the suits was intoxicating.

Selenne had briefed them on the mission that the Illuminate had been planning, a mission that would only be possible with the help of Sam and his friends and their new weapons. If it was successful, it could permanently tilt the tables of the war in their favor. That didn't change the fact that it would be the seven of them against an army.

"They all look like they're enjoying themselves," Mag said as she walked up to Sam. "You, though, not so much. Don't suppose you want to tell me what's bothering you, huh?"

"I'm not sure," Sam said with a frown. "Just the usual, I guess."

"The usual being trying to work out how to save everyone from becoming a casualty of a war between two alien races," Mag said with a wry smile. "Which, I suppose, is kind of weird, when you stop and think about it."

"I try not to worry about it too much anymore," Sam said, shaking his head slightly.

"I don't believe that for a second," Mag replied, looking up at him. "In fact, I don't think I've ever met anyone who worries about things more than you."

"Hey, someone has to," Sam said.

"Maybe, but it doesn't *always* have to be you."

"Yeah, I know." Sam sighed. "It's just that none of us

ever asked for any of this. I don't just mean us here; I mean all of us . . . everywhere. Humans."

"It's not the first time that innocent people have been caught up in a war," Mag said. "It's not only your responsibility, you know, and you're doing everything you possibly can. Just because you were unlucky enough to have that thing stuck in your head when you were a baby doesn't mean you're responsible for the safety of everyone on the planet."

"I know," Sam said. "I just think that if we don't look out for humanity, no one else will. Definitely not the Voidborn, but maybe not the Illuminate either. And if I'm honest, that's what worries me more."

"Yeah, well, don't worry," Mag said with a grin. "I'm keeping both eyes firmly fixed on our blue friends here. Nice to know I'm not the only one who doesn't trust them. Speak of the devil."

Selenne was walking across the room toward them, a smile spreading across her face as she approached.

"Hello, Sam," Selenne said. "I was wondering if you would have time to talk with me."

"He's all yours," Mag said. "I'll catch you later, Sam. I'm going to go and check on Stirling."

"Your companions are surprisingly resourceful and tenacious," Selenne said when Mag had gone. "I have seen Illuminate warriors with less resolve. They are adapting to the weapons with impressive speed."

"We've all become fast learners over the past couple of years," Sam replied. "We've had to."

"Yes, I suppose you have . . ." Selenne suddenly looked sad and slightly distracted. "Many have paid the price for the Voidborn's madness. Perhaps what we are preparing to do here today will change all that."

"Or it could just be a suicide mission," Sam said, looking at her and raising an eyebrow. "Let's face it: it could go either way."

"We are confident that the device we detected at the Voidborn site is the correct target," Selenne replied. "If we are successful . . . if *you* are successful, it could be a critical step toward ending this war once and for all. We have to try."

"I'm not saying we shouldn't. I just don't want to lose anyone else."

"Sometimes losses are inevitable in war. Believe me, I understand the burden of leadership."

"I'm not their leader, though," Sam said, gesturing toward his friends busily training at the other end of the room.

"They think you are," Selenne replied. "Sometimes that's all that's important. In my experience, the greatest leaders are the ones that don't want to lead."

"Oh, that's definitely me," Sam said with a chuckle. "Honestly, I'd rather be just about anywhere else right now."

"And yet here you are, and that's what matters." Selenne turned and looked him in the eye. "In my experience, the universe has a way of giving you exactly what you need only when you *most* need it. Call it fate, call it destiny if you will, but it is a gift that one would be foolish to reject. If it were not for your abilities, the gift that Suran gave you, we would not be able to strike back against the Voidborn. You give us hope, Sam, which is something the Illuminate have not had for a very long time. I am honored that you have allowed me to bond with your weapon so that I may assist you in the battle ahead. Apart we stand no chance; together we can defeat the Voidborn once and for all."

"I suppose, but—"

"Sam!" He was interrupted by Mag's panicked yell as she ran back into the room. "It's Stirling. I think he's getting worse."

Sam ran toward her and followed her down the corridor to the docking bay. The pair of them sprinted up the boarding steps of the Scythe, running through the bridge and heading for the rear compartment. Sam raced over to Stirling's stasis pod, quickly examining the holographic display floating above the glowing chamber. He didn't have anywhere near enough medical training to understand what many of the numbers meant, but the fact that most of them were highlighted in red couldn't be a good thing. A moment later Anne ran into the room, pushing Sam to one side and studying the display carefully.

"He's crashing," she said with a sudden edge of panic in her voice. "Is there anything you can do for him? Whatever you did to fix Will's ankle—can you do the same thing for him?"

"I will do what I can," Selenne replied.

She walked toward the stasis chamber, which slid silently open as she approached. Raising a single hand above Stirling's prone body, she closed her eyes as a glowing stream of particles flowed from the wall of the Scythe next to the pod. The bright ribbon of nanites moved quickly through the air, settling on Stirling, flowing up and over his chest and into his nose and mouth. Selenne's face was a mask of concentration as she continued to hold her hand out in the air over the old man's body. She stood there, immobile, for several long minutes as Stirling twitched and convulsed on the bed. Eventually, she opened her eyes, looking over at Sam.

"I'm sorry," Selenne said, "his injuries are too severe. Our nanites were not designed to repair human physiology. His injuries are too extensive, I have done all I can. He is dying."

"No, there's got to be something else you can do," Anne said, shaking her head in denial. "You traveled across the stars, you built machines like this." She waved at the walls of the Scythe. "There must be something . . ."

"Sam," Stirling said suddenly, his voice little more than a strangled whisper.

Sam hurried to his side and crouched down beside the stasis pod, taking the doctor's hand as he slowly lifted it from the bed. Stirling tried to say something, his voice virtually inaudible. Sam leaned in closer, bringing his ear within inches of the doctor's mouth. Suddenly, he felt Stirling's grip tighten as he whispered a single phrase into Sam's ear.

"Don't trust them."

The doctor gave a single pained grunt, his body convulsing one last time before his grip on Sam's hand went loose. His war was finally over.

"What did he say?" Jay asked as he came over and stood beside his friend.

"It doesn't matter," Sam said, glancing over at Selenne. "I'll tell you later."

"What are we going to do now?" Jack asked, as they gathered solemnly around Stirling's body. Without him, there would never have been a resistance movement at all. In fact, they would have been lying unconscious in a Voidborn dormitory somewhere in London if it had not been for his efforts.

"We take the fight to the Voidborn," Sam said, feeling something suddenly harden in his gut. "We go out there and we kick their asses off this planet once and for all." He turned toward his friends. "We do it for Stirling, we do it for Liz, for Rachel, for Adam, for Jackson, for Toby, for Tim, for every last person we've lost. We go out there and make the Voidborn pay a hundredfold for every drop of blood they've spilled. That's what we do." Sam looked at each of them in turn. He no longer saw the children they'd been two years ago; now he saw a hardened group of veterans whom he would have followed into hell. That he was *going to* follow into hell, he reminded himself. "We have a war to win."

7

Sam rocketed through the night, the flat, scrub-covered desert floor racing past just a couple of feet below him. The others were spread out behind him, traveling at hundreds of miles an hour, their suits automatically following the slight undulations in the terrain. A projected display inside his helmet told Sam that they were now just a couple of miles from their target and he felt his mouth turn dry. They all knew what this meant: they had to succeed in their mission or there would be nothing to stop the Voidborn from laying waste to the Earth. The stakes could not have been any higher and there still seemed far too few of them to succeed, even with the undoubted advantages that the Illuminate nanite armor provided.

Remember the plan, General Indriss said in their heads. *Keep them scattered and off balance*.

Let our warriors guide your actions, Selenne said. *Use their experience to supplement your own instincts. Remember, they have fought the Voidborn many times before.*

"We've had the odd tussle with them ourselves," Jack said, his voice clear in Sam's earpiece.

"Yeah, maybe we'll even teach you a thing or two," Anne said.

"Approaching target," Mag whispered. "Ready when you are."

"Roger that," Sam said. "Twenty seconds."

Sam sent his suit shooting over the edge of the drop, before diving toward the floor of the canyon far below. There, the Colorado River continued its ceaseless task of carving a massive channel out of the desert. Sam leveled out as the canyon floor raced up to meet him. He skimmed low over the water, almost close enough to reach down and touch its surface. The others followed in tight formation behind him, the Illuminate bonded with their suits guiding them safely to their destination. They were now just seconds from their target and Sam found himself silently praying that their approach had gone unnoticed. Stealth was unimportant once they reached their target, but the element of surprise would be essential.

Sam banked hard, sending his suit racing around a tight bend in the canyon, hugging the wall. Seconds later they saw what they'd been looking for. The massive structure spanned the gap between the canyon walls far above, and the giant bulging oval of black crystal at its center hung suspended like some form of monstrous chrysalis, glowing with a deep crimson light. A scarlet beam fifty feet wide seared downward from the crystal, blasting into a deep bore hole in the canyon floor. The canyon walls on either side of this central span were covered with Voidborn structures dug into the rock face, all of them swarming with Hunters and Grendels. Dozens of drop-ships were also circling overhead, providing aerial defenses for the Voidborn platform.

Sam's suit systems automatically tracked and targeted the Voidborn ahead of him, highlighting their positions throughout the structure. The tactical data was instantly shared between all of their suits, their Illuminate copilots allocating targets for each of them based on threat levels and range.

"That's a lot of Voidborn," Jay said with a low whistle.

"Okay, guys," Sam said as his suit plotted an attack vector ahead of him, "you know the drill. Shock and awe."

A split second later, the Scythe screamed past overhead, shooting across the top of the glowing hub in the center of the Voidborn hive, missing it by just a few feet. The response from the drop-ships buzzing around the structure was immediate; they banked sharply to intercept the Illuminate vessel and raced after it as it rocketed away down the canyon.

"Hit 'em," Sam said, willing his suit to accelerate and

feeling the odd sensation of benefitting from years of another being's experience as he swooped through the outer structures of the Voidborn base, missing the black crystalline buildings by what seemed like inches. He powered through the outer defenses, green energy bolts sizzling through the air around him as the Hunters at the outer perimeter began to react to the Illuminate warriors that shot past them, their armored suits weaving this way and that, diving through and between the fortifications.

Air brakes flared on the back of Sam's suit and he landed hard, the nanites of his armor absorbing the impact as he slid across the ground and pointed both hands at the Hunter that was shooting at him. The bracers of his armor flashed with blue light and a searing beam shot from each of his clenched fists, punching straight through one side of the Hunter's silvery shell and out the other. The Voidborn creature exploded in a shower of dark green liquid and Sam spun around as he felt the ground shake. A Grendel charged toward him, its blade-tipped tail sweeping through the air. Sam fired the beam weapon again, punching a hole in the giant creature's chest as his other arm morphed into a glowing rectangular shield with which he blocked the Grendel's whipping tail, its razor-sharp tip glancing off it in a shower of sparks. Without thinking, Sam willed his other arm to shift into a long, flat-bladed sword, its edges crackling with blue fire. He fired the suit's boosters and closed the few feet to the staggering Grendel, dark green fluid gushing from the hole that Sam's weapon had created. Sam swept the blade upward, putting all the energy from the short burst of speed into the swing. The sword tore through the Grendel's abdomen, slicing upward and out of the top of the hulking beast's shoulder. The Grendel gave a single strangled roar and toppled forward onto the ground, where it lay twitching. Sam spun around, watching as his friends and their Illuminate passengers tore into the Voidborn defenses, explosions and flashes of bright blue lighting up the base.

More Hunters flew toward Sam. He launched himself straight upward, firing his beam weapons while sweeping his arms in a wide arc and slicing through several of his predators at once. Suddenly, Sam's suit jinked to the left as a green bolt of energy arced through the air where he had been hovering just an instant before.

"Thanks," Sam muttered inside his helmet.

You're welcome, Selenne's voice said in his head.

It was a bizarre sensation, like having a kind of active sixth sense that was always one step ahead of you. The feeling of barely controlling his own actions was unsettling, but seeing as Selenne had probably just saved his life, Sam felt inclined to roll with it for now.

"Lots of angry Voidborn!" Jack yelled in his ear. "Anyone want them?"

Sam watched as the suit tagged with Jack's name shot

past overhead with a swarm of Hunters in hot pursuit. Jack banked hard, plotting a course between Anne and Nat, who were dropping into flanking positions on either side of him. An instant later all three of them rolled onto their backs, firing their weapons to form a web of intersecting beams and cutting the pack into ribbons, chunks of Hunter shell tumbling to the ground in showers of sparks. Jack, Anne, and Nat broke formation a moment later, each racing off toward fresh targets.

"Don't let up," Sam said. "We have to keep them off balance."

"Anything from Mag yet?" Jay asked with a growl, the sounds of his weapons firing and then something exploding nearby in the background reaching Sam's ears.

"Nothing yet," Sam said, "so keep them busy if you can."

Mag scratched at her ear for the twentieth time in the past five minutes. The nanites that made up the Illuminate earpiece she was wearing directly stimulated her eardrum, making the alien device completely silent to the outside world. It also gave her the creeps. She poked her head out from the shadowy alcove in the superstructure on the top of the Voidborn base. As they'd hoped, the Scythe's noisy flyby had distracted the Voidborn from the tiny figure dropping out the hatch in its belly. The trick now was to make sure that she remained undetected. The

Scythe had vanished from view, but the sounds of battle from far below were all she needed to hear to know that her friends were doing everything they could to provide a distraction. She crept quickly across the top of the massive glowing pod at the center of the canyon-spanning structure, flitting from shadow to shadow with inhuman speed and agility. She searched frantically for some sort of doorway or opening, anything that would grant her access, but could find no obvious way inside.

"Okay," Mag whispered, "looks like there's no way in up here. Plan B it is."

"Copy that," Sam said. "Bringing the Scythe around for another pass. Stand by."

Mag heard the distant whine of multiple drop-ship engines and the Scythe came shooting back down the canyon toward her with a swarm of the daggerlike ships still in close pursuit. The Voidborn ships' cannons blazed as the Scythe bobbed and weaved through the hail of fire, splashes of light dancing across its rear energy shields as they absorbed the hits it could not dodge. Mag ducked down behind a solid-looking wall as the Scythe dived toward her with its forward cannons firing. The energy blasts tore into the upper surface of the Voidborn structure, sending clouds of debris flying into the air. Mag covered her head with her arms, ducking further behind the cover of the wall. The Scythe shot past just above her with the pack of drop-ships screaming after it, still in close pursuit. She waited a few seconds to ensure there was no sign of any new Voidborn forces and then dashed out from her hiding place toward the chain of glowing craters that the Scythe's attack run had carved out of the ground in front of her. She peered down into one of the jagged holes and saw an opening that looked like it would be just wide enough for her to crawl inside.

"Good job I'm not claustrophobic," Mag muttered to herself before jumping into the crater. She got on her hands and knees and slid slowly into the opening, barely able to squeeze her shoulders into the narrow crawl space. She pushed herself forward with her feet, trying to keep her breathing under control as she followed the dull crimson lights that pulsed through its dark translucent walls. As she slowly edged her way down, she couldn't shake the feeling that she was moving through the body of some giant alien creature.

"Think happy thoughts," Mag whispered, the sounds of the distant battle getting more muffled as the temperature in the tunnel grew warmer and the air started to smell like hot metal. She reached a junction and chose the path that most of the lights racing through the walls seemed to be following. Soon she saw a red glow reflecting around the curved walls of the passageway from a light source somewhere up ahead. She crawled around the bend, shuffling forward with her elbows and knees, and let out a sigh of relief as she saw a glowing opening in front of her at the end of the tunnel. She slid out of the shaft and into the dimly lit corridor, feeling the floor vibrate with not only the force of the distant explosions outside, but also a deep throbbing hum that pulsed through the structure like a monstrous heartbeat. There was no sign of Voidborn activity anywhere nearby and Mag could only hope it would stay that way. For the moment at least, the distraction outside appeared to be working.

She crept along the corridor, moving silently toward the source of the pulsing sound. As the sound got louder she noticed that the scarlet lights in the walls were also increasing in brightness and frequency. She hoped that meant she was heading in the right direction and she continued along the passage, hugging the wall as the corridor grew wider and wider before opening up into an enormous chamber that was lit from within with searing red light. As she stepped out onto the walkway running around the sides of the cavernous space, her mouth dropped open. The spherical chamber was at least two hundred yards across, the curved walls stretching up to a vaulted ceiling far above her. The walls blazed with lightning-bolt arcs of crimson energy that raced toward the equator of the spherical room before lancing out toward the giant machine that appeared to be levitating in the center of the vast space. The floating structure looked like a giant inverted cannon, pointing straight down at the base of the chamber, a torrent of energy streaming from its barrel with a rumbling, thunderous roar.

Mag felt the hairs on her arms stand up with the static charge in the air. She moved toward the edge of the walkway, looking down into the yawning pit before her and watching as the thundering beam of energy drilled a seemingly bottomless channel into the canyon floor far below. The raw power that was being directed through the apparatus was breathtaking to behold.

"Well, looks like I found it," Mag said quietly into her comms unit. She continued around the walkway, which spiraled toward the upper reaches of the chamber. Mounted on top of the cannon-like machine was a huge throbbing red crystal that sent a crimson stream of energy arcing up to another platform toward the top of the chamber.

"Roger that," Sam replied in Mag's ear. "Report as soon as the beacon is in place."

"Will do," Mag replied. She continued to walk toward the top of the chamber, running her hand over the smooth bumps of the black walls. Their texture here was different from elsewhere in the base, smoother and more organic, and the bumps were slightly warm to the touch. She looked up toward the platform near the ceiling of the chamber and broke into a jog, feeling increasingly confident that there were no Voidborn forces nearby. As she got closer she could see the patterns of scarlet lightning dancing across the underside of the platform where the beam of energy from the crystal below struck it. Mounted in the center of the upper surface of the platform was a device she had only ever seen once before, during their final battle with Talon in Tokyo. It was a massive black sphere suspended within a dangling web of cables with a glowing red portal at its base. That was Mag's target, the central Voidborn command node for the entire American continent. She walked slowly toward it, her unnaturally acute senses still alert for any sign of Voidborn forces. She reached into one of the equipment pouches dangling from her belt and pulled out a small white disc with a fine pattern of blue light etched into its surface. She reached out toward the black crystalline surface of the command node and attached the small device to its surface.

"Beacon placed," Mag said. "Ready when you are!"

"Understood," Sam replied in her ear. "Get clear, I'm starting my run."

Mag ran back down the walkway, heading away from the command node. As she made her way toward the base of the chamber she noticed a flicker of movement out of the corner of her eye and glanced over toward the smooth chamber walls. She blinked twice, trying to clear her vision as the patterns on the walls seemed to shift and blur in unusual ways. It took a moment for her to realize what she was actually looking at and then she felt a sudden chill in the pit of her stomach.

There was nothing wrong with her vision; the walls

were moving: the countless millions of Voidborn swarm creatures that lined the chamber walls were beginning to stir and shift. She backed away from the wall, her eyes wide with terror as the first few skittering creatures began to scurry across the walkway toward her.

"Sam!" Mag yelled. "You have to—"

She never got time to finish her sentence. A black tentacle formed from countless thousands of the swarming creatures lashed out from the wall, slamming into her and sending her flying off the edge of the walkway. She felt a moment of sickening free fall before she slammed into the smooth crystalline wall sloping down toward the thundering beam of the energy drill. She clawed frantically at the slope, her razor-sharp talons scratching against the rock-hard surface, finally managing to stop her slide just a few feet from the drop-off to the canyon below. She could feel the heat of the energy beam on her back as she looked up at the walkway fifty feet above her. The Voidborn swarm began to pour over the edge of the walkway, surging down the smooth slope toward her. There was nowhere to run.

Sam whirled around, swinging the massive blade protruding from his right arm and slicing the Hunter that was buzzing through the air toward him clean in two in a shower of green blood. An instant later, a Grendel landed with a thundering crash just a couple of yards away from him, dropping from one of the structures overhead. Sam managed to raise one arm, the nanites of his armor forming a shield at the speed of thought as the Grendel swiped at him. The shield absorbed the worst of the impact but the force of the monstrous blow still sent Sam flying. He slid across the ground, slamming into a nearby wall. As the Grendel charged toward him, he rose to one knee, trying to force himself to his feet. He barely had a chance to raise his shield again before the creature was upon him a second time. Again the shield absorbed the worst of the blow, but Sam could feel himself weakening in the face of the relentless assault, despite the amplified strength the Illuminate nanites granted him. The Grendel raised both its massive claws, bringing them together for one final blow. A split second later, there was a flash of light and the Grendel's head was instantly vaporized by a pair of blinding white beams. Jay landed next to Sam in a cloud of dust as the decapitated Grendel toppled slowly to the ground.

"You looked like you could use a hand," Jay said, and even though Sam could not see his face, he knew that his friend was grinning inside his helmet.

"Thanks," Sam said, taking Jay's hand and letting his friend pull him up from the floor. "Mag's planted the beacon. I'm calling in the Scythe."

"Want a wingman?" Jay asked, looking up at the giant Voidborn structure far overhead.

"It can't hurt," Sam said, "but if this goes to plan, we'll

have all the backup we could ever need in just a couple of minutes."

The Scythe is inbound, Selenne said. *ETA fifteen seconds*.

Sam nodded at Jay and sent his own suit shooting vertically into the air, powering upward and heading straight for the center of the Voidborn structure, with Jay close behind him. In the distance he could see the Scythe rocketing toward them from the other direction, its shield still just holding up under the relentless barrage of the pursuing Voidborn ships. He adjusted his own path slightly to put himself on a direct collision course with the Illuminate ship and the pursuing pack of Voidborn interceptors. At the speed they were both traveling, the distance between Sam and the Scythe closed in the blink of an eye, collision now inevitable. As Sam plowed into the front of the Scythe, the ship disintegrated into a swirling cloud of energized plasma, unleashing a shock wave of energy that slammed into the pursuing Voidborn ships, tearing them to pieces and sending them cascading toward the canyon floor far below. The swirling cloud of superheated energy that was all that remained of the Scythe hung in the air above the Voidborn hive, flaring almost too brightly for Jay to look at directly. For a second or two the cloud swirled chaotically, but then slowly it began to coalesce into a single bright mass. At the center of the boiling sphere of energy, Sam felt the subtle influence of Selenne as he fought to control and guide the massive swarm of Illuminate nanites that had once made up the Scythe.

The cloud continued to solidify as it dropped toward the central Voidborn structure, forming a vaguely humanoid shape. Jay watched as a pair of massive armored feet crunched down onto the top of the black crystalline hub. A giant Illuminate warrior, four times the height of a Grendel, appeared from the cloud and raised its fifty-foot-long sword above its head. The massive weapon came crashing down, hacking through the outer layers of the Voidborn hive's superstructure. The giant warrior then reached down and peeled back a massive section of the hull. Safely encased inside the enormous machine, Sam fought against the strange sense of disorientation that came with suddenly feeling like he was a hundred feet high. He concentrated instead on tearing his way into the Voidborn base, heading straight for the waypoint inside it that indicated the position of the beacon Mag had placed just a few moments earlier.

"Okay," Jay said quietly, watching as the giant mech ripped into the Voidborn base, "maybe you didn't need a wingman after all."

"I could do with a hand here," Nat's voice said suddenly in Jay's ear, sounding slightly frantic. "I've got Grendels."

"Roger that," Jay said. "How many?"

"Erm . . . all of them, I think," Nat replied.

"Understood," Jay said, the display in his helmet

highlighting Nat's current position. "On my way. Anyone else who's in a position to help should provide backup. Sam's nearly at the target."

"I'll be with you in ten seconds," Jack said. "Just mopping up over here."

On top of the Voidborn base, Sam tore through what he thought was the final bulkhead separating him from his target, bright red light pouring from the open wound that he had inflicted on the giant structure. He ripped at the tattered edges of the breach, widening it just enough for him to force his way inside, then dropped into the chamber below, the clawed feet of the Illuminate mech encasing him fighting for purchase as he landed on the smooth, sloping surface of the chamber walls. He glanced up at the platform at the top of the cavernous space, his target clearly marked on the heads-up display inside his helmet. A split second before he could issue the mental command that would send the giant machine he was piloting soaring to the top of the chamber, something slammed into his back with enough force to knock him clean off his feet. He tumbled down the smooth slope at the bottom of the chamber, rolling toward the massive drilling beam while desperately grabbing for anything to hang on to. The clawed feet of the mech left long gouges in the wall of the chamber as he finally managed to slow and then stop his descent.

Sam shot a glance upward and immediately saw what it

was that had just struck him in the back. Rearing into the air above him was a swarm of the same creatures that had attacked London, the skittering insectile machines crawling over and around each other, forming a solid mass. He dived to one side as a huge tentacle speared out from it, crashing into the ground where he'd been crouched just a moment before. He had no time to dodge as the tentacle whipped toward him, slamming into the chest of his mech and sending him flying backward. He crashed into the fragile walkway, smashing it to pieces, and raised his arm, willing the Illuminate nanites that it was made from into the shape of a cannon. He fired a searing bolt into the seething mass and the beam vaporized countless thousands of the Voidborn creatures, sending the heaving swarm recoiling across the chamber walls. Sam took advantage of the momentary retreat to transform the Illuminate mech's other arm into an identical weapon before firing again, the twin beams slicing through the surging Voidborn horde.

"Oh God, no." Sam spotted a limp form lying on a section of the undamaged walkway thirty yards away. "Mag!"

Sam felt a sudden hot rush of anger, and let out an enraged howl and charged at the Voidborn swarm.

Sam, Selenne said, *no, you can't fight . . .*

Sam wasn't listening. Without even properly understanding how, he channeled a massive energy charge into the right hand of his mech, swinging its balled fist into the center of the mass of skittering creatures. There was a huge violent discharge of energy as Sam's blow struck home, whipping through the swarm in a searing white explosion. The swarm retreated for a second and then surged back toward him with renewed speed and aggression, slamming into him like a tidal wave. He staggered backward, flailing against an enemy that he could barely hit as it swept over and around him, dragging the enormous mech to its knees despite its colossal strength. Sam felt the horrible sensation of individual swarm Drones burrowing their way into the mech's armor plating, scratching and clawing their way inside. He continued to struggle fruitlessly as the hissing wave swept over his head and everything went black. Then came a moment of panic before he heard Selenne's calming voice in his head. She said just two words.

Star Lance.

Immediately Sam understood what she meant. He willed the Illuminate nanites around him back into their original form, hoping that they still had the power required for what Selenne was suggesting. For an instant Sam found himself floating inside the cockpit of the Scythe, the black mass of the Voidborn swarm scratching and clawing at the armored glass outside. A split second later the Star Lance drive fired and everything went white. The Scythe was instantly transformed into a bolt of pure white energy that erupted up and out of the swarm, spearing toward the top of the chamber. Sam materialized on the upper platform in a blinding flash of light, the Illuminate nanites that had once composed the Scythe cascading to the ground around him, their glow fading, their power reserves spent. Sam staggered forward, trying not to think about the limp body lying on the walkway far below. The only possible way he could help Mag now was to complete his mission. Her life and the life of every last person on the planet depended on it. He half walked and half fell the last few yards toward the Voidborn central command node, stretching out his hand and thrusting it into the glowing crimson portal at the base of the black crystalline sphere.

Now! Selenne whispered inside his head. *Open the Bridge. Set the Illuminate free.*

8

Sam ignored the burning waves of agony shooting up his arm and triggered the implant inside his head. He was struck by a sudden crackling explosion of red lightning, which sent him flying backward from the command node before landing hard.

He slowly staggered to his feet, backing away from the command node as the red portal at its base flared angrily with a screeching whine that was rapidly increasing in pitch. He had absolutely no idea if their desperate plan had worked. Behind him there was a shriek of tearing metal as the Voidborn swarm surged up and over the edge of the platform, tearing away the guard rail. It seethed toward the command node, then recoiled from it as if repulsed by some kind of invisible force field.

Sam leapt over the edge of the platform, engaging his

armor's flight systems, and flew down toward Mag's crumpled body, scooping her up before flying up and out of the massive tear in the dome above him. He landed on the roof, lowering Mag to the ground as gently as he could.

"Sam!" Jack yelled over the comms system. "The Voidborn, they . . . Oh no."

The others landed all around him as Sam knelt down next to Mag, cradling her head in his arms.

The suit's sensors indicate that she is alive, Selenne said inside Sam's head, *but she requires immediate medical attention. She has been infected with Voidborn nanites. Let me work.*

Sam suddenly felt a sensation that was quite different from any that he had previously felt Selenne exert over him. This wasn't subtle coercion; this felt like she was hijacking his body completely. An instant later a stream of glowing particles began to radiate from the hand Sam was using to support Mag's head, spreading across her face and into her nose and mouth.

"Defensive line!" Jay yelled as the Voidborn swarm began to pour out of the tear in the hive superstructure fifty yards away. As the others ran to join him, he raised both his arms, energy beams lancing out and slicing into the black mass as it swept toward them. The others followed Jay's lead, laying down a withering barrage of fire at the tide of tiny scurrying monsters. The swarm slowed its advance beneath the relentless assault, but still it kept coming.

I need more time, Selenne said. *Your friend's physiology is . . . unique. I am being forced to make certain assumptions about the best way to treat her.*

Sam felt a moment of despair as he watched his friends start to fall back, retreating before the seemingly unstoppable advance of the swarm. Time was the one thing they did not have.

From nowhere a hail of blue energy bolts rained down upon the leading edge of the Voidborn swarm, vaporizing it and sending the main bulk recoiling backward. Sam's head snapped around; he looked over his shoulder, his mouth hanging open with surprise at the astonishing sight before him. Hundreds, possibly thousands, of Hunters were swooping down toward the top of the Voidborn structure, the energy cannons mounted on their backs blazing. The sickly green glow that had illuminated their shells up until just a few minutes before had been replaced with a deep blue. Behind the Hunters, pounding across the ground toward Sam, were at least a dozen Grendels, glowing with the same blue light.

"It worked," Sam whispered to himself.

Yes, Selenne said in his head, *I believe it did*.

Sam had succeeded in opening the Bridge between the Illuminate Heart and the Voidborn control node. Now every last Voidborn in North America, whether it was a Hunter or a Mothership, was under the control of a very old, probably very angry Illuminate warrior. Sam watched as wave after wave of Hunters tore into the black mass while the Grendels formed a protective cordon around him and his friends. A minute later it was over, as the Hunters mopped up the last scuttling remnants of the swarm. Against all the odds, they had succeeded. Now they had an army.

Your friend's condition is stabilizing, Selenne said, and Sam looked down at Mag as her eyes flickered open.

"Ow . . . everything . . . ow," Mag groaned.

"Take it easy," Sam said, feeling a flood of relief. "I think you got into a fistfight with a Voidborn swarm."

"Yeah, it feels like it," Mag said with a pained wince.

She should recover fully, Selenne said. *Her hybrid anatomy makes her unusually strong*.

"Help me up," Mag said, after taking a couple of long, deep breaths.

"Are you sure you're okay to stand?" Sam said with a slight frown.

"Don't mollycoddle me, Riley," Mag said as she held on to his arm for support and slowly climbed to her feet. "I feel fine."

The others gathered around them as the final glowing remnants of the Illuminate nanites flowed in a flickering ribbon from Mag's arm before being reabsorbed into Sam's hand.

"You're okay?" Jay said with a broad but slightly confused-looking grin.

"Looks that way," Mag replied, returning his smile. "Though I think I've got Sam to thank for that."

"Don't thank me," Sam said, shaking his head, "thank Selenne. Without her I don't want to think about what might have happened."

"You be sure to thank her for me," Mag said, tapping the side of Sam's head and smiling at him.

Illuminate forces are reporting in from across the continent, Selenne said, her voice clear in all of their heads. *It would appear that our mission has been a complete success. There are no signs of any Voidborn forces moving to counterattack.*

"We did it, buddy! You took over the control node; we've got ourselves our very own army," Jay said, punching Sam playfully in the shoulder. "This is it. Now we can take the fight to the Voidborn."

"Yeah, we did," Sam said with a smile, "but it's not over yet. What about the Sleepers? Is there any change in their condition?"

No, Selenne replied after a couple of seconds, *the Illuminate controlling the Drones that attend the sleeping humans are reporting that they still appear to be in distress.*

"It didn't make any difference at all?" Will asked with a confused frown. "But that must mean that whatever's causing this isn't connected to the Motherships. Which means—"

"That we might just need this army we've acquired," Sam said. "This isn't over yet."

"I'm beginning to wonder if it ever will be," Nat said with a sigh. "So what exactly—"

The rest of Nat's question was drowned out by a thunderous roar as a chain of massive blazing projectiles slammed into the canyon floor less than a mile from where they were standing. The shock waves from the impacts tore outward, vaporizing the nearby Voidborn structures in clouds of billowing black dust. The concussive blast of the explosions hit them a moment later, sending Hunters spinning through the air and even staggering the Grendels. Sam grabbed Mag, wrapping his arms around her, his armor expanding to form a protective shield. Jay and the others were blown off their feet, the flight systems in their suits fighting desperately to right them as they spun through the air.

Sam gritted his teeth as there was another series of explosive impacts at the other end of the canyon, sending more shock waves smashing into them from the opposite direction. He hunkered down, feeling the nanites of his armor hooking into the crystalline black floor, anchoring him in place. It was at least thirty seconds before the rumbling dissipated and an eerie calm fell over the area around Sam. His heads-up display highlighted the positions of his friends scattered nearby, but the billowing clouds of ash and dust were making it impossible to see more than a few feet in front of him.

"Are you okay?" Sam said as he looked down at Mag.

"I think so," she replied with a cough, the smoke irritating her lungs. "What the hell was that?"

"I'm not sure," Sam replied, "but I've got a horrible feeling it might be the same thing that happened in London yesterday. Could you help me find the others?" Sam stood up, the nanites in his suit releasing their grip on the Voidborn structure with a crackling sound. "Come on, this way!"

He hurried through the swirling, acrid fog, heading for the nearest blip on his visor. He stepped to one side as a Grendel loomed out of the fog, stomping past him, and a group of Hunters raced overhead.

"Did the Illuminate see anything?" Sam asked.

No, Selenne replied. *There are Illuminate units approaching the impact sites now, but whatever attacked us came from nowhere as far as the Voidborn sensors were concerned.*

"That's what worries me," Sam muttered to himself.

A moment later Anne came sprinting out of the cloud and almost ran into him.

"Did you see what it was?" Sam asked urgently. "Did you see what hit us?"

"No," Anne replied, shaking her head, "it all happened too fast. I know what it felt like, though."

"Yeah, me too," Sam said, hoping he didn't sound as nervous as he suddenly felt.

"Sam, look!" Mag yelled, pointing over his shoulder. Sam spun around and spotted Nat's armor suit just visible through the haze, half buried under a collapsed section of the Voidborn superstructure. Without a word he sprinted toward his fallen friend, with Mag and Anne just two steps behind him. He knelt down next to Nat and gently shook her shoulder.

"Hey, you awake?" Sam asked.

"Yeah," Nat replied groggily after a second or two. "I feel like I'm stuck, though. I think you're going to have to help me out from under this."

"Okay," Sam said. "Mag, we'll lift this thing, you pull her out, okay?"

Mag gave a quick nod and bent down, grabbing both of Nat's hands, ready to haul her out.

Sam grabbed one end of the huge black crystalline slab that was pinning his friend to the floor and Anne grabbed the other, the nanites in their armor boosting their strength to inhuman levels as they both heaved upward.

"That's it!" Mag yelled, feeling Nat start to move. "I've got her."

Mag hauled Nat clear with a grunt. As soon as she was out of the way, Sam and Anne let go of the slab and it slammed back down onto the ground.

"Thanks," Nat said as she climbed to her feet. "Where are the others?"

"I've got blips for Will and Jack," Anne said, spinning around as she scanned for her friends. "Nothing for Jay."

Sam suddenly realized that she was right; he could see

the blips that she was talking about but there was no sign of Jay anywhere.

"Jay, Jack, Will, sound off!" Sam snapped, broadcasting to his friends, feeling a sudden chill in the pit of his stomach.

A couple of seconds later Will's voice replied, sounding slightly shaky.

"I'm okay. I got knocked off the top of that thing. Took a bit of a tumble but the suit saved me."

"Roger that," Sam replied. "Could you get back up here as fast as you can?"

"On my way," Will replied.

"Jack? Jay?" Sam asked again, but there was still no response from either of them.

"Oh God, no," Nat suddenly whispered, and Sam spun around to look at whatever it was she had seen. As the billowing clouds thrown up by the impacts began to disperse, it became horribly clear exactly what it was that had caused them. Half a dozen massive black cylinders, identical to the ones that had fallen on London, were towering over the desert at each end of the canyon, standing in scorched, smoldering impact craters.

"How quickly can you get more Voidborn reinforcements here?" Sam asked Selenne.

The nearest Mothership that we control is twenty minutes away, Selenne replied.

"Okay, pull back all of our remaining forces in the

vicinity," Sam said quickly. "We need everything we have here, protecting the control node. Those things could swarm at any moment."

I'll marshal our forces into a defensive perimeter, Selenne said. *I suggest you and your friends stay as close to the control node as possible. You may be our last line of defense.*

"Okay, let's move!" Sam yelled, running back toward the massive tear in the roof of the Voidborn structure that led down to the core below. He tried not to think about the fact that there was still no sign of Jack or Jay; right now he had to focus on the most clear and present danger.

Sam watched as Grendels moved into defensive positions around the opening in the roof, their hulking black techno-organic bodies glowing with the blue light that indicated they were under Illuminate control. They suddenly seemed a very inadequate defense against the threat they now faced. A second later, Sam heard a voice in his ear garbled by static.

"Repeat that last transmission," Sam said, "repeat, say again."

"Anyone . . . this . . . seeing what I'm . . ."

Sam felt a sudden surge of relief; it was unmistakably Jack's voice.

"Jack!" Sam yelled back. "Are you okay? Repeat your last message. Your transmission's breaking up."

"Above us!" Jack yelled back, his transmission suddenly clear to them all. "Up in the sky, what the hell is that?"

They all looked upward in perfect unison as an enormous shadow raced across the top of the Voidborn base toward them. In the sky directly above, a ship larger than anything any of them had ever seen before was slowly descending. It would have dwarfed even a Voidborn Mothership, but its design seemed quite different from the Voidborn vessels they had encountered before. At its center was a giant glowing red eye ablaze with crackling bolts of crimson energy that shot outward to the ring of clawlike black structures surrounding it. The rest of the hulking vessel's main body was covered in flowing, rib-shaped structures that pulsed from within with a deep red glow. Sweeping out from the central superstructure were massive pylons, lit up by the coruscating scarlet lightning bolts that arced between them. Sam felt the hairs on the back of his neck stand up as the giant vessel dropped toward them. A very simple, very old, but very insistent part of his brain was telling him to run and hide under the nearest rock.

There was a sudden earsplitting screech from the enormous ship and the giant black cylinders at both ends of the canyon began to disintegrate into black waves that swept across the desert floor in the direction of the Voidborn base.

"Selenne," Sam said, "what is that thing?"

I have no idea, Selenne replied. *I . . . We have never seen anything like it*.

"Whatever it is, it must be the same thing that dropped those things on London," Jack said. "Which puts it right at the top of my to-shoot list."

Sam glanced around at the nearby Grendels flexing their claws and the Hunters sweeping through the air overhead. He took a deep breath, pushing his concern for Jay to the back of his mind and focusing instead on this new threat.

"Whatever that is," Sam said, "I don't think it comes in peace. Hit it with everything you've got."

His friends opened fire on the monstrous ship. Sam launched into the air, weaving crazily, hoping that his wild maneuvers would stop the ship from being able to lock its weapons onto him. He raised his arms, triggering his beam weapons, the bolts searing into the hull of the behemoth as Sam closed the distance between them, pushing his suit to its maximum speed. The others were not far behind him, rocketing toward the huge vessel, their guns blazing. As he sped toward it he could not help but feel intimidated by its overwhelming scale, his shots striking home but seeming little more than meaningless pinpricks.

"Everyone follow my lead!" Sam yelled. "Concentrate your fire on my target. Let's see if we can actually do some damage to this thing."

Sam banked hard, racing along the flank of the giant ship and heading straight for the base of one of the winglike spines jutting out the side of it. He raised both his hands, concentrating the beams on a single spot, the hull of the giant ship glowing white hot where his weapons struck home. The others opened fire as they too banked toward Sam's target, their own beams of energy lancing out and striking the ship in precisely the same location. There was a small rippling chain of explosions across the base of the pylon as the concentrated beams tore into the ship's hull, and Sam led the others back around for another attack run.

Swarms of Hunters were now swooping at the alien ship as it continued its descent toward the Voidborn control node, the Grendels below still tightening their defensive cordon around the tear in the roof of the structure. As he made another dive at the vast ship, Sam noticed the black wave of the swarm sweeping up the walls of the canyon and toward the central span of the core structure. At the speed they were traveling, he could see they would reach the control node in a matter of minutes. If the swarm succeeded in destroying the control node, they would lose their control over the Voidborn forces and everything they had done would count for nothing. He accelerated again, swooping toward the damaged area of the pylon, raising his arms to fire.

The bolts of crimson lightning that struck Sam seemed to come from nowhere, arcing from the giant ship's hull and enveloping him in a crackling blood-red energy field.

Sam let out a piercing scream as every nerve ending seemed to light up with excruciating pain, his body convulsing as the surface of his armor morphed into chaotic, angular shapes. He began to tumble through the air, barely conscious, his connection with the Illuminate technology that had been keeping him aloft suddenly severed. He hardly noticed the other crackling bolts of energy that lanced out toward his friends, who frantically tried to dodge the sudden hail of fire. As he finally surrendered to unconsciousness, Sam felt something catch him, arresting his plummeting descent and pulling him toward the alien vessel. He was faintly aware of being surrounded by a bright red light, which was blinding in its intensity, before everything faded to black.

Mag sprinted across the top of the Voidborn structure, vaulting over the piles of debris that lay scattered in her path. In the air above her, her friends fought a desperate battle for survival and she was powerless to help them.

"Never wanted to be a bloody superhero anyway," she growled to herself as she leapt over the burning remains of a Grendel that had been struck down when the swarm cylinders had impacted barely a minute earlier. She tried to ignore the battle going on around her and focus on the scent trail that she was tracking. Jay might not be responding on comms, but he was somewhere nearby, she could smell it. She ran past the cordon of Grendels, the trail leading toward the hole that Sam had torn in the roof of the core chamber. She looked down into the cavernous room and spotted a figure lying prone on one of the half-collapsed walkways toward the bottom. She dropped through the tear, landing silently on the control node platform and sprinting down the nearby walkway. When she reached Jay's immobile armored body, she knelt beside him and gently rolled him onto his back. His helmet was still sealed and there were black scorch marks all down one side of his suit, its surface melted and glassy. There was no way of telling how badly injured he was while he was still encased within his armor, and Mag could see no obvious way of opening it. She gently shook him, trying to wake him, not knowing quite what else to do.

"Come on, Jay," Mag said. "I'm definitely not giving you permission to be dead, do you hear me, soldier? So you'd better just wake the hell up."

She felt an overwhelming flood of relief as Jay gave a low groan, his helmet moving slightly. A few seconds later his battered faceplate melted away and Jay slowly opened his eyes.

"Did you have a nice sleep?" Mag asked him with a relieved grin.

"What hit us?" Jay said with a confused frown. "I got knocked flying by that shock wave and fell through that hole." He gestured toward the tear in the ceiling as he slowly sat upright. He looked down at the scorch marks on his armor. "I'm guessing I probably landed on that big glowing crystal over there. Whatever happened, I can't feel anyone up here anymore." He tapped the side of his head. "Looks like I've lost my copilot."

"Is this thing still working, then?" Mag asked, waving toward Jay's armor.

"Guess there's only one way to find out," Jay said, getting unsteadily to his feet.

"Whoa there, big guy." Mag grabbed him and helped him to stand. "You might want to take it easy for a minute or two."

"Not sure a rest break is an option at the moment," Jay said with a pained groan. "Let's see if I can get this thing off the ground, shall we?"

Mag took a step back as Jay closed his eyes, concentrating hard, trying to remember what the suit felt like to fly when he had the luxury of Illuminate assistance. A moment or two later he felt himself gently rising into the air, his feet slowly coming off the ground.

"Okay, that's still working at least," Mag said. "So how about you give me a lift up there"— she jerked a thumb toward the ceiling—"and we get back in this fight."

"Sounds good to me," Jay said.

Jack screamed in frustration as he saw Sam's floating body vanish through the glowing red portal that had opened in the ship's hull. He dived toward the hatch as it began to close, willing it to stay open just long enough for him to make it through behind Sam. Jack would never know whether it was his own instincts or those of the Illuminate bonded to his implant that jinked his suit a foot to the left as the energy beam lanced out from the hull. That tiny maneuver was the only thing that prevented the bolt from striking him dead center. Instead, it just glanced off his right shoulder and fried the systems controlling the nanites on that side of his suit. He felt a sickening lurch in his stomach as the flight systems in his armor went haywire, and he plummeted toward the ground far below, spiraling wildly out of control.

"Jack!" Nat yelled in alarm as she saw her friend get hit. She aborted her attack run, banking sharply and diving after him. She accelerated hard, her controlled power-dive rapidly closing the distance to his free-falling body. She could feel the Illuminate warrior bonded to her implant subtly guiding her flight path as she rocketed toward the canyon floor, weaving in and out of the Hunters that were swooping toward the approaching swarm. She closed the last couple of yards to Jack's plummeting body, stretching out her hand and grabbing on to his ankle, the nanites of her glove bonding to Jack's suit and strengthening her grip. She felt sudden dramatic deceleration as air brakes flared on her back, her armor shifting to help slow their descent as she fought to pull out of the terrifying dive. They were too close to the ground and traveling way too fast to stop in time, but her last-second maneuver meant they hit the ground at an angle, the impact bone-jarring but not fatal. They tumbled and slid across the desert floor in a cloud of dust before crashing into the side of one of the Voidborn buildings at the base of the canyon wall.

"Nice catch," Jack said with a pained groan.

"Are your weapons systems online?" Nat asked as she staggered to her feet.

"My Illuminate tells me they'll be back up in just under thirty seconds," Jack said. "But my flight systems are fried."

"Tell your Illuminate to concentrate on getting those weapons systems working," Nat said, raising her arms and leveling her own weapons at something behind Jack with a growl. "We're going to need them."

9

Mag wrapped her arms around Jay, hanging on tightly as he shot up through the hole in the chamber roof and back out into the chaos that was unfolding on the top of the Voidborn structure. An outer perimeter of Illuminate Hunters was swooping and diving toward the leading edge of the swarm as it advanced along the span of the giant bridge-like structure, the energy cannons on their silvery upper carapaces firing constantly.

"Who's that up there?" Mag yelled, pointing up at the two suits of Illuminate armor that were buzzing around the giant ship overhead.

"I've got no idea. My HUD's not working properly," Jay said, peering up at the tiny figures that were dwarfed by the massive vessel they were attacking. "Have you got comms?"

"Yeah, give me a sec," Mag said, tapping her Illuminate

earpiece. "This is Mag calling whoever it is that's attacking that giant spiky thing above us, sound off!"

There was a moment's silence and then Anne's voice replied, the sounds of weapon fire loud in the background.

"Roger that, Mag, this is Anne. It's me and Will . . . aahh!" She let out a sudden pained grunt and cursed under her breath. "It's getting a little busy up here. We're going to need a lot more firepower if we're going to have any chance of stopping this thing."

"There's no way we're taking it down," Mag replied, "not without some Mothership support anyway." Mag looked down the length of the span as the outer defensive line formed by the Illuminate Hunters gradually retreated toward them, slowing but never halting the advance of the swarm. The massive vessel overhead seemed only concerned with firing defensively at the Illuminate armor suits that swooped around it; it wasn't attacking the Voidborn facility below at all. "Fall back and help protect the control node," Mag said. "If we can hold that, we can let the Motherships worry about that thing when they arrive."

"You don't understand," Anne snapped back in Mag's ear. "That thing's got Sam."

"What do you mean it's got Sam?" Mag yelled, turning toward Jay, his eyes widening as he heard what she said. "What happened?"

"We don't know," Will said, joining the conversation. "It was just sitting there and then Sam went in for an attack run and it opened fire on him. He got hit and then some sort of tractor beam seemed to pull him inside. Jack tried to save him, but he got hit too and Nat went down into the canyon after him."

"Okay, understood," Mag said, looking up at the giant vessel above her. As she watched, the colossal ship started to move, climbing back up into the sky, slowly at first but steadily accelerating. It was leaving, with Sam on board. "Keep firing. Try and slow that thing down and keep it distracted at the same time if you can."

"Roger that," Anne replied. "On it."

"Jay," Mag said, her mind racing, "we have to get on board that thing *now*. Has your suit still got enough juice to get us both up there?"

"Let's hope so," Jay replied. "Come on." He put his arms around Mag again and tilted his head back, the helmet of his suit re-forming as he turned his face up toward the massive ship that was climbing into the sky overhead. He concentrated hard, willing the suit to lift into the air once again, before quickly increasing thrust, accelerating hard and sending them streaking up toward the strange alien dreadnought.

Mag hung on to Jay with all her might, pressing her face into his chest as the ground dropped away beneath them, the wind whipping past her at hundreds of miles per hour as they rocketed straight up. She felt her claws digging into the armor on the back of Jay's shoulders as she clung desperately to him, glancing up to see that the giant alien ship was now just five hundred feet above them. She knew that Jay couldn't slow down if they were going to catch it, but she didn't know how much longer she could hold on to him at the speed they were traveling.

They shot up past the flanks of the giant ship, flying close to its segmented hull as Jay searched frantically for somewhere to land. He was starting to feel tiny variations in the levels of thrust from the suit and he didn't need his Illuminate copilot to tell him that his badly damaged armor was starting to malfunction. Meanwhile, Anne and Will concentrated their attacks on the opposite side of the huge ship, focusing less on causing any specific damage and more on providing as much of a distraction as possible. Jay could only assume that the lack of any defensive fire aimed in his direction as he raced low over the hull meant that the diversion was working. He dived into one of the narrow gaps between the massive, shifting outer plates of the hull, his eyes struggling to adjust to the relative darkness as they flew through the shadowy ravine, its walls lit from within with a dull red glow. He swooped to the bottom of the trench, touching down gently as Mag released her vice-like grip with a relieved sigh.

"Let's not do that again," Mag said, letting out a long, deep, slightly shaky breath. "Ever."

"Judging by the way that my suit was acting in the last

few seconds there," Jay said, "we're not going to be flying again anytime soon." He looked up at the strip of bright blue sky above, framed by the alien vessel's crystalline black superstructure. "Which could make getting back down interesting . . ."

"I'm not so worried about how we get off this thing at the moment," Mag said, looking around at the monolithic black slabs that formed this section of the hull. "In fact, I'm actually more concerned with how we get inside it."

They suddenly both stumbled, fighting to regain their balance as the ground beneath their feet seemed to shift. The whole section of the hull on which they were standing appeared to undulate for a moment and then several of the nearby slabs split apart, clouds of white vapor gushing out from within.

"Come on," Mag said, gesturing for Jay to follow her as she sprinted toward the new opening in the hull. The cloud of steam cleared as she approached and Mag peered inside, seeing a narrow shaft beyond, its grilled walls and ceiling dripping with moisture. After a few yards the passageway disappeared into darkness, a low, rumbling hiss the only clue as to what might lurk in the shadows beyond.

"Seriously?" Jay asked, staring into the cramped, damp tunnel. "Does this look like an entrance to you?"

"Nope," Mag said with a grin, baring her razor-sharp fangs. "And that's exactly why it's perfect."

"I was afraid you were going to say something stupid

like that," Jay said, shaking his head. "I suppose you want me to go first too, don't you?"

"Well, you are the one wearing the armor," Mag replied with a crooked smile.

Jack spun around just in time to see the energy beam from Nat's wrist strike the leading edge of the swarm as it rushed toward them.

"We could do with some backup here!" Jack yelled into his helmet's comms system. Wherever Nat's weapons struck, the swarm was temporarily driven back, only to surge forward in another area. It was like trying to hold back the tide with a shotgun. The swarm rushed to one side, sweeping up the canyon wall, attempting to flank Jack and Nat, while more Illuminate-piloted Hunters swept down from overhead, their weapons blazing as they joined the fight against the seething black mass.

"We're going to be surrounded if we're not careful!" Nat yelled, maintaining her withering barrage of fire on the swarm, determined to slow it down even if she could not stop it.

"Can you fly me out of here?" Jack asked quickly. "We need to get back up top and help protect the control node. If we lose that, this is all over."

"Yeah, I think I can get you up there," Nat said with a nod, vaporizing a swarm tentacle as it lashed out toward her. "We're going to need to stay away from that huge ship, though. There's no way I can dodge the fire from that thing if I'm carrying you."

"Actually, that might not be an issue," Jack replied, opening fire as the Illuminate inside his head informed him that his weapons systems were finally back online. "Look. It's moving away."

Nat glanced up and saw the giant alien vessel climbing into the sky, with Sam on board. She could see Will and Anne still flitting around it, diving in and out of its colossal superstructure, the bright white beams of their weapons flaring. The effects of their attacks seemed negligible at best as the vast ship pulled away.

"Come on," she said, stepping behind Jack and threading her arms under his, wrapping them tightly around his chest. "I'll fly, you shoot."

The Illuminate bonded with Nat subtly helped her to compensate for Jack's additional mass as they flew over the seething black tide below. Jack fired his weapons into the swarm, carving furrows in the dark mass, which closed up again just as quickly. Nat adjusted her course, angling up toward the spanning structure, then dropping down next to the tear in the core chamber roof. She watched as the swarm surged forward along the span toward them. It was now barely fifty yards away from the front line of Grendels that were the control node's last line of defense. The Illuminate-controlled Hunters continued to lay down fire on the creeping mass, but Nat could see that despite the accuracy of their fire, they were doing as much damage to the superstructure as they were to the swarm itself. Suddenly the germ of an insane idea formed inside her head.

"Selenne, come in, can you hear me?" Nat yelled into the comms system, shouting to make herself heard over the deafening sounds of battle surrounding her.

Selenne is not responding, the voice of General Indriss replied. *Do you require assistance?*

"Yes," Nat snapped back, "we need every Hunter you can spare right now."

That will weaken our defensive line considerably, General Indriss said. *What exactly do you intend to do?*

"Buy us some time," Nat replied. She explained the plan as quickly and efficiently as she could.

I cannot decide if you are brilliant or insane, General Indriss said when Nat had finished.

"A little of both if you ask me," Jack said, shaking his head.

It's risky but it could work, the general said. *As it stands, we are fighting a losing battle. This might be all we need to hold out until the Motherships arrive.*

The general began to issue orders to the rest of the surviving Illuminate Hunters throughout the canyon that were engaged with the swarm but not actively defending the control node. First dozens and then hundreds of the silvery, jellyfish-like Drones dived toward the Hunters that were already fighting to hold back the swarm as it advanced. The swooping pack divided in two, with one half dropping below the suspended core of the Voidborn hive, where they landed, inverted, on its underside. Their tentacles snaked through the crystalline structure of the building's outer walls, attaching them to its surface like giant limpets. The Illuminate controlling these Hunters boosted the power to their Drones' antigravity generators, pushing them to their very limits. At the same instant, the fresh wave of reinforcements that had joined the Hunters already attacking the swarm all opened fire simultaneously. Their target, however, was not the tide of tiny skittering metallic creatures, but the ground ten yards in front of the swarm.

The effect of the sudden, concentrated barrage of fire was instant and catastrophic. A section of the giant bridge-like structure disintegrated in a series of searing white explosions as the sustained torrent of energy bolts carved through the floor and supports below. Nat felt the ground lurch beneath her feet as the span was suddenly severed and fiery explosions erupted from the disconnected part of the bridge, which was beginning to lose its increasingly futile struggle with the forces of gravity. The blue lights within the shells of the Hunters attached to the underside of the core chamber glowed fiercely as their antigravity generators collectively fought to support the massive weight of the colossal structure, which was now only attached to the canyon wall at one end. The Hunters in the air continued to pour fire on the unsupported section of the span covered by the seething black mass of the swarm.

There was a sudden shrieking groan as the supports carved into the canyon wall that were bracing that part catastrophically collapsed, unable to support its weight. With a thunderous roar, the rest of the swarm-covered section plummeted toward the ground far below, slamming into Voidborn buildings in a fiery explosion of debris, filling the canyon floor with a thick, impenetrable cloud of black dust. Back on the top of the remaining half of the Voidborn structure, Nat and Jack felt the floor beneath their feet lurch again and there was an ominous-sounding groan as the massed Hunters on the underside of the structure fought to keep it from collapsing.

"I can't believe that actually worked," Jack said, shaking his head in disbelief.

"That makes two of us," Nat said. "But we're not safe yet." She turned and looked at the other end of the structure, which was still firmly attached to the canyon wall. At the moment there was no sign of the swarm climbing the canyon wall toward it, but something told her that it would only be a matter of time. She couldn't shake the feeling that they were just delaying the inevitable.

"Wow!" Will said as he dropped to the ground next to Nat and Jack. He walked past the hovering Hunters and leaned out over the ragged, severed edge, peering down at the smoldering clouds of dust far below. "You guys don't mess around, do you?"

"There wasn't really time for subtlety," Nat said. "We need to move our forces and reinforce the other end of this thing. We're not out of the woods yet. Have you guys seen any sign of Mag or Jay?"

"That's what we were doing up there," Will said, as Anne dropped down beside him. "We were trying to keep that thing busy while Jay and Mag snuck on board."

"While they did what?" Jack asked, his eyes widening in surprise.

"Did they make it?" Nat asked.

"I'm not sure," Anne said, shaking her head. "Jay's armor was malfunctioning, so we couldn't get a fix on his position. I'm pretty sure they managed to land on that thing, but then Mag's tracker just vanished. I've got no idea what happened to them after that."

"Well, let's hope they did get on board," Jack said, looking up at the tiny black dot in the sky that was all that was visible now of the giant mysterious vessel as it vanished into the heavens. "Because right now, I think they're the only chance Sam's got."

10

Sam felt cold, smooth stone against his face as he drifted back into consciousness. He struggled to reconstruct his memory of the past couple of minutes. He could recall flying up toward the giant alien ship, but beyond that, nothing. His eyes flickered open and all he could see was blackness, and for a horrible moment he thought he'd been blinded, but after a few seconds he realized that there was the tiniest glimmer of light somewhere nearby, just enough for him to make out black shapes looming in the shadows around him.

He pushed himself up onto his knees, trying to ignore the throbbing pain in his head. The only thing he could hear other than his own breathing was a low, almost subsonic throbbing sound that seemed to come from somewhere beneath the ground. As his eyes continued to adjust to the darkness, Sam could make out more and more details of the room around him. He could see now that the dark objects were huge columns of twisting, faceted black glass, within which sinuous *things* writhed and twitched horribly. Sam recoiled from one of the columns as something inside it seemed to react to his presence, slamming against the glass with a wet thud. He continued to walk slowly and quietly through the shadows, staying as far away as possible from the columns. Ahead of him, a sheer black wall appeared from the darkness. Sam walked toward it, reasoning that if he followed it along far enough, sooner or later he should find a door.

"Assuming there is a door," he whispered to himself. He reached out and placed one hand on the wall, jumping back with a startled cry as it responded instantly to his touch. The surface seemed to disintegrate in front of him, revealing an enormous wall of crystal clear glass, through which light flooded into the room. Beyond the window, the deep blue disc of the Earth glowed brightly in the darkness of space, breathtakingly beautiful, but very, very far away.

Sam suddenly noticed patterns of red light dancing on the wall around the window. He turned and saw a column of fire materializing in the center of the room, its deep red flames sending shadows the color of blood flickering across the floor. The column seemed to glide toward Sam and he instinctively backed away until he felt his shoulders press against the smooth, cold glass of the window. The flames drew nearer and nearer and yet Sam could feel no heat from them; if anything they seemed to bring a deathly chill to the air.

When the column of fire was only a few yards away from Sam, it stopped advancing and, spinning very quickly, collapsed in on itself with a sudden bright flash. Sam winced, screwing his eyes shut, almost blinded by the intensity of the flare. He slowly opened them again, letting out a gasp as he saw a towering figure standing before him. Superficially, the creature looked like an unusually tall Illuminate warrior, but instead of bone-white plates of armor it was clad in shards of glistening obsidian crystal that glowed from within with a deep red light. Its armor was topped by a pair of elaborate crested pauldrons that framed the alien being's monstrous head. Where its eyes should have been, scarlet flames burned, tongues of fire flickering across its jet-black skin, reaching toward its temples. Instead of an Illuminate's nose, there was just a pair of reptilian slits, and below that a wide, lipless mouth that spread wide in a sinister rictus, revealing long, jagged, daggerlike teeth.

"Greetings, child of Suran," the monstrous creature said. "I have been so looking forward to meeting you." Its voice was sinister and unsettling, deep and multilayered, like many voices speaking in perfect unison. The creature took a single step toward Sam, looming over him and flexing the talons of its massive clawed hands. "I believe you have something that belongs to me."

"Who are you?" Sam croaked, his mouth suddenly dry.

"I am the Primarch," the creature replied, "and you will give me what I want, human, or I will burn your world to ash."

"I don't understand," Sam said, shaking his head. "What is it that you think I've got?"

"Something that was taken from me a very, very long time ago," the Primarch replied. "Something that will finally allow me to destroy the hated Illuminate once and for all. Your father stole it from me and then hid it inside your skull." The Primarch reached out with one of its massive clawed hands, gently running the razor-sharp tips of its talons along the side of Sam's head. "It is called the Bridge and you are going to give it to me."

"I'm not giving you a damn thing," Sam said, wincing as he felt the Primarch's claws suddenly pressing harder into the side of his skull. "If you want it, you'll have to take it."

"If it were that simple you'd be dead already," the Primarch snarled, gripping the back of Sam's head. "Suran was many things, but he was no fool. No, the Bridge is bound to you; only you may use it."

"Well, it looks like you're out of luck, then," Sam said defiantly, gritting his teeth as the Primarch tightened its grip. "I'll die before I help you."

"You seem to be laboring under the misapprehension that I'm giving you a choice," the Primarch said with an evil smile as it twisted Sam's head, forcing him to turn and look out through the window. "Allow me to demonstrate."

The view through the window suddenly shifted, the Earth racing toward them as they seemed to fly down, getting closer and closer to the surface. First it focused on Europe and then on the United Kingdom, zooming in still further until eventually an aerial view of London filled the screen.

"I believe this is your home," the Primarch said as Sam felt a chill run down his spine. "You never did find the rest of your family, did you? Your mother? Your sister? Don't worry. I found them for you."

An instant later a pair of display panels opened next to the aerial view of London, both of them showing live video feeds. Sam gasped in surprise as he saw what was displayed on the panels. One showed the writhing, agonized body of his mother, and the other, his sister, who was clawing at the air as if trying to fight off some invisible attacker.

"Perhaps, to prove my good intentions, I should end their suffering?" the Primarch asked.

"If you think I'm going to help you just because you offer to release my mother and sister, then you're wrong," Sam said, trying to hide his emotions. The truth was, he hadn't seen either of them since the day of the Voidborn invasion and, until a few seconds ago, he'd had no idea whether they were even alive or dead. There were countless Sleeper dormitories across London and searching all of them would have been impossible. He'd always told himself that the best way to ensure their safety would be to defeat the Voidborn, but to see them like this, enduring whatever it was that was tormenting the Sleepers when he was so powerless to help them, was its own form of torture.

"You misunderstand me," the Primarch replied. "I didn't say I was going to release them; I said I was going to end their suffering. In fact, I'm feeling so generous, I'm going to end the suffering of every living thing in that city."

An instant later, a light brighter than the sun flared in the center of London as the Voidborn Mothership's core detonated over the city. The raging furnace of the earthbound star that had been created by the core's collapse consumed and annihilated everything within a five-mile radius. Beyond that, a devastating, blazing shock wave spread out across the rest of the city, flattening everything in its path above ground level and scorching the earth with a ceaseless roaring inferno. Less than a minute later, all that remained of the ancient capital city was a ten-mile-wide crater surrounded by a trackless wasteland of smoldering rubble.

"No!" Sam said with an anguished sob.

The Primarch released its grip on him and Sam dropped to his knees, his palms on the glass. Everything and everyone that had been part of his life before the

Voidborn invasion had just been obliterated.

"What have you done?" Sam gasped, feeling the hot sting of tears in his eyes as his world shrank down to a tiny white-hot core of grief and pain.

"Erased ten million barely evolved apes from the universe," the Primarch said with a sneer. "I have done and *will do* far worse."

"I'll kill you," Sam said, his voice hoarse with grief. "I swear to God, if it's the last thing I do, I'll watch you die."

"Empty threats," the Primarch said. "Now give me the Bridge."

"No," Sam hissed, climbing to his feet and turning to face the Primarch. "I'll never help you. After what you've just done . . . I'd rather die."

"You still don't understand, do you?" the Primarch said. It gestured at the window again, the display zooming in on an aerial view of another sprawling city. "I believe this place was once called Shanghai. Twenty-four million humans packed into such a tiny space. Such a pity. What a waste."

"Please . . . don't . . . ," Sam said, knowing with a horrible certainty now that the Primarch did not bluff. "You can't . . ."

"Don't be so childish, human. You know now that I can and that I will," the Primarch replied with a sneer. "The choice I offer you is a very simple one. Give me access to the Bridge and let me end the Illuminate once and for all and I will spare your people. Refuse me and I will force you to watch as I erase your species from existence."

"So you'd have me trade our lives for theirs?" Sam snapped back. "Either way, that's genocide."

"Yes, I'm giving you a very simple choice: it's you or them," the Primarch growled. "Now choose!"

Sam stared at the city on the screen. It was an impossible choice. He did not doubt for an instant that the Primarch would carry through with its threats. The insane creature was right about one thing: the choice that Sam now faced was terrifyingly simple and utterly stark. He had no way of knowing if the Primarch had any intention of honoring its agreement, but only one of the two choices before him offered either of their two species any hope of survival whatsoever.

"Okay," Sam whispered, knowing in that instant that whatever happened now, he was damned. "I'll do it . . . God help me . . . but I'll do it."

Sam, please don't do this, Selenne said, her voice barely a whisper inside his skull.

The response from the Primarch was instantaneous and violent. It rounded on Sam with an enraged roar, grabbing Sam's head with both hands as crimson lightning arced from its fingertips. Sam let out a scream; it felt like something inside his head was on fire.

"How dare you!" the Primarch bellowed as it forced Sam to his knees, bolts of scarlet energy dancing from its fingertips and across Sam's skull. "How dare you bring one of the Illuminate *here*!"

Sam didn't even hear the Primarch, all of his senses overwhelmed by the searing pain inside his head. Then the torture stopped as quickly as it had begun. The Primarch stepped away from Sam, a look of satisfaction on its face. A swirling blue cloud contained within a cage of crackling red fire hovered above its outstretched hand.

"Selenne?" the Primarch said, sounding surprised. "You were a fool to come here inside this child. What did you hope to achieve?"

"I hoped I might be able to reason with you, Sabiss," Selenne replied, the swirling blue cloud pulsing with light in time with her voice. "You were a being of reason once."

"The time for negotiation passed millennia ago," the Primarch replied, shaking its head. "And the creature you knew as Sabiss is long, long dead."

"He is not dead," Selenne replied. "He stands before me."

"You murdered him!" the Primarch screamed, its voice suddenly filled with rage. "Yes, Selenne, you killed him, but you have no idea how long it took him to die. You and Suran were just the same, always desperate to make the next discovery, to explore the new frontier. You both lied to me; you told me the transfer process was foolproof, that there were no risks, that it would be an eternity of dreamless sleep. You sent me to the stars on a journey that lasted millennia, but I did not sleep. Something happened that meant I *could not* sleep." Sam heard the unmistakable fragile note of insanity in the Primarch's voice, its tone becoming ragged and high pitched. "Even I don't know when Sabiss died, Selenne. Was it after a hundred years of drifting in the void? A thousand years? Ten thousand years? Can you even begin to imagine that, Selenne? To be lost, truly, hopelessly lost? Adrift in a ship that you cannot control, still awake, still aware, trapped for eternity." The Primarch's final words came out as a malevolent hiss.

"By the Illuminate," Selenne gasped, genuine shock, horror even, in her voice. "We didn't know, Sabiss; we couldn't have known. Suran and I were your friends. We thought the Primarch was lost. When we received its final transmissions, we were certain that it had been destroyed. The final damage reports that the Primarch broadcast were catastrophic. We had no idea that you were still adrift out there and that the hibernation protocols had malfunctioned. We would have kept searching, no matter how long it took, until we found you. . . ."

"Oh, but the Illuminate did find me, Selenne," the Primarch said, barely contained fury in its voice. "Or at least their automated colony vessels did, seventeen thousand years later. Do you want to know what sustained me in that perpetual dark, Selenne? I'll tell you. It was the belief that the only reason the Illuminate had never rescued me from my endless torment was that something terrible had happened to our civilization. I told myself that was why no one had ever looked for me, because you were all *dead*. But then, when the automated colony ships found me and repaired the Primarch, allowing me to hijack their systems, I discovered the truth. I was not the last of my kind; I had just been forgotten. So I took those colony ships and used their nano-forges to create a new species. A warrior species forged in the furnaces of the heavens, the instrument of my final revenge, the Voidborn."

Sam slowly got to his feet. He reached out with his mind to the Illuminate nanites throughout his body, willing them to re-form his armor.

"You're wasting your time," the Primarch said, turning to Sam. "No Illuminate weapons will work on board this ship unless I will it. That's why Selenne cannot physically manifest." It gestured toward the swirling blue cloud trapped within the energy cage hovering in the air nearby. "I make the rules here."

"I don't understand," Sam said. "I never opened the Bridge for you. How did you bring Selenne here physically? She . . . she was supposed to be safe."

"Safe in the Heart, you mean?" the Primarch asked. "Locked away in Suran's precious sanctuary? You and your little resistance force were responsible for sabotaging my first attempt to retrieve it. The loss of the core drill in London was . . . irritating, but not as irritating as not knowing how you did it. I couldn't risk sending any more of my forces deployed on this planet against you, at least not until I was sure you wouldn't steal any more of my ships. And now it appears that you and your friends are about to destroy my new drilling rig, having hijacked a whole continent's worth of my forces." The creature walked toward Sam, towering over him, flexing its massive clawed fingers as crimson lightning flickered between them. "As I say, irritating."

Sam swallowed hard, mentally preparing himself for fresh waves of agony as the Primarch raised its hand to the side of his head once more.

"But none of that matters anymore," the Primarch said, lowering its monstrous head toward Sam's ear, its voice dropping to a low, sinister whisper. "Because you brought me something that is much, much more precious. You see, once you open the Bridge to the Heart for me, the Illuminate's sanctuary becomes their prison. A prison from which there is no escape and of which I am the only warden. There will be no need to retrieve the Heart physically anymore. In fact, it can stay precisely where it is. The Illuminate will be trapped in a nightmare that I completely control. Their torment will last an eternity, just as mine did."

The Primarch walked around Sam, running its claws across his shoulder blades, just hard enough for him to feel their tips digging into his skin.

"Oh, I am sorry. None of that answers your question,

does it?" the Primarch said with a sly smile. "You have not yet physically released the Illuminate from the Heart, so how could Selenne possibly be here? Let me guess. She told you that she was just a voice in your head, there to help and advise. But it was actually rather more complicated than that, wasn't it, Selenne? Would you like me to explain it to our friend here?"

"Please, Sabiss," Selenne said, "there's no need—"

"SABISS IS DEAD!" the Primarch bellowed, roaring at the caged Illuminate, the dark, faceted surface of its armor flashing with bright red light. It spun back toward Sam, jabbing a finger toward Selenne. "Do you want to know how she got here? She hitched a ride. At some point she must have blended her own nanites with yours. How did she manage to persuade you? Was it so you could better control their weapons? Just like the Illuminate, to hide poison inside a gift. When I found her hiding inside you, she was comfortably coiled around your central nervous system. Now, why on earth would she have done that? Unless, of course, she was planning a hijack of her own."

Sam glanced over at the Illuminate cloud, waiting for Selenne to deny the Primarch's accusations.

"The silence of the guilty, I fear," the Primarch said with a sadistic grin. The creature leaned in close to Sam, its voice dropping to a conspiratorial whisper. "Oh, but the Illuminate are guilty of so much more. So many lies,

lies on top of lies, lies under lies, lies as far as the eye can see. Isn't that right, Selenne?" The Primarch whirled around, shouting the question at her. "There's one really big lie though, isn't there? One great, big, black, festering deception. I wonder what would happen if we told your friend here the truth about that?" The Primarch walked right up to the caged swirling cloud. "You must have heard us talking as you hid inside the child. Did you hear him? He actually seemed to care that he would have to destroy the Illuminate to save his own species. I wonder if he'd feel the same way if he was to discover what you actually had planned for this planet. Shall we find out?"

"Don't do this, Sabiss, I'm begging you," Selenne pleaded, her voice suddenly sounding desperate. "You will bring doom to our people."

"*Our* people?" the Primarch spat. "They should have died out millennia ago. The Illuminate have always clung desperately to life, though, haven't they, Selenne? Which brings us back to the humans."

"What are you talking about?" Sam asked angrily, suddenly sick of feeling like a playing piece in a game that he didn't quite understand. "What has all of this got to do with us?"

"Absolutely everything," the Primarch replied. "I think it's time that humanity finally learned the truth about the Illuminate, don't you?"

* * *

Jay and Mag walked through the dark, cavernous corridors of the alien ship, trying very hard to make as little sound as possible. The walls and floors around them were made of a smooth, dark rock that was warm to the touch and throbbed with a regular, pulse-like vibration. They had not seen a sign of a single living creature since they had managed to get on board, and it seemed like they had been walking for miles along the featureless corridors in their search for Sam.

"I'm starting to think this wasn't such a good idea," Mag said. "This place is enormous. We're never going to find him."

"We'll find him," Jay said. "We just need to keep searching."

"You did notice how big this thing was when we were flying up here, didn't you?" Mag asked.

"Yeah, I know but . . ." Jay stopped for a moment, looking at Mag with a slightly confused frown. "Erm . . . you do know you're glowing, right?"

"I'm what?" Mag replied.

Jay gestured toward the breast pocket of her jacket, which was lit up from within, a yellow glow showing through the weave of the fabric. She reached into her pocket and pulled out the test tube containing the handful of inert nanites that she had gathered up from the fallen Servant in London. Except they obviously weren't quite so inert anymore. The glowing particles were all clumped at one end of the tube, which she could feel vibrating slightly in her hand. As she flipped the tube, the particles raced back to the other end, as if they were trying to head in that specific direction.

"Is that . . . ?" Jay asked, gesturing at the tube.

"Yeah, this is some of what was left of the Servant," Mag replied. "And it wasn't doing this earlier, I'll tell you that much. It seems to want to go that way, though." She turned slowly around, the glowing nanites shifting within the tube to remain pointing in the same direction. "Shall we find out where it wants to go?"

"I guess it's better than wandering randomly," Jay said with a shrug. "Let's be careful, though. For all we know, that stuff is leading us toward the biggest group of Voidborn it can find."

Mag gave a quick nod before holding the tube in front of her, using the movements of the nanites to give her an idea which direction to head in. After ten minutes she and Jay rounded a bend in one of the endless corridors and saw a faint golden light somewhere up ahead.

"You see that?" Jay whispered as they approached a doorway. The yellow light that was flickering on the corridor walls was coming from the room beyond.

"Let's check it out," Mag said, her nose twitching as she sniffed the air. She could smell nothing but the faint, lingering odor of burnt metal that seemed to hang in the air everywhere on the alien ship. The pair of them slid along the wall, creeping up to the doorway until they were close enough for Jay to poke his head around the corner.

"Whoa," Jay said under his breath as he saw what was hovering in the center of the room. The Servant hung suspended in the air in a shaft of white light. She was still recognizable as the Voidborn that had served and protected them during their time in London, but the glowing nanites that made up her body seemed to swirl in tiny chaotic storm clouds, yellow sparks flickering within them. Her head was thrown back, her mouth agape as if frozen in a perpetual scream and her eyes open wide, still burning with a fierce yellow light.

"Is that . . . ?" Mag asked as she followed Jay into the room.

"Yeah, I think it must be," Jay replied. "Unless you know any other golden Voidborn that you've not been telling us about?"

"Nope, just the one," Mag said as she walked over to the pedestal, leaning in and examining the floating body of the Servant more closely. "What do you think's happened to her?"

"Your guess is as good as mine," Jay replied, shaking his head and looking up at the floating Voidborn. "Whatever it is, it doesn't look good." If the Servant had any idea that the pair of them were there, she was showing no sign of it.

"So what do we do with her?" Mag asked.

"I don't know," Jay said, rubbing his forehead and

frowning. "She might be able to tell us where Sam is. I don't know about you, but I'm starting to think that we could run around this ship all day and never find him."

"Aye, I know what you mean," Mag said, looking up at the vaulted ceiling far above them. "I'd not really thought about how big this thing was when we stowed away, to be honest."

"So, the question is, how do we get her out of this thing?" Jay said, raising his hand toward the beam of light. "What the . . . ?"

A stream of blue particles had begun to flow from Jay's fingertips and into the beam of light, twisting and entwining itself within the scattered, swirling structure of the Servant. Jay went to pull his hand away, but Mag grabbed his wrist, holding it in place.

"Wait, Jay, look!"

Within the shaft of light, the swirling streams of blue particles started to draw the scattered remnants of the Servant's body back together, the features of her face and body sharpening and becoming clearer as her form continued to coalesce. Within seconds, the Servant was restored, her head tipping forward and her mouth closing. She raised her eyes again and looked first at Jay and then at Mag, her head tilted slightly to one side.

"How may I be of assistance?" the Servant asked, a wary smile appearing on Jay's face as Mag released his wrist and he lowered his arm.

"You can start by telling us who you are," Mag said. "And, more importantly, who you take orders from."

"I am the Servant of the Illuminate," she replied. "You are both companions of the Illuminate and as such I am duty-bound to serve you too."

"Aye, that's Golden Boobs, all right," Mag said, using the rather unflattering nickname that Rachel had coined for the Servant not long after her first appearance.

"So how do we get you out of . . ." Jay waved vaguely at the column of light that the Servant was trapped inside. "Well, whatever this is."

"The energy distribution node that provides power to the stasis field is nearby," the Servant replied. "If you look along the wall to your left, you should be able to identify it."

Jay spotted a crystalline disc mounted on the wall in the direction the Servant had instructed them to look. It was a couple of yards in diameter and its surface was covered by a crackling red energy field that discharged along weblike energy conduits that disappeared into the wall behind it.

"Okay, I think I found it," Jay said, walking over to it. "How do I switch it off?"

"I believe that the regional application of sufficient kinetic energy should prove effective," the Servant replied.

"The what of what?" Jay asked, with a confused frown.

"Oh, come on, Jay," Mag said, pulling the handgun from the holster on her hip. "She means hit it with something." Mag raised the pistol and fired three quick shots into the device mounted on the wall. It exploded in a shower of sparks and an instant later the shaft of light surrounding the Servant vanished. The Servant slowly dropped to the ground and stepped off the pedestal. As the final echoes of the gunshots faded, the sound of a low, wailing alarm siren could be heard somewhere in the distance.

"I believe your actions may have drawn unwelcome attention," the Servant said to Mag calmly. "I would advise evasive relocation."

"Yeah," Jay said, looking around nervously as the alarm continued to blare. "I think you might just be right. Let's get the hell out of here."

"Hold the line!" Jack yelled, searing white energy beams lancing out from the weapons mounted on the back of his forearms. "Don't let them push you back." He fired again, sending more bolts into the massive wave of Drones surging up the canyon wall toward the one end of the Voidborn structure that was still firmly secured in place. There were just too many of them and he knew they would not be able to hold them back forever. Now it was just a case of trying to buy themselves as much time as possible. Beyond that, they could only hope for a miracle. As the swarm surged up the sheer rock face, it swept under the giant Voidborn structure, disappearing from view beneath it.

"What are they doing?" Anne yelled as she and Will ran toward the edge of the span, leaning over and trying to see exactly where they had gone. They could just make out huge clumps of the swarm forming on the main supports that held that end of the structure in place. There was a sudden screeching sound and then a loud, ominous crunch. A moment later one of the supports gave way in an explosion of black crystalline shards, sending billions of the bug-like Drones cascading down into the canyon below. The whole colossal structure gave a sickening lurch, and the Hunters supporting the control node struggled to compensate for the sudden massive shift in its center of gravity. Anne and Will fought to keep their footing as the ground bucked wildly beneath their feet.

"They're going to bring this whole thing down," Will yelled, triggering his armor's flight systems and rising into the air. "We've got to try and keep the swarm away from those supports." A moment later, he dived under the massive structure, firing at the heaving masses of tiny creatures. Showers of them dropped away as his beams struck home, only to be replaced by countless thousands more surging up the canyon wall behind them. He kept firing, despite the apparent futility of his actions, as Anne and Nat hovered beside him, adding their own beams to the withering field of fire he was laying down. Their combined bombardment was marginally more effective but it still seemed only to be delaying the inevitable.

"I need every Hunter we can spare down here now!" Nat yelled into her comms system. "Have them concentrate all their fire on the swarm attacking the supports." A moment later another one of the supports began to crumble, chunks of it dropping away as its structural integrity failed. Illuminate-controlled Hunters began to pour over the edge of the superstructure above them, sweeping down toward the swarm as it continued to devour the massive bracing structures. The humans and the Hunters both had to choose their targets carefully, trying to drive the swarm back without further damaging the supports beneath them with their own fire.

"How long until the first Illuminate Mothership gets here?" Will yelled over the deafening roar of weapon fire around him.

"My Illuminate's telling me it's going to be at least five minutes," Jack replied in his ear.

"Roger that," Will replied, feeling his mouth go dry inside his helmet. He looked at the rapidly disintegrating support structures and the tiny skittering black creatures swarming over them.

There was no way they'd last that long.

* * *

"What do you mean, the truth about the Illuminate?" Sam asked the Primarch, who was towering over him with a sinister grin.

"I mean that you have been lied to, right from the start," the Primarch replied. It turned back toward the energy cage within which Selenne was trapped. With a wave of its hand the cage disappeared and the swirling cloud of glowing blue dust coalesced quickly into the robed form of Selenne, dressed just as Sam had last seen her at the Threshold.

"These beautiful, luminous creatures of light," the Primarch sneered. "Do you really think this is their true form? Or could it just be that they chose a shape that humans would trust? Hoping that you would believe that such luminous beings could only be your friends, possibly even your saviors?" It turned back toward Sam, its fiery eyes suddenly blazing with increased intensity. "They are *no such thing*." The words came out as little more than a growl.

Sam glanced over at Selenne and she looked away from him, refusing to make eye contact.

"You see," the Primarch continued, "the Illuminate understood that my Voidborn had infinite patience and that they would continue to scour the universe until they knew with certainty that the Illuminate's hated presence had been erased from existence for all eternity. So they needed somewhere to conceal themselves, a hiding place where even I would never find them."

"You're not telling me anything I don't already know," Sam spat back at the Primarch angrily. "I've heard this all before. We know about the Heart. The Illuminate never lied to us about it."

"Oh, I'm not talking about the Heart," the Primarch replied. "That was only ever a temporary measure. They knew that I would find it eventually, no matter how well hidden it was. No, they needed a more *permanent* solution. Hidden in plain sight. Somewhere I would never think to look." The creature placed one massive hand on the side of Sam's head, the claw at the tip of its thumb pressing into the center of his forehead painfully. "Inside you."

"I don't understand," Sam said, sounding slightly bewildered. "What do you mean, inside me?"

"Oh, not just you," the Primarch replied with a vicious smile. "Inside all of you."

"All of us?" Sam said, frowning in confusion. "I still don't understand."

"Do you know how many Illuminate consciousnesses are stored inside the Heart?" the Primarch asked, taking its hand away from Sam's head and turning back toward Selenne. "No? Then let me tell you. Seven billion. That was all that was left of a species that once numbered in the trillions, reduced at their end to compressed memory engrams, just ghosts stored away inside an indestructible tomb. Seven billion. An interesting number, I'm sure you'll agree."

Sam stared at the Primarch, a vague notion of what the horrific creature was talking about starting to form in his head.

"Let me ask you this," the Primarch said. "Do you really think it's a coincidence that all of these terrible misfortunes should befall your planet just as its native population reached a similar number?"

"What are you saying?" Sam asked quietly. He feared he knew exactly what the Primarch was implying, but he didn't want to believe it.

"What I'm saying is that your friend over there"—the creature gestured toward Selenne, who was standing silently with her head hung low—"is really no friend at all. They chose this planet as a hiding place for one reason and one reason only. Life. Rich, abundant, ubiquitous life. A verdant jewel of a planet with an already partially evolved higher-order primate life form that was just beginning to claw its way toward civilization. A species that could be steered, manipulated, prepared."

"That's not true. It was the Voidborn that manipulated our history," Sam said, "not the Illuminate. You've been here for thousands of years."

"Who told you that?" the Primarch asked.

"A friend," Sam replied angrily, the pain of Stirling's death still feeling like a fresh wound. "He told me everything about how the Voidborn had tried to manipulate human history, how they recruited him and my father to help prepare the Earth for the invasion and how they turned against you when they discovered what you were really planning."

"Don't be so naive," the Primarch said. "Do you really think Suran told your friend the truth? These creatures have manipulated your entire society for millennia. Is it really so hard to believe that they could deceive just one man? As I said before, lies within lies, it's the Illuminate way."

"I don't believe you," Sam snapped angrily. "It wasn't the Illuminate that invaded our world. It wasn't the Illuminate that turned every person on this planet into a mindless slave." His voice became louder as he grew angrier and angrier. "It wasn't the Illuminate that killed my family. That was *you*!"

"You still don't understand, do you?" the Primarch said, shaking its head. "They were already dead. One way or another, it was just a matter of time. It wasn't my Voidborn who created the technology that enslaved your people. All that the Motherships did was alter the control signal that the Illuminate were broadcasting, even if they had not yet used it to exert their control over your planet. It was *their* signal that robbed your people of their free will. The Voidborn merely intercepted it when they arrived and altered it to suit their own purposes. If they had not, the Illuminate would have eventually assumed control of your species, as they had always intended to do. That is why I have inflicted such torment on the humans sleeping below.

The sensory overload caused by their agony makes it impossible for consciousness transfer to take place. As long as the humans suffer, the Illuminate are unable to possess them, even with the Bridge. Any attempt would cause fatal neural shock. That's all humanity ever was to the Illuminate, the perfect hiding place, a lowly species on a backwater world. It would never have occurred to me to look for the Illuminate within you. They would have simply erased humanity from existence in a heartbeat and overwritten them as if they were no more than junk data. A new life for them at the expense of the lives of every last one of your kind. Your consciousnesses erased and replaced in an instant, as if they had never existed at all. So spare me your indignant talk of genocide," the Primarch said, turning toward Sam with a sneer. "Because what your *friends* intended to do to you was just as bad. Perhaps worse. And best of all, it was all your father's idea."

"No . . . I can't . . . I won't believe that," Sam said, shaking his head, not wanting to entertain the idea that what this monstrous creature was telling him could be the truth. His mind raced, trying to rationalize what the Primarch had told him. The more he thought about it, the more it all started to make sense, whether he wanted it to or not. He had always wondered why the Voidborn had gone to the trouble of enslaving humanity when it would have been much simpler to wipe them out.

"Tell him, Selenne," the Primarch said, looking toward the captured Illuminate. "Tell him that everything I have just said is a lie. Tell him that the Illuminate had nothing but humanity's best interests at heart." The creature walked up to her, staring down at her as she turned away from it. "Except you can't, can you? Because you know as well as I do that everything I have told this child is the truth." It faced Sam again, pointing a single claw-tipped finger at Selenne. "So now you see your *allies* for who they really are and perhaps, just perhaps, you are beginning to understand why they have to be destroyed."

His initial reaction had of course been to assume that the malevolent creature standing before him was lying, but if that were true, why did Selenne say nothing? A memory from just a few hours before leapt into his head unbidden. It was something one of the Illuminate, General Indriss, had said to Jay when they had first visited the virtual world within the Heart. The general had called Jay something odd in the heat of the moment; the word had been strange enough that it had stuck in Sam's head. It had been meant as an insult, a single word said with a dismissive sneer.

Vessel.

At the time, he had dismissed it as some quirk of the Illuminate language, its true meaning lost on him, but now . . . Sam felt something almost like vertigo as the implications of what he had just learned began to sink in.

There was nothing left to fight for. If he didn't open the Bridge for the Primarch, the monstrous creature would scorch the surface of the planet. London would just be the start. He suddenly realized that the desperate battle his friends were presumably still fighting far below was meaningless. Even if they were somehow victorious, all they had done was hand control of an army to the Illuminate, a species whose only hope of survival was the effective murder of every last human being on the face of the Earth. Sam suddenly felt something he hadn't felt for a very long time. Not since the very first earliest days of the Voidborn invasion. Despair.

"It's all true, isn't it?" Sam said, staring at Selenne, his voice filled with anger.

She looked up at him, her face a mask of grief.

"Yes," she whispered, "all of it. We have lied enough. Here, at the end for both our species, you at least deserve the truth."

"This, all of it, it's . . . it's your fault," Sam said, feeling a hot rage building in his chest. "This is because of you, everything—the Voidborn, the invasion, Rachel, Adam, Stirling, all the dead. London . . . Damn you . . . My family . . ." His voice cracked as he felt the sting of tears in his eyes, grief suddenly overwhelming him. He turned back to the Primarch.

"I'll open your damn Bridge for you on one condition. If I help you destroy the Illuminate, you leave the Earth and never come back. Humanity has suffered enough."

"You are hardly in a position to negotiate, human," the Primarch replied. "But you may rest assured that when I have finished with the Illuminate, it will bring an end to my interest in your meaningless little planet."

Sam knew it was only the slimmest hope of survival for humanity, but that had to be better than no hope at all.

"Then show me what you want me to do."

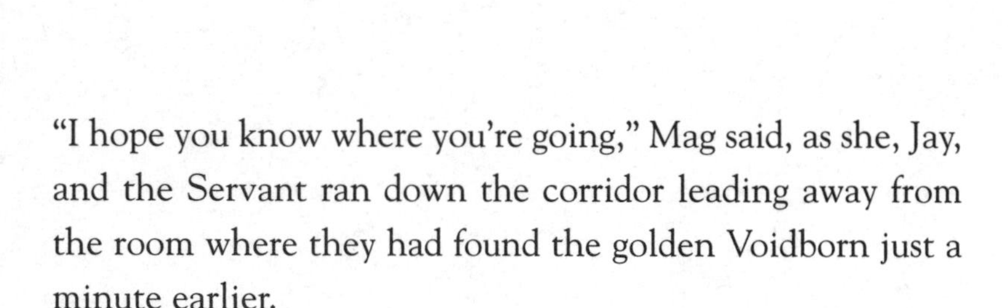

11

"I hope you know where you're going," Mag said, as she, Jay, and the Servant ran down the corridor leading away from the room where they had found the golden Voidborn just a minute earlier.

"I share a bond with the Illuminate," the Servant replied. "My own nanites are still integrated with his system, despite the recent physiological changes he has undergone."

"What do you mean, your nanites . . . Oh, yeah, right, his arm," Jay said, sounding slightly out of breath.

Sam had lost his arm in their first encounter with the Servant, when she had still been loyal to the Voidborn. The golden, shape-shifting limb that had replaced it was composed of the same nanites that made up not only the Servant, but also all of the Voidborn units that were part of the London Mothership. It had been one of the first indications that there was something both strange and unique about Sam.

"Whoa, whoa, whoa," Mag said, pulling to a sudden stop and waving for quiet. "Can you hear that?"

"Hear what?" Jay said. "There's nothing . . ."

But there was something. A scratchy, hissing sound that was coming from somewhere behind them and slowly increasing in intensity. It was a sound that had become horribly familiar to both Mag and Jay over the past couple of days.

"That'll be the guard dog," Jay said, shooting a worried glance at Mag.

"We are on board a Voidborn vessel in high Earth orbit; it is most unlikely that a Terran canine is pursuing us," the Servant said matter-of-factly, her head tipped slightly to one side.

"Yeah . . . No . . . You see, that's just a figure of . . . Never mind," Mag said, shaking her head. "Point is, we need to get out of here now."

"Mag's right," Jay said. "We need to find Sam. Show us the quickest route to him."

"Understood," the Servant said with a nod. "Follow me." She set off at a sprint, with Jay and Mag close behind her.

In the darkness, somewhere behind them, the swarm that had been summoned by the release of the Servant gathered speed in pursuit of its new prey.

* * *

"Fall back!" Anne yelled, watching as the others took up new positions behind the outer line of Illuminate Grendels defending the gaping hole that led to the core chamber below. The swarm had now completely engulfed both the top and the underside of the span, and the giant structure was beginning to lean precipitously. The cutting beam beneath the core sputtered and died; its control systems had finally failed due to the cumulative damage the structure had suffered, and a chain of small explosions ran through the underside of the span. They all felt a sickening jolt and heard a low rumble from the far end as something beneath the heaving mass of the swarm finally gave way.

"Will, grab Jack and get airborne!" Nat yelled.

Will gave a quick nod and took off into the air, rocketing toward Jack and scooping him up off the ground just as the massive Voidborn structure dropped fifteen feet in one sudden, heart-stopping lurch. Nat and Anne launched themselves into the sky, watching helplessly as the Grendels stranded on the top of the building struggled to maintain their balance. A series of huge explosions came from the far end of the structure and finally it lost its battle with the Voidborn swarm and gravity. The Hunters attached to the underside of the core chamber fought pointlessly to keep its colossal weight suspended, their antigravity generators screaming in protest and then overloading in showers of sparking, fiery debris. The doomed building plunged toward the canyon floor far below, the core within active until the end, burning bright with chaotic, violent discharges as it fell. It smashed into the Voidborn buildings that covered the canyon floor, now barely visible beneath countless millions of skittering swarm Drones.

Nat, Anne, Jack, and Will raced up into the sky, climbing as fast as their suits would safely allow, pushing them to the limit. Below them, the Voidborn core imploded, instantly vaporizing everything within five hundred yards, whether it was Voidborn or Illuminate controlled. Nat slowed her ascent, staring down in horror at the devastation below. The canyon was a hellish, blazing wasteland with a giant crater at its center, and as she watched the few Hunters that had survived the explosion tumble from the sky, their tentacles flailing limply, severed completely from Illuminate control, she could only assume that exactly the same thing was happening all over North America; their final, desperate gambit had failed.

"What do we do now?" Anne asked quietly as she dropped into a hover beside her friend and joined her in surveying the catastrophe below.

"You tell me," Nat replied, shaking her head. "There's no point in us staying here now."

"So where *do* we go?" Will asked as he rose up alongside them, hanging on tightly to Jack.

"Honestly?" Nat replied. "I have absolutely no idea."

* * *

"Kill them and bring me the bodies!" the Primarch snapped at the dozens of tiny crawling swarm Drones that scurried across the surface of its hand and forearm. The Drones dropped to the floor as the Primarch lowered its arm, skittering away into the darkness. "It seems some of your friends have a death wish."

"What do you mean?" Sam asked with a confused frown as the Primarch shoved him hard in the back, sending him staggering down the corridor ahead of it. Selenne walked along beside Sam in silence, her head hung low. "Who's here?"

"It hardly matters," the Primarch said with a growl. "They're already dead. My swarm Drones are far more efficient hunters than the previous generation of Voidborn. Your friends will not escape them."

Sam said nothing, but he was secretly encouraged by the fact that the Primarch could not instantly locate whoever it was who had managed to get on board. The fact that it needed to rely on the swarm Drones to find the intruders suggested the creature was not perhaps as omniscient as it would like to appear. This was not much of a weakness, but it was something.

"You are privileged, human," the Primarch said, shoving Sam into the massive chamber at the end of the corridor. "Very few creatures have ever seen this."

Sam's eyes widened as he tried to make sense of the

scale of the colossal machine in front of him. The walls of the vast space were lined with larger versions of the nano-forges that Sam had seen on board the Mothership above London. Dozens of streams of white-hot liquid poured from the massive crackling portals on the front of the huge cylindrical structures before cascading down the slope that led to the center of the chamber. There, the streams collected in a bubbling pool, strange alien shapes forming and then melting back into its boiling surface as Sam watched. Above the pool a giant silvery black ball was slowly rotating. It was formed from countless writhing snakelike creatures, their intertwined, segmented bodies sliding over and between each other.

"The Voidborn Nucleus," the Primarch said, stepping out onto the suspended walkway that led to the center of the chamber. "Once, these were Illuminate constructor nanites, designed to prepare new worlds for Illuminate colonists ahead of their arrival. Now they are mine, the Voidborn in their purest form, the clay from which I built my armies."

Again, Sam heard the slight manic edge to the Primarch's voice. There was no doubt in his mind that the creature's grasp on sanity was fragile at best, but Sam couldn't tell if it was something that he could exploit or if it simply made the Primarch more unpredictable and therefore dangerous.

"I didn't come here for a guided tour," Sam said. "Let's get on with it."

"I have waited millennia for this, human," the Primarch said as it moved across the walkway toward the hovering silver ball. "I will savor the moment for as long as I wish."

Sam followed behind the towering creature, his mind racing. There had to be something he could do, some way of derailing the Primarch's plan. Despite what he had told the Primarch a few minutes earlier, he had absolutely no intention of granting the insane creature access to the Heart if he could possibly help it. At the same time, if it really did come down to a choice between humanity and the Illuminate, Sam knew exactly what he would be forced to do. What he had to do now was somehow come up with a way of ensuring he didn't end up in that nightmarish situation.

As they walked closer to the giant squirming silver ball, Sam could see that the snaking creatures were in fact writhing chains of much smaller machines. When they were within just a couple of yards of the Nucleus, Sam could see that those smaller devices were themselves made up of even tinier networks of intricate machine work. It was the perfect illustration of exactly how the Voidborn worked, their nanites building upward from the microscopic level to the macroscopic. Horrors made of dust.

"This is the Voidborn," the Primarch said, raising one of its giant clawed hands toward the squirming mass. "In our purest form, nothing but unfettered potential. With it, we can become anything, create anything, destroy anything . . . whatever is required. We are the true heirs to the stars, not you, Selenne, and certainly not these fragile, organic life forms with their fleeting, useless lives."

"Sabiss, these things are machines," Selenne replied, walking slowly toward the Primarch with a look of terrible sadness on her face. "You were lost and these machines found you. You . . . your vessel was damaged and these machines simply did what they were programmed to do: they repaired you as best they could. The Primarch was supposed to be our first proper step into the universe, a pioneer vessel, exploring and building homes for us among the stars so that we could all follow in your footsteps."

"All lost in the darkness," the Primarch said, without turning to face her. "I remember nothing before that."

"I do," Selenne replied, her voice sounding desperate. "I remember you, Sabiss. I remember the man you were. I remember you designing your ship, the Primary Architect. That was what you were intent on calling it, until Suran convinced you that you needed to call it something shorter. You're not the Primarch, Sabiss, you're the man who designed it, built it, and ultimately piloted it, but you are *not what this ship has become*."

"I do not expect you to understand," the Primarch replied, its back still turned to her. "No, you *cannot* understand. You might think you can imagine what it would be like to drift through nothingness for an eternity, your eyes pinned open, awake and yet dreaming of a sleep that will never come, but you can't. You can't imagine what that forces you to become."

As the Primarch spoke, a stream of glittering black dust began to pour from its hand, rushing toward the slowly rotating sphere before being absorbed into its endlessly shifting coils. A few seconds later, the surface of the Voidborn Nucleus began to split and divide, the dark squirming mass opening to reveal a ball of red energy that flared with the brightness of a tiny sun.

"Perhaps watching your people burn will be enough to give you a true taste of horror," the Primarch said. "Come here, human."

Selenne shot a pleading glance in Sam's direction and he suddenly felt sick to his stomach as he realized they were out of both time and options.

"Sabiss, I'm begging you, please," Selenne pleaded with the creature. "I know you're still in there. The colony ships that found you were simple machines with basic programming. The Voidborn are intelligent: they plan, they reason, they think. That had to come from somewhere, Sabiss. That had to come from you!"

She reached toward the Primarch, her outstretched fingertips brushing its arm. Without warning, the creature whirled around to face her, a single outstretched hand held out in a clawlike grip, as if crushing some invisible object in its palm. The response from Selenne was instant, her face contorting in a rictus of agony as her body began to shift and morph horribly, taking strange, nightmarish forms.

"We are Voidborn!" the Primarch bellowed, its voice suddenly filled with insane rage. "We are many; we are one, indivisible, eternal! We will outlive the night and when there is nothing left but us, we will still endure." Its words came out in a manic torrent, as if something within the creature had finally snapped. "This child will open the Bridge and the final tattered remnants of your people will be mine to do with as I please. The cursed light of the Illuminate will be erased from the universe forever and only we, the Voidborn, will remain."

Selenne let out a bloodcurdling scream, collapsing to the ground, writhing in agony, while the Primarch tightened its fist in the air above her, as if crushing the life from her body. The creature raised its other hand, jabbing a finger toward Sam.

"Come here, boy," the Primarch snarled. "It is time for you to play your part."

Sam stared back at the monstrous creature, knowing in his heart that defiance at this point would be an act of utter futility, but determined, all the same, not to let the Primarch see any sign of the fear that was churning in his gut.

"I'd tell you to go to hell," Sam spat back, "but I think you already went there and something else came back."

"Do not test my patience," the Primarch said. He clenched his fist and Selenne's body disintegrated in a flash of blue light, crumbling into a pile of inert gray dust. "Your only ally is gone, trapped once again in her self-made prison. Perhaps you would like a taste of what Selenne was experiencing." Suddenly Sam felt a hideous stinging sensation throughout his body as the Primarch took control of the Illuminate nanites that coursed within him. "Now open the Bridge between the Nucleus and the Illuminate Heart. I have waited long enough."

Sam gritted his teeth, feeling the Primarch exerting its malign influence over the nanites within him, like a horrible gnawing itch deep inside his body. He knew that he couldn't resist, even if he wanted to.

"The time has come," the Primarch said with a vicious smile. "My victory is at hand."

"I just want to remind you that it was your idea to come here," Jay said, his voice ragged with exertion as he sprinted down the corridor. Behind him the leading edge of the swarm swept around the corner, traveling so fast that it washed up the opposite wall like a wave before rushing after them. It was now only thirty yards behind them.

"Nope, definitely your idea," Mag said with a nervous glance over her shoulder as she ran.

"The Illuminate is less than two hundred yards away," the Servant reported calmly, effortlessly keeping pace with Mag and Jay. Jay risked a glance back toward the swarm; it was gaining on them too quickly.

"He should be just up ahead, then," Mag said. "I'm not sure he's going to be pleased to see us with this lot in tow, though."

Jay knew what she meant: the swarm wasn't going to stop chasing them just because they'd found Sam. They rounded another corner and saw the corridor opening out into a massive chamber at the far end.

"I believe the Illuminate is within the chamber ahead," the Servant said. "I am detecting power signatures of a scale and type quite unlike anything I have seen before. I believe it is safe to assume that whatever is contained there is vital to the operation of the Voidborn."

"Yeah, just like Riley to get himself into the maximum amount of trouble possible," Jay said, panting. "Is he alone in there?"

"No, I do not believe so," the Servant replied as Jay and Mag picked up the pace, sprinting still harder to stay ahead of the voracious black wave pursuing them. "I am detecting a power signature identical to the one that I encountered when I was first interrogated by the Primarch."

"Great," Jay said, gritting his teeth, the exertions of the past couple of hours pushing his stamina to its limits.

They sprinted out onto a walkway that passed between two massive Voidborn nano-forges. The towering machines produced glowing torrents of fluid that flowed into huge channels carved in the basin far below. Jay and Mag didn't have time to stop, even if they'd wanted to. The swarm poured out onto the walkway behind them, hundreds of the creatures tumbling into the torrent of white-hot liquid flowing below. The losses seemed inconsequential to the swarm, as it surged down the walkway after Mag and Jay, still gathering speed.

"Jay, look!" Mag yelled, pointing at the platform suspended in the center of the chamber. A giant silver ball hovered in the air above it, its surface seeming to shift and warp in an unsettling way. A towering, monstrous creature clad in gleaming black armor stood next to the sphere, its hand raised as if to strike down the tiny figure standing defiantly before it.

"Sam!" Jay screamed.

The Primarch turned toward them, letting out an enraged roar, baring its long, black daggerlike teeth.

"What is that thing?" Mag yelled as they sprinted toward the platform.

"That is the Primarch," the Servant replied, "the creator of the Voidborn, or so he claims."

Mag felt something snag at her leg with a quick tentative tug and then felt a sudden vicious wrench as something with superhuman strength pulled her feet out from under her. She gave a startled yelp before she was slammed into the cold, hard surface of the walkway. She flipped over and felt a wave of panic as she saw the dozens of tiny black insectile creatures that were clamped around her foot, their collective grip tightening as she watched, holding her in place as the main body of the swarm swept toward her. She yelled out to Jay for help and he spun around, his eyes going wide as he saw the swarm wave rear up above Mag, ready to smash down and crush the life out of her.

On the platform, Sam saw what was about to happen and in that instant the world seemed to slow down. He saw the Servant, her eyes flaring with the same yellow light he had last seen in London. In that tiny fraction of a second, before the swarm smashed down on Mag, their eyes met. He did not need to speak for the Servant to understand his wishes; he never had. He just formed a single thought.

Save her.

The response from the Servant was instantaneous. In the blink of an eye her humanoid form dissolved into a glowing golden cloud that flew into the swarm, disappearing within it and sending explosions of golden light rippling through the heaving mass of tiny robotic creatures. The swarm flailed wildly, as if trying to shake off some unseen attacker. The flares of golden light within its writhing body seemed only to get brighter as its movements became more violent. Mag quickly scrambled backward across the floor and Jay ran toward her, helping her to her feet. They both sprinted for the platform, trying to put as much distance as possible between themselves and the hissing, thrashing swarm. In its final moments, the swarm seemed almost to turn against itself, twisted clawed tentacles lashing out and ripping chunks from its own body. The heaving black mass gave one last screaming hiss and then exploded, glowing particles cascading down toward the pool of white-hot raw nanites below. No trace of the Servant remained.

Sam watched as his friends hurried toward the platform, the damaged walkway creaking ominously as they ran. He could not understand what had just happened. Why had the nanites that composed the Servant's body had such a violent effect on the swarm? Why was she not a slave to the Primarch like the rest of the Voidborn? There had to be something different about her, something special, something . . .

"Riley," Sam whispered to himself, "you idiot."

Sam stared down at his arm and with an effortless thought changed its color, shifting it from its normal skin tone to a reflective golden color. He glanced up at the Primarch, who was watching Jay and Mag approach and had not noticed what Sam had just done. The nanites that had replaced Sam's arm after their first battle with the Voidborn in London had never been truly Voidborn or Illuminate. Thanks to the experiments his father had conducted on him when he was just a baby, Sam had somehow co-opted the Voidborn nanites when he took over the Mothership. The Servant too had been altered by the experience. That had to be what had allowed her to destroy the swarm.

Mag and Jay dived for the platform as the walkway, weakened by the swarm's death throes, finally gave way behind them. As they scrambled to their feet, the Primarch strode toward them, its hideous face a mask of fury.

"How dare you bring that poisonous thing here, to this chamber," the Primarch roared as Mag and Jay retreated before it. "I shall strip the flesh from your bones for what you have done."

"Stop!" Sam yelled. "If you hurt them, I'll never help you. You can burn every city on the face of the Earth but I will *never* open the Bridge for you if anything happens to them."

"You would risk the lives of billions for these two?" the Primarch said, turning toward Sam. "How very human of you. Very well. Open the Bridge now and I will spare them. Any further delay and you watch them both die."

Sam replied with a nod. "What do I need to do?"

"Come here," the Primarch said, pointing a single clawed finger at the ground in front of him. Sam walked slowly toward the towering creature, his head bowed. The Primarch placed a hand on each side of Sam's head and closed its eyes. "Now," the Primarch hissed, "open the Bridge to me."

Sam took a deep breath. He drew his arm back, its color shifting from pink to gold as his fingers shifted shape, flowing and then melting together to form a vicious curved blade. Sam thrust his arm forward with all his might, driving the serrated weapon between the black crystalline plates of the Primarch's armor and deep into the creature's gut. The Primarch howled in pain, releasing its grip on Sam's head. It delivered a vicious backhanded blow to the side of Sam's face, sending him flying across the platform and slamming into the raised dais that the Nucleus hovered above. The Primarch clutched both of its massive clawed hands to the wound in its belly, looking down with an expression of startled horror. Visible between the Primarch's fingers was a faint golden glow.

"You human filth!" the Primarch screamed, stomping toward Sam, who, still stunned by the force of the blow, was struggling to push himself up onto his knees. The Primarch grabbed him by the neck and lifted him above the ground. Sam swung wildly at the creature with the golden blade, but the Primarch blocked the clumsy attempt effortlessly with its free hand, clenching it into a fist and whipping it back, delivering another vicious blow to Sam's jaw. Sam's human hand clawed desperately at the Primarch's fingers as they tightened their grip on his throat. A fringe of blackness began to encroach on his field of vision as his brain was starved of oxygen, the Illuminate nanites within his body powerless to defend him while within range of the Primarch's malign influence.

"What have you done to me?" the Primarch demanded, its hand tightening still further on Sam's throat, threatening to crush his windpipe. "What is this poison?" The Primarch held the hand that had just been pressed against the wound in its abdomen up in front of Sam's face. Tiny golden particles swarmed across its surface. "Did you truly think you could harm me, here, of all places?" An instant later a billowing cloud of jet-black nanites streamed from the spinning sphere at the center of the platform, swirling around the Primarch. The golden glow that was emanating from the wound Sam had inflicted began to fade as the Voidborn Nucleus healed its master.

"You have just doomed your species, human," the Primarch hissed, bringing Sam's face close to its own. "I will lay waste to this world and when I have finished, and all that remains is rubble floating in the void, I will retrieve the Illuminate Heart from its ruins. I have all eternity to unlock its secrets. I want you to die knowing that what awaits humanity is horror and death and *it's all your fault.*" The Primarch raised its massive clawed hand high above its head. "Now die!"

Mag emptied the clip of her pistol into the Primarch's back, the hollow-point rounds blowing chunks out of the creature's armor. The Primarch tossed Sam to one side, momentarily distracted by the unexpected attack.

"Damn," Mag said quietly, as the hammer clicked down on an empty chamber. Sam staggered to his feet, watching helplessly as the Primarch strode toward Mag and Jay. He saw the fear in his friends' eyes and in that instant knew that there was only one thing he could do. He summoned the last reserves of energy in his battered body and sprinted toward the raised dais at the center of the platform.

"Sam, no!" Jay yelled.

Sam threw himself into the Voidborn Nucleus. He felt a single instant of searing pain and then nothing.

"Oh God, no," Mag gasped, as the swirling vortex of Voidborn nanites consumed her friend completely, ripping his body to pieces.

The Primarch stopped in mid-stride, a shudder running through its massive body as it turned back to the Nucleus, taking a single unsteady step toward the hovering sphere. The crackling ball of red energy at its center began to flare chaotically, crimson lightning bolts arcing out from the core, leaving glowing scars in the surface of the platform around it. One of the violent discharges lanced out and struck the Primarch, searing a smoldering trail in its armor and making the creature howl in pain. The Nucleus began to spin more and more quickly, its shape shifting and distorting chaotically as it began to emit a hideous screeching roar that steadily increased in pitch and intensity.

"We have to get out of here!" Jay shouted at Mag, struggling to make himself heard over the shrieking noise coming from the Nucleus.

"I'm not leaving without Sam!" Mag screamed back at him.

"He's gone, Mag," Jay said, shaking his head and grabbing her by the arm. "You know no one could have survived that. Come on!"

He pulled her toward the walkway on the other side of the platform. He had no idea where they were going, but something told him they needed to get as far away from the Voidborn Nucleus as possible. He tried not to think about the fact that there might not be *anywhere* safe on board the giant ship.

As they approached the walkway, Jay glanced back at the Primarch. The massive creature seemed to have completely forgotten about them. It was staggering toward the howling vortex that had formed around the Nucleus, its clawed feet leaving long scratches in the platform surface as it fought to reach the rapidly spinning sphere. Jay tried not to think about what had just happened to Sam as he pushed Mag along the walkway, fighting back the sudden wave of grief that threatened to overwhelm him. They had to survive if Sam's death was going to count for anything. The pair of them didn't look back as they ran, desperate to escape the colossal chamber while they still could.

Unable to accept it had lost control, the Primarch continued to claw its way to the Nucleus, desperately stretching out its hand toward the chaotically spinning mass as the cataclysmic forces it was generating finally tore the platform beneath it apart. The Primarch gave a final enraged scream and tumbled toward the white-hot pool of raw Voidborn nanites far below. It hit the surface of the liquid with a massive splash, thrashing in torment for a few seconds before vanishing below the bubbling surface.

Jay and Mag felt the ground lurch beneath their feet. The walkway collapsed and they both clung on to the handrail for dear life as it slammed down onto the sloped surface of the huge basin that formed the floor of the chamber. They half rolled and half slid down the slope toward the searing pool at its center, coming to a halt just a few yards from the lip of the bubbling crucible.

"Are you hurt?" Jay asked Mag with a pained groan.

"I'm okay," Mag replied, pushing herself to her feet and staring up at the Nucleus. "I don't think there's much point in running anymore, Jay." Jay looked up at the chaotically spinning vortex above them. The shrieking noise it was emitting was now deafening, massive bolts of crimson lightning arcing out from it in all directions. "It's been fun, big guy."

Without warning, the pool of raw nanites exploded upward in a shower of boiling liquid. Jay and Mag tried as best they could to back away from the pit, both watching in horror as *something* dragged its twisted body out of the searing lake, before slowly climbing to its feet.

The Primarch stood before them, its face hideously scarred by the white-hot nanites, sections of its armor twisting and flowing where the tiny machines blindly reconstructed it into chaotic new forms. The hideous creature took several long, slow strides toward Mag and Jay. Its fang-lined mouth opened wide and it let out a single bellowing roar as the searing liquid splashed across its face, warping its features. Whether it was in pain or rage, it was impossible to tell, but as it stomped toward them one thing was clear on its face: *hatred*.

"Your friend has achieved nothing," the Primarch said, its voice a malevolent, gurgling rasp. "All of this, everything you see around you, this ship, every Voidborn on your cursed planet, is *me*. He may destroy this body or even this ship, but while one Voidborn remains, I live. All of this will be rebuilt, your pathetic species will be erased from history. and we will rule the stars; nothing can change that. So now you will die knowing you have lost."

Above them, there was a sudden, painfully loud thump and for an instant it felt like something had sucked not just all of the air but all of the sound out of the room too.

The Voidborn Nucleus instantly stopped its chaotic flailing rotation, seeming to bulge and expand for a split second before imploding down to an impossibly small and bright white point of light. That single point then drifted slowly down toward the bubbling pool of raw nanites, vanishing below its glowing surface. The Primarch appeared to flinch for an instant, its hand touching its forehead as it took a single, hesitant staggering step toward Mag and Jay.

No.

The voice was plucked from the air as if it had come from an invisible person standing right next to Mag and Jay. The Primarch wheeled around to face the bubbling pit, an expression of horror spreading across its face. Something began to rise slowly from the surface of the pool, a vaguely human shape with its head hung low, streams of white-hot liquid pouring off it. It came to rest, floating three feet above the surface of the pool. As the Primarch watched in horror, the figure solidified, the lines of its features and the armor it was wearing becoming clearer.

"It can't be," the Primarch said with a strangled gasp of disbelief. "That's impossible! I watched you die."

"Everything dies eventually," Sam replied. "Even you."

He floated forward through the air, before dropping to the edge of the pool and walking toward the Primarch. His features were neither fully human nor Illuminate, but a strange hybrid of the two, while the crystalline black armor he was wearing seemed to be almost Voidborn in design.

"What have you done, human?" the Primarch said, its voice desperate as it staggered backward, retreating from Sam with a bewildered expression on its face.

"Can you feel it?" Sam asked, his expression neutral as he walked toward the hideous creature. "In here." Sam tapped a finger against the center of his chest.

The Primarch continued to move away from Sam, shaking its head in disbelief as its eyes went wide.

"I cannot feel them," the Primarch gasped. "My Voidborn . . ."

"No," Sam replied, looking the Primarch straight in the eye. "My Voidborn."

The Primarch launched itself at Sam with an enraged howl, its massive claws swiping through the air toward him. Sam didn't even flinch; he simply raised one hand into the air and the Primarch was instantly frozen in midstrike, hovering inches above the ground.

"All of this is mine now," Sam said, taking a single step toward the creature and bringing his face close to the Primarch's as it struggled fruitlessly against the invisible force that was holding it in place. "Including *you*."

"Release me, child," the Primarch spat. "Or are you too much of a coward to face me as a warrior?"

"Don't be ridiculous," Sam replied. "I'm not going to fight you." He gave the tiniest wave of his hand and the

Primarch's arm, still raised for a killing blow, lowered to its side. "I don't need to."

"No!" the Primarch screamed. "I will not let you take my Voidborn from me!"

"So now you understand," Sam said, a cold edge of distilled rage in his voice, "how it feels to lose *everything*." He walked around the frozen Primarch. "Now I have a gift for you." He raised his hand again, holding it above the Primarch's head. "You brought agony to the Earth and I think it's time you had a taste of it yourself."

Sam reached out to the Voidborn with a thought; the act of connecting with the alien hive-mind was completely effortless. He sought out the devices scattered around the surface of the Earth that were twisting the Illuminate control signal and instantly brought an end to the suffering of every Sleeper on the face of the planet. Around the world the enslaved masses of humanity dropped back into a deep, dreamless sleep, their torment brought to an end as quickly as it had started.

"Do you know how it felt?" Sam asked the Primarch, his voice a whisper. "No? Let me show you." With a thought, Sam inflicted the same searing agony on the Primarch that humanity had been feeling for the past few days. The creature let out a ragged, howling scream as overwhelming waves of pain seared through its body. Sam relented after a few seconds, releasing the Primarch from its torment. "You're going back to the dark, Sabiss, but this time you won't be alone; you will have that pain for company for all eternity."

"No," the Primarch gasped. "Anything but that, anything. You can't send me back to the darkness, please . . . no . . . If you have any mercy within you . . ."

"I'll show you the same mercy you showed ten million people in London," Sam said without a hint of emotion. "I'll show you the same mercy you showed my family." Sam raised his hand.

"Then destroy me!" the Primarch screamed. "If you would punish me for what I have done, then kill me. You said you would watch me die!"

"And I will," Sam replied. "One day."

Sam clenched his open hand into a fist and with a hideous scream the Primarch seemed to fold in upon itself, the nanites that composed its body swirling inward, compressing relentlessly. A moment later a black crystal, no bigger than a man's thumb, hovered in the air where the Primarch had once stood. Sam reached out and plucked the crystal from the air, examining it for an instant before tossing it into the glowing pool of raw Voidborn nanites. He turned toward Mag and Jay, who were slowly climbing to their feet and dusting themselves off. They still had slightly wide-eyed, bewildered expressions on their faces as he walked toward them.

"Are you both okay?" Sam asked.

"You're asking us?" Jay replied, shaking his head in

disbelief. “Man, we thought you were dead. When you jumped into that thing and . . . well . . . It looked like it ripped you to pieces. What happened?”

“I’ll explain later,” Sam said. “Let’s go home first.”

“Is that it, then?” Mag asked, looking around the massive chamber. “Did we win?”

“No,” Sam replied, “we didn’t.”

His shape shifted as the Voidborn armor he had been wearing vanished and his normal human features returned. “There’s something I have to tell you. It’s about London. . . .”

“What happened to them?” Anne asked, crouching down beside Will.

“No idea,” Will said, staring at the tiny insect-like Drone in the palm of his hand. “They’re all like this.” He tossed the swarm Drone back into the knee-high drifts of identical and equally inert creatures that covered the canyon floor around them. He, Jack, Anne, and Nat had been about to evacuate the area when something happened to the swarm. It was as if someone had just switched them off, the entire swarm deactivating at precisely the same instant.

“You sure these things are dead?” Jack asked, prodding at another heap of the Drones with the toe of his boot.

“Well, it’s impossible to be completely certain,” Will said, “but they’re not showing any signs of reactivation. That’s a positive sign.”

"Hey, don't get me wrong," Jack said. "I much prefer them this way. I'm just wondering what happened to them."

"Maybe whoever sent them didn't need them anymore after they kicked our asses," Nat said with a sigh.

"That is a possibility, yes," Will replied. "A pretty depressing one, though."

"Still, doesn't answer the question of what we're supposed to do . . ." Jack fell silent mid-sentence as a massive shadow suddenly swept across the canyon floor. They all looked upward as the mysterious alien vessel that had vanished with Sam, Jay, and Mag on board barely an hour ago descended quickly toward them.

"I don't know about you guys, but I think it would be a really good idea if we got the hell out of here," Jack said.

"Yeah," Anne agreed. "I think you might just be right."

Will ran over to Jack, wrapping his arms tightly around his friend's waist and activating his own suit's flight systems, sending them both shooting into the air. Nat and Anne were right behind them, powering up from the canyon floor and rocketing into the bright blue sky. As the giant ship dropped toward them, the two girls weaved evasively through the air, hoping to distract the massive ship's attention away from Will and Jack, whose comparative lack of agility made them far more vulnerable.

"Where do you think you're going?" Jay asked, his voice clear across the comms system.

"Jay?" Nat asked. "Where are you? Are you still on board that thing?"

"Yeah," Jay replied, "this is probably going to sound a little weird . . ."

It took a couple of minutes for Jay to explain to the others what had just happened on board the alien vessel. It dropped into a hover above the canyon, a portal opening above the giant glowing red eye at its center. Nat was the first to land on the platform, relieved to see Jay, Mag, and Sam all walking toward her, looking relatively unscathed.

"I'm so happy to see you guys," Nat said. "When this thing flew off with you on board, I thought . . . we all thought that we'd never see you again. I can't believe that . . . What's wrong?"

Nat stopped abruptly as she saw the expressions on her friends' faces. She did not yet understand the terrible truth. The war had indeed been won, but the cost had been almost too high to bear.

"We need to go home," Sam said. "There's something you all have to see."

Sam walked through the empty streets of the Illuminate city. Unlike the last time he had visited the Heart, he was not wearing the body of some dead Illuminate. Now he could wear whatever body he wanted. He walked into the gleaming tower and through the beautiful entrance hall inside, before stepping into the beam of light that would transport him to the council chamber. As he stepped out, a frown passed across his face.

"There's no point hiding," Sam said to the empty room. "I can wait forever if needs be."

The chamber lit up with blue light and Selenne appeared in front of him, wearing her council robes.

"I thought I'd find you here," Sam said, staring at her. "I came to tell you what I've decided."

"Sam, please—"

"I don't want to hear any more of your lies, Selenne," he said, shaking his head.

"Then tell me, what do you intend to do with us?" Selenne asked.

"I have to make sure that my world is protected from you," Sam said. "You understand that, right?"

"Sam, we meant you no harm, we would never have—"

"I said no more lies, Selenne," Sam replied angrily, his eyes flaring with red light.

"It doesn't have to be like this," Selenne said. "We can coexist now that the Voidborn are gone. We can help humanity, give you our technologies, whatever you need. We—"

"Enough," Sam said. "I didn't come here to hear you beg, Selenne. I came to tell you my decision. The Earth is ours. This world"—he gestured to the city beyond the council chamber windows—"is yours. You will never leave this place again."

"No, please, Sam, this world is not real," Selenne pleaded. "You cannot leave us here, trapped in a dream!"

"It's a kinder fate than the one you had in mind for us," Sam replied. "Good-bye, Selenne."

"No, Sam! Wait!"

But Sam was already gone.

12

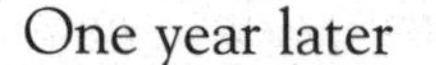

One year later

Jay walked down the drop-ship's boarding ramp, pulling at the uncomfortably tight collar of his shirt. Mag came toward him with a broad grin on her face, throwing her arms around him and hugging him hard.

"You do know you look super hot in a suit and tie, don't you?" she said.

"I feel like I'm wearing a straitjacket," Jay replied with a sigh. "I'm just glad that I've only got to keep this ridiculous getup on for an hour or two."

"Oh, stop moaning," Mag laughed. "The others are dying to see you."

He followed Mag through the immaculately maintained

park, its sweeping paths surrounded by manicured lawns and carefully tended flower beds. The half-dozen close protection agents who were surrounding them at a respectful distance did their typically terrible job of being invisible. As they walked, the people who were wandering around the park looked furtively in their direction, whispering to each other as they passed. Jay wondered if he'd ever get used to it. He'd decided a while ago that he'd rather fight a dozen Grendels than have to put up with people treating him like he was some kind of celebrity, but it wasn't like he had a lot of say in the matter. He was, after all, one of the six most famous people on Earth.

"Mr. Sawyer," said the sharply dressed man who was waiting at the entrance gate as they approached.

"Jay," he replied, "please. No one calls me that."

"Sorry . . . erm . . . yes, of course," the man said. "I'm so glad you're here. The dedication ceremony is about to begin. Please follow me." He gestured for them to accompany him through the entrance, leading the pair into a lawned area that was lined with seats, most of which were now occupied with conspicuously important people and dignitaries of one description or another.

"Just make sure I don't end up talking to the prime minister again," Jay said quietly to Mag as the man led them between the rows of seats toward the front of the lawn. "She bores me rigid."

"I'll keep an eye out for you," Mag said with a smile. "Don't worry."

"Jay!" Nat squealed with excitement as she saw him approaching. She and Anne ran down the aisle between the seats, almost knocking him over as they both hugged him. "I thought you were still in China?"

"I was," Jay said with a smile. "They've got most of the power grid back up now. They think they're going to be ready to wake the next group of Sleepers within a month. There was no way I was going to miss this, though. Even if it did mean a couple of hours of handshake duty."

"You've just lost me some money," Jack said with a grin, hugging Jay. "I bet this lot you wouldn't show today."

"Like to keep you guessing," Jay said, clapping his friend on the back. "Besides, I wanted to see what you'd been up to. How're you getting on with the reconstruction?"

"Slowly," Jack said. "Come on, I'll show you." He gestured for Jay to follow him and the pair of them walked past the lectern and screen that were set up in front of the rows of seats and toward the railing at the end of the lawn. Beyond the barrier the lawn disappeared and the ground dropped away in a steep slope. The London crater extended ten miles into the distance, its opposite side barely visible through the haze. All around the edge of the crater, new buildings were under construction and Jay could just make out the Voidborn Hunters swarming around their skeletal steel frameworks.

"Those things still make me nervous," Jay said.

"We don't call them Hunters now obviously," Jack said. "They're just construction Drones. But yeah, I do know what you mean. At least we don't have to worry about the person controlling them anymore."

"I guess not," Jay said quietly.

"Is he coming today?" Jack asked.

"I've got no idea," Jay replied. "I haven't seen him in months."

"He's busy, I suppose," Jack said. "Will saw him last month. A dam collapsed in Canada and he showed up there to help with the rescue efforts. Will didn't speak to him, but . . ."

"Let's get back," Jay said, after staring down into the crater for a few seconds.

They walked back to the seating area and took their places in their reserved seats at the front.

After a couple of minutes, the crowd fell silent as the prime minister took the stage. She stood there for a moment and then addressed the crowd.

"Ladies and gentlemen," she said, "we have come here today to unveil the London Memorial, and while this is inevitably a time of sadness and reflection for us all, we should also take this opportunity to recognize the bravery of the people we are so lucky to have join us here today. . . ."

An hour later, the ceremony was over and Jay was

studying the list of names carved into the slab of black marble on the monument in front of him. The others had left for the reception that was taking place in a marquee nearby. He stood there alone, his bodyguards standing near the entrance to the garden and keeping a wary eye on him. To most people, they were the names of heroes, names that would be found in history books for centuries to come, but to him they were dead friends.

"Hello, Jay," Sam said.

Jay spun around to see his friend standing just a couple of yards away, as if he had simply appeared from thin air.

"I didn't think you were coming," Jay said, trying to keep the emotion from his voice.

"I wasn't going to. I don't like coming here."

"None of us do. I'm glad you did, though. I've missed you, Sam. We all have."

"I've had a lot to do," Sam said. "There's a world to fix."

"Yeah, I guess there is," Jay replied. There was something different about his friend and there had been ever since the defeat of the Primarch. He was cold and distant, not at all the person Jay had once known.

"It's Nat's birthday next week," Jay said. "She's having the biggest party imaginable, of course. It would mean a lot to her if you came."

"I'll try to be there," Sam replied.

"No, you won't," Jay said. "What is it, Sam? What happened to you?"

"Everything." Sam looked at Jay with a haunted expression. An instant later he vanished, leaving just a faint cloud of glowing particles hanging in the air.

Jay turned back to the memorial.

"There's one name missing," he whispered to himself.

Far above the Earth, someone looked down on his home planet, feeling the input from the countless Voidborn below that worked tirelessly to restore the war-torn world.

He wasn't Sam Riley anymore. He wasn't the last of the Illuminate. He wasn't the Primarch of the Voidborn. He was all of those things.

The humans below were slowly being roused from their long sleep, as their society rebuilt itself to a point where all the Sleepers could finally be woken once more. Until then he would stand guard over the planet below, help it rebuild, help it grow. Watching over humanity.

And then, when the time was right, he would lead his people to the stars.

After spending ten years as a video games designer and producer, **Mark Walden** left the games industry to write and be a full-time dad to his daughter, Megan. He studied at Newcastle University, where he received a BA in English literature and an MA in twentieth-century literature, film, and television. It was there he met his wife, Sarah. He lives in the United Kingdom.